Praise for A.J. Park

'Splendidly twisty, with a compelling inner momentum, it keeps its secrets until the final pages'

DAILY MAIL

'A real page turner. I finished it in one go!'

MARTINA COLE

'A.J. Park is a master of suspense who knows how to keep readers hovering tensely over the edges of their seats'

SOPHIE HANNAH

'A gripping read'

THE SUN

'Riveting, fast-paced, and full of twists and unforgettable characters . . . I absolutely could not put it down'

CHRIS MOONEY

'Twisty, layered and compelling. A genuine page turner, A.J. Park has a big future in British crime fiction'

M.W. CRAVEN

'Tightly plotted, well-drawn characters and an edge-of-your-seat page turner'

CATHY KELLY

'A great thriller that will keep you turning the pages late into the night'

LUCA VESTE

'A fantastic read! It's a superbly gripping and brilliantly twisty tale'

SIMON LELIC

After studying literature, linguistics and Spanish at university, A.J. Park trained as an English teacher and actor. He has edited magazines, and taught English, media studies, drama, and English as a foreign language in secondary schools across England and abroad. He was also a competitive fencer for seven years.

By A.J. Park

The First Lie
Don't Speak

DON'T SPEAK

A.J. Park

First published in Great Britain in 2021 by Orion Fiction,
an imprint of The Orion Publishing Group Ltd.,
Carmelite House, 50 Victoria Embankment
London EC4Y 0DZ

An Hachette UK Company

1 3 5 7 9 10 8 6 4 2

Copyright © A.J. Park 2021

The moral right of A.J. Park to be identified as
the author of this work has been asserted in accordance
with the Copyright, Designs and Patents Act of 1988.

All rights reserved. No part of this publication may be
reproduced, stored in a retrieval system, or transmitted
in any form or by any means, electronic, mechanical,
photocopying, recording, or otherwise, without the
prior permission of both the copyright owner and the
above publisher of this book.

All the characters in this book are fictitious, and any resemblance
to actual persons, living or dead, is purely coincidental.

A CIP catalogue record for this book is
available from the British Library.

ISBN (Mass Market Paperback) 9781409187479
ISBN (eBook) 9781409187486

Typeset by Born Group
Printed and bound in Great Britain by Clays Ltd, Elcograf S.p.A.

www.orionbooks.co.uk

Wiola

Maya

Max

'Make our faces vizards to our hearts,
disguising what they are.'

'I am in blood
stepped in so far that, should I wade no more,
returning were as tedious as go o'er.'

Macbeth, William Shakespeare

I

He knows what she likes to do, has become familiar with her routines, her likes and dislikes. He has watched and waited and prepared for this moment.

For the start.

Time – delaying the inevitable for so many years – has only intensified the anticipation and the excitement that stems from this moment.

It's Friday night. She always goes out on Friday nights. Always the same nightclub in town and with the same three friends. They're all undeniably pretty girls, and they dress for one purpose – attention – but he only has eyes for one of them. *For her.* It's as if the others aren't even there when he's watching them.

In recent days, he's got closer to her, and she hasn't been suspicious of a thing. His confidence has increased; now, for the past day or so, he's been parking his car directly across the road from her parents' house. He'll be facing her when she walks out of the front door, while she walks down the path, as she opens the gate and says goodbye to her family for the last time.

He will be only metres from her and she will be clueless about what fate the hours to come will bring.

She always leaves at 9 p.m. and today is no exception. Her front door opens inward, the light from the hallway streaming out, joining the moon's feeble attempt to light the street. It's a dark, wet evening. Although it stopped raining an hour ago, the whole area remains covered in puddles. Of course, she's not dressed for the weather; that would be inappropriate for a nightclub. And of course he's pleased that she has chosen to leave the house in a state of near undress.

She steps out, slowly, her long slim legs tightly wrapped in a short black dress. She moves carefully along the path, careful to avoid the puddling rainwater.

He follows her as she moves and he imagines how touching her will feel. She opens the gate and steps onto the pavement. While his eyes bore holes into her, she gazes ahead.

As she walks along the pavement, she pulls out her mobile phone. His eyes are able to cast a slow look along the length of her body, absorbing, appreciating, salivating, before she leaves his sightline.

Now it is time to move; he can't let her get far away from him. This is only the first stage and there can be no delay.

The second and third stages are already planned, so delay cannot be an option.

At the end of the street, he predicts she will turn left. Because of the weather, he's hopeful she'll take a shortcut. And, indeed, it looks like that's what she's doing, for she turns left instead of right. That means walking through the park. The route home in the early hours is when he thought he'd have his chance to act, but now an unexpectedly earlier opportunity seems to be presenting itself.

His breathing quickens. He won't have to wait, after all.

He starts the engine and moves slowly down the street, passing her after a few moments. The view afforded him as he approaches her, then the side view, reinforces his feeling that he has made the right choice.

Silly girl, hasn't a clue. She doesn't notice him – doesn't give herself a chance because her eyes are glued to her mobile phone.

An almost immediate right turn, then another left and, about a hundred yards ahead, he spies the entrance to the alleyway that leads into the park. It's surrounded by trees, and the nearest houses, which are beyond the fences that line both sides of the alleyway, are some distance off; their large back gardens put plenty of space between them and the fences.

He stops the car right next to the entrance to the alleyway and switches off the engine. From the glovebox, he removes a pair of latex gloves, a hand towel and a bottle containing what he calls his *magic*. After pulling on the gloves, he steps out of the car and pours a good amount of the liquid onto the towel. Its stench is pungent, and he's pleased he's outside of the car. He leaves the car unlocked and partly opens the rear door on the passenger side.

About halfway along the path is a great elm. Residents wanted to cut it down years ago, but its age meant that it had to be protected. They had warned that it added potential danger to the alleyway; it was at its deepest and darkest point, after all.

But no, the local council knew better, and silly teens, unwilling to walk just a little bit further, wouldn't heed the warnings – this was their favourite shortcut.

Perhaps, after tonight, that might change.

He stands near the end of the alleyway until she appears in the distance. How, even in shadow, her hips sway. He could recognise her, from her shape alone, at a mile's distance.

Stealthily, he makes his way along the alleyway and positions himself between the elm and the fence. Then he waits, his heartbeat quickening the whole time, as the anticipation becomes so great that he feels his heart might burst out of his chest.

It's going to happen again. It's been such a long time.

The time of waiting, of living a lie, is over.

After several minutes, footsteps break the silence. They grow louder, louder, as she gets nearer, nearer.

His heart must surely explode, it's beating so fast. Racing, pounding so much that, for a moment, he fears she might hear it. Revealed to his victim by his own heartbeat.

One step, two steps, three steps, and then she's here. She passes him. Four steps, five steps. Eyes still glued to the phone, headphones on, hips still swaying. He counts down, *Three, two, one*, then he steps out from behind the tree. He can't resist a grin; he's never been so pleased. Everything he has planned, it's all coming together. Nothing can go wrong; he feels invincible.

He takes a step forward, as she does, and within seconds he's walking in sync with her. They share four steps before she senses something isn't quite right – a change in the wind, perhaps, or the atmosphere around her, the darkness starting to envelop – for she lowers her phone and lifts a hand as if to remove a headphone from an ear. But before her hand can touch it, his left hand reaches around her neck and pulls her towards him, as the right hand places the hand towel over her mouth and nose, over most of her face. He snatches sharply at her and pushes the towel so hard he might suffocate her, but he's desperate to keep her quiet, to prevent her from screaming, so he keeps hold and applies all the pressure he can muster, until the few physical struggles she made at the start subside and, finally, she falls limp in his arms.

Removing the towel, he twists his neck round so that he can see into her face. He eyes her from her eyes to her lips, then along the line of her entire body.

I have you now.

He wants to place her on the ground and have his way with her right here, but he can't risk them being stumbled upon. He lifts her – she's surprisingly light – and carries her towards his car, a threshold of sorts, one that marks the start of their private time together.

He pulls the car door open with a spare finger and places her on the back seat. It's an awkward movement, and the car is low, which makes his back twinge in discomfort, but he manages to get her in, placing her comfortably, he hopes, before closing the door. He knows he'll have at least half an hour to get her into position, before he'll apply more ketamine to the towel and use that to keep her exactly where he wants her.

Where he will keep her till the very end.

Once Upon a Time

The dark figure steps into the doorway, a shadow cutting off the bright light of the hallway. It's something she recognises, of course, something that has become familiar; a hulking figure, broad, engulfing.

The blackness spreads wider as it enters the room. Growing larger, it comes closer and nearer to the bed.

She cowers under the covers, the same as always, yet always with nowhere to go. Attempting to hide is futile. There's no fighting against this. Against him. That she knows what's about to happen only makes it worse. She knows who it is, why he's here and what he's going to do to her.

The silhouette becomes one black mass when he's within a metre of the bed, and his hand reaches out towards her. A metre becomes inches, becomes centimetres.

And just as he leans down over her body and his hand pulls back the duvet under which she's taken shelter, her heartbeat quickening, thudding, ready to burst through her chest, his face emerges out of the pitch-dark, becoming clear, surrounded by the light from the hallway.

Then she screams.

She always screams.

2

The phone ringing startles me awake and I turn to face Edward, knowing that from his face I will always receive comfort.

He isn't here.

Groggy, I turn to the bedside table where I usually leave my phone for the night.

'Amelie Davis,' I say, trying to sound wide awake.

What time is it?

I squint in an attempt to clear my vision and the red illuminated numbers come into focus: *5.40*.

'It's Lange,' the voice says. Detective Chief Inspector Lange, my superior at work. 'The body of a young woman, possibly a teenager, has been found in Hampstead Heath. How soon can you get there?'

I sit up abruptly. 'About forty minutes,' I say.

'Okay. I'll ask Hillier to meet you there. Take charge of the scene, then call me to give me a debrief. I'll be there as soon as I can, but it won't be for a couple of hours.'

He's gone before I can expel a sound.

I lower the phone onto my lap and turn back to Edward's side of the bed. *What day is it?* I think. *Where is he?* I lift up the phone and select his name on the speed dial. My finger lingers for a moment over the call button.

Where are you? Then: *Were you with me here last night?*

I had a couple of glasses of wine, but that was all. Surely. So why can't I remember? Why is my head not clear?

I look back at the phone screen and decide against it. I flick the screen and it goes black. I pull myself out of bed and, in the en suite bathroom, wash my face quickly; maybe that'll help. I dress and head downstairs. When I enter the kitchen, I walk straight to the wall calendar.

Birmingham.

For the last two days. Edward is due back home this evening. How can I have forgotten? There was a time when I had a picture-perfect memory.

I turn away from the wall and stop. On the kitchen counter is an empty wine bottle and, behind that, another bottle, which is half empty.

I lift up the half-empty bottle and stare at its label. I read the words. I sniff the head of the bottle. Its scent is rancid. *This is what I drank last night?* I place it under my lips and twist the bottle, teasingly. *Maybe just a sip to get the day started.* I slowly tilt my head back. *Just a taste.* I let the liquid enter my mouth, but then I stir, wondering what the hell I'm doing. I dash to the sink and spit. Half of what comes out of my mouth ends up on the windowsill. Sighing and appalled at myself, I wipe the surface with a cloth and rinse the sink clean. Then I look again at the bottle.

I have to stop.

I turn the bottle upside down and deposit what's left of it into the sink.

3

Hampstead Heath, London

A large corner of the park has been cordoned off by uniformed officers. As I hold up my warrant card and say, 'Detective Sergeant Amelie Davis,' one of them answers, 'Along that path,' and he points. 'You should see some activity deep into a wooded bit. You'll find her in there.'

'Make sure no one else comes in except for Detective Constable Ryan Hillier.'

'He's already in there.'

'Oh,' I say, glancing at my watch. That's when I notice it's taken me almost an hour and a half to get here. *Where did I lose all that time?* 'Good,' I add casually. 'No one else comes in, then, until I say otherwise.'

'Yes, ma'am.'

I lift the cordon marker and enter under it. The path is slippery from all the mud and water that has amassed on it. The path curves and I see another cordon marker in the distance. As I walk, I scan left and right. Plenty of escape points for whoever is responsible. A place that's probably busy in the daytime. Countless footprints, but useless for any investigation purposes due to the sheer volume we're likely to find.

Which is possibly why this location was chosen.

A slim, tall, dark-haired figure, Hillier, who's about five years younger than me, lifts up his head and sees me as I approach. I've worked closely with him for just over a year now. He's a good detective and I like working with him very much. He says something to the uniformed officer who lifts a second cordon for me and then steps aside so that I can enter.

Instantly, I spot something on the ground approximately ten metres away. It's half hidden under some overgrown bushes and vegetation. Four large trees form a sort of perimeter around it.

'Body dumped or killed here, what are your thoughts?'

Several crime-scene investigators, kitted up in their blue outfits, are on their knees, combing through the shrubbery and mud.

'Dan thinks killed here.'

'Amelie.' Daniel Emerson, the lead crime-scene investigator with whom I've worked on and off for the past eight years, appears from behind the nearest tree. He's bald and very fat, so each step looks like it's a struggle.

'Dan.' I realise there's a pointlessness to our greeting, but it's part of the process we go through, after these years of working together in usually horrific circumstances. Saying each other's names helps, somehow; it makes the unfamiliar, which each murder most certainly is, a tiny bit familiar, providing an odd sense of comfort when it's most needed.

'Ryan says you think she was killed here.'

'I think so. Six to eight hours ago, I estimate. There's a big mess around the body. Signs of lots of activity.'

'Such as?'

'Intercourse.'

'Intercourse?'

'Yep. Knee marks from when he was on top of her, I'd guess. Traces of semen, both inside and out.'

'He's brazen.'

'Oh, yes,' Emerson says.

'Which likely means no criminal record,' I tell Hillier. 'Certainly no samples on file. Otherwise he'd practically be announcing himself to us and there aren't many people that foolish or stupid.'

'Ready to have a closer look?' Emerson asks.

Ready as I'll ever be. It never gets any easier.

'Sure,' I say. After I have kitted up, I follow Emerson along a narrow police-made path to where the body is.

'Remember to keep inside the markers,' he says, telling me what I already know. There's something reassuring in hearing the familiar.

I stop several feet away from the body. It's as though a brick wall has appeared in front of me, which won't let me pass.

I can see her from here. I can see exactly what she looks like.

Long blonde hair, beautiful blue eyes, raised cheekbones. A slim figure. Curvy for her age. Long legs, nicely tanned. Black high heels. A short black dress, the bottom of which has been lifted and lies scrunched around her pelvis. I can see semen stains on her outfit. Black underwear is wrapped around her neck.

'Any clue as to who she is?'

'No ID on her.'

'Wright and Anderson are trawling missing persons' reports,' Hillier adds, 'but it's probably too early to find anything. They're going to keep tracking anything that comes in.'

I approach. Slowly, tentatively, cautiously.

I don't want them to see my apprehension. It's not because I'm afraid – I'm used to seeing all kinds of horrors. It's just . . .

Arriving by the body, I stand next to her feet.

So pretty.

I look deep into her eyes. She looks so peaceful. Whatever he did to her, he was careful not to harm her face.

Her beautiful face. Lovely smooth skin. A good sense of fashion. Lots to show off, which she clearly understood, judging by how she is dressed. So much potential. So much life ahead of her.

Taken from her in an instant.

I draw my gaze along the corpse. 'When will you be able to get her in the lab?' I ask Emerson.

'By late afternoon, I hope.'

'Give me a buzz when you're ready.'

4

It's almost 4 p.m. when I arrive at Emerson's workspace, the morgue in Charing Cross Police Station. I haven't had lunch, even though I'm famished, and that's probably a good thing under the circumstances; years ago, I learnt the hard way that morgues aren't places to visit after a filling meal.

Daniel Emerson's office is located deep in the bowels of the police station. It's closed off by a heavy wooden door. There isn't a pane of glass in it, so it cuts him and the secrets of the morgue off from the rest of the building.

I knock and his voice calls out something indecipherable. Tentatively, I enter and ask, 'Are you decent?'

'Always,' he answers.

Placed before him on the inspection slab is the young woman. Perhaps *girl* would be more appropriate – we still don't know who she is or how old she is, but she's definitely young. There's a sheet covering her body from the waist down. Her skin is pale, her long blonde hair fanned out beneath her head and shoulders, almost like a pair of angel's wings, and her eyes are now closed. I walk towards her, slowly, trying not to look too closely at her, unable not to.

'What have you found?' I ask.

Emerson is entering some details onto a computer, which sits atop a desk against the wall nearest to the slab. He pushes back, rolling on his chair, and stands. 'High levels of ketamine, according to initial test results, so she was incapacitated when he killed her.' *No chance to fight back.* 'We're currently running a more detailed toxicology analysis and will hopefully have a more complete picture in a day or so. Semen in the vaginal tract.'

'As we thought.'

'Nothing that matches anything on the database yet, but here's where it gets interesting. I found two different semen samples.'

'As in *two* men?'

'Yes, as in. And as if that's not disturbing enough, there's one more tabloid shocker headline to share with you. I need to carry out some more testing to be certain, but the signs are that there are both pre-mortem and post-mortem deposits of semen,' he says.

'You're kidding? I've never encountered such a thing.'

'I have,' he says simply.

I step to the side of the slab, standing only inches from her. I bend down, running my eyes up and down her body. *So young. So much like . . .*

It's hard to take.

I bend close to her and study her face.

'Show me her eyes,' I request.

Emerson carefully lifts the lids.

Yes, just as I . . .

Blue eyes. Big oval eyes. So pretty. I stare intently, so intently I get lost in them.

Just like . . .

Dead eyes.

Just like . . .

Blonde hair, blue eyes, tall, slim, leggy.

Everything about her, just like . . .

And, in an instant, dead, her life ripped away. Once so full of vibrancy, now lifeless on a slab in the basement of an old rundown building in London.

'How can someone do this, Daniel?'

He leans back, hands on hips. 'Remember, I spend more of my time with corpses than with people. They make more sense to me now. People don't make any sense at all. I arrived in hell a long time ago and don't understand what's upstairs.'

'You've got to give me something more I can work with. Hairs, anything?'

'Several. We're running everything through HOLMES.' HOLMES, the Home Office Large Major Enquiry System, has the ability to explore names, dates, details and connections, however small, between a crime and all the others on its database.

'And –'

'We can only wait. We're being patient. Like every other time we have the pleasure of standing here together.'

'I know,' I say. 'I just need something.'

'And as soon as we have it, you'll be the first person I let know.'

'So you'll call?'

'You know how lonely I get,' he jokes.

I don't smile. All I can muster is a nod.

I take one more look. Dead eyes. *They look just like . . .*
I back away. 'I've got to do something,' I say.
Just like me, years ago.
'I've got to find him.'

5

I've returned to the major incident room of the MIT. The MIT is the Major Investigation Team. There are desks spread sporadically throughout the large open space. At the far end is DCI Jonathan Lange's office. I knock on the closed door.

A sound emanates from within. I take that as a sign to enter.

'What's new?' DCI Lange says without looking up at me, reading documents and signing them. He's in his mid-sixties with grey-white hair on the sides of his head and slight wisps of what seem to be streams of cotton crisscrossing over the top's shine.

Knowing how tetchy he can be, I remain standing so that I can leave sooner rather than later. I explain everything I've just learnt from Emerson.

'That all?' he says, offering a quick, casual glance in my direction before resuming his reading and signing.

'At the moment, yes.'

'Well, then,' he says, signing and dotting something on a page, 'drop by when you have something more to tell me.'

'Sir,' I say and start to leave.

'Oh, and Davis,' he adds as I pull open the door.

'Yes, sir.'

'I thought you said forty minutes this morning.'

I hesitate, my back to him.

Before I can respond, he adds, 'Ninety minutes seems a little long to drag your slim behind out of bed. You haven't suddenly put on a lot of weight from what I can see.'

I turn to face him. 'Traffic,' I say. 'It was, erm, worse than I expected.'

'Of course it was,' he says. 'But, next time, find a way around it. Make sure forty minutes means forty minutes. Imagine if Hillier had had a coffee waiting for you. It would have gone cold. Would have been a shame to waste it.'

And with that, he lowers his head and continues reading and signing.

Taking this as an indication of conversation over, I return to the main MIT workspace. The office space I have, which I share with Ryan Hillier, is a small area off the end, opposite Lange's office. Next to my office is a large boardroom, which is where I head next. I spend time gathering all the paperwork we've generated, then pile it on the long rectangular table so that I can sort through it, displaying what I think is necessary on the large wheelie whiteboard that's pressed up against the largest of the walls. On the whiteboard, under the heading *Unidentified*, I've displayed a map of Hampstead Heath, with the location where the body was found circled in thick red marker, and I've penned up details including when she was found, by whom, along with a description of the body and the scene around it, as well as Emerson's estimated time of death. I display on it pictures that have just been sent over by the crime-scene photographer.

Detective Sergeant Katherine Wright puts her head around the door. 'How are things, Amelie?' she asks. She's a couple of years older than me and sports a new short haircut and a slightly forced smile, but she's friendly.

I stop writing on the whiteboard and turn to her. 'Tired,' I say, giving an honest answer. If anyone knows what I feel like, it's her. I know I can always be honest with Katherine.

'Me too,' she says. 'Still, there's been a development. We've had a report of a sixteen-year-old daughter going missing last night. She left for a nightclub and didn't return. Parents say her friends said they didn't see her at all last night. Description they've given matches and so does the photo they've sent through. They're coming in to identify the body.'

6

I arrive at the home of Sid and Margaret Cunningham, a sprawling five-bedroom detached property that's partly shielded behind a gate and high walls, close to Hampstead Heath. About an hour ago, they formally identified their daughter, Fiona, as the victim of – well, I don't know yet. The victim of a psychopath, that's all I'm clear about right now.

Sitting in my car in front of an imposing gate, I press the buzzer and a female voice announces, 'The Cunningham residence.'

After introducing myself, I'm buzzed in and drive along the long driveway. I park behind a BMW and a Jaguar, get out of the car and climb the steps to the towering front door, which opens before I press the doorbell.

'Detective Davis?' a woman in her early thirties says.

I nod.

'Thank you for coming.'

I step forward, taking the woman's hand. 'May I enquire who –?'

'I am Mr and Mrs Cunningham's housekeeper, Brenda Leech,' she says, with a hint of pride in her voice. 'Miss Price will be with you shortly.'

'Miss Price?'

She nods. 'That's Mr Cunningham's personal secretary. Please follow me into the drawing room.'

The old manor house is impressive. The ceilings are high and large gilt-framed paintings adorn most of the walls.

'Can I get you a cup of tea?'

'No, thank you.'

'Detective,' a woman announces loudly from afar. I turn in the direction of her voice and see she's approaching at speed, a diary clasped in her hand and pressed against her chest. 'I'm Nadine Price. Thank you for coming.' She doesn't extend a hand.

'I'm here to see Mr and Mrs Cunningham. Please can you let them know I'm here?'

'Oh, they know,' she says, animatedly. 'They won't be long. Can you follow me to the dining room?'

She leads me along another long corridor at the end of which is a set of tall white double doors. She turns the handle and opens the doors impressively, revealing a dining table that could probably seat twelve. Cabinet upon cabinet line the opposite wall, plates and other items of tableware on display in each one. In the corner, there's an ornate golden globe on wheels, no doubt filled with expensive bottles of alcohol.

'Please take a seat. They won't be long. Are you sure we can't get you a cup of tea?'

'No, thank you,' I say. I'm eager to get underway.

When Sid Cunningham appears, he looks as grand as his house, outdone only by his wife who comes in shortly after him. Both are dressed as if ready for an evening at the opera.

'I'm afraid, detective, we haven't much time,' Sid Cunningham says. 'My wife and I have an event we must attend.'

'I'd like to talk about your daughter,' I tell him, thinking that'll be enough to highlight the importance of my visit and to impress the need for their time to be given to me. 'I'm sorry if it's too soon to talk about her.'

'It's not too soon,' Margaret Cunningham says, her voice lilting on a shrill note.

The couple sit at the opposite side of the table.

'What would you like to know?' Sid Cunningham asks.

'What is your line of work?'

'I'm the CEO of a multi-national oil firm. May I ask what that has to do with anything?'

'I need to consider whether there might have been a financial motive. You have a stunning house.'

'Thank you.'

'And sometimes that can attract very bad people. Did your daughter have access to large sums of money?'

'She had access to money,' he states. 'All she had to do was ask.'

'Do you know if she had any money on her the evening she was killed?'

'She always carried money,' adds his wife. 'She was a sensible girl. In case she found she needed to make her own way home if one of our drivers couldn't collect her, for example, money was a necessity.'

'What were her plans the night she was killed?'

'She was going out with friends, as far as I'm aware,' Fiona Cunningham's mother explains. 'A nightclub, I believe.'

'Even though she was only sixteen?'

'Young girls will go where young girls want to go. Besides, she was very mature for her age and she looked older than her years.'

'How do you know that's where she was going?'

'That's what her last post said.'

'Post?'

'She posted pictures online. She was a blogger. Her influence was growing quite rapidly, actually. She kept her followers up to date about her activities and her last post – oh, what did it say?' Margaret Cunningham removes a mobile phone from her handbag and taps the screen, then reads, 'Nightclub time. Night night.' Her focus remains on the screen. It looks like she's been caught by a realisation. Perhaps that she will never see the girl in the photo again.

'What did you mean by influence?' I ask.

'She – what is the word, darling? Worked with?'

'Collaborated,' her husband clarifies.

Margaret Cunningham places her phone on the table and shuffles as if to compose herself. 'Yes, that's right. She collaborated with a number of companies. They would send her some items, clothing and what not, and she would go to fashionable places in London and photograph herself with those items and then post them on her Instagram account. It's all the rage nowadays. Followers see those items and then want them, apparently.'

'And what do you mean by her *influence*?'

'It's her profile,' Margaret Cunningham says slowly. 'It was increasing. She has several thousand followers. Have you seen our daughter, detective?'

An image of Fiona Cunningham lying naked on the slab in the morgue flashes before my eyes. I peer down at the dining table. 'I have,' I say softly.

'Then you will know she was an exceptionally beautiful girl,' her mother says proudly. 'Companies wanted to work with her. Girls her age want to be like her. That's what influencers are. People others aspire to be like. That's what my daughter was.'

'Do you have any pictures I can take a look at?'

'They're everywhere, detective.' She lifts up the mobile phone and flicks at the screen. 'Here,' she says, handing it to me.

There's picture after picture of an exceptionally beautiful girl. So full of life. I scroll down the Instagram page. 'Truly beautiful,' I say. Looking up, I encounter Margaret Cunningham beaming with pride, but there's also something arrogant in her appearance. It's something I can also detect in Fiona Cunningham's eyes in her online pictures. She knew she was attractive and she knew people would envy her when they saw the pictures. Perhaps she even wanted people to be envious. It's an unattractive quality in complete contrast to the attractive image she conveyed.

'Thank you,' I say, handing back the phone and making a note of her Instagram username. 'Did Fiona have a boyfriend?'

'No.' An immediate response from her father, delivered somewhat sharply.

I cock my head. 'And how do you know that?'

'I know my daughter.'

'But she was sixteen. Sixteen-year-olds go out alone. How could you possibly know what she was up to all the time?'

'I trusted her. She would have told us.'

'What makes you say that?'

His wife interjects. 'We were very close.'

Something in that statement and the way she says it doesn't ring true. The atmosphere in the house, too, is probably much more of a true indication of the way this family lives. I feel nothing but cold emanate from the place, and from them. *Something empty*, I think. Rich people in denial. Or pretending.

'Did she ever have any boyfriends you were aware of?'

'None at all,' her mother says.

'Such a beautiful girl and no boyfriend, *ever*?'

'She wasn't interested. She was too focused on her studies.'

'What were her plans for when she finished school? She would have had to make a choice at the end of this academic year.'

'She would have studied for her A levels and then gone to university,' her father says. 'We already had the best ones lined up to take her.'

'How can that be?' I ask innocently. 'She'd still have had two years of A level study to complete.'

'She would get through comfortably,' he stresses knowingly. *Money and status*, I realise. *They can get you anywhere.* 'She would have been well taken care of.' He closes his eyes and slowly shakes his head. 'And now . . .'

'Is something the matter?'

'Nothing's the matter, Detective,' Margaret Cunningham says. 'Tell her, Sid, tell her nothing's the matter.'

'It's fine, really.'

'It's fine,' his wife repeats.

'But it's not really, is it?' he says sharply, wincing and bringing a fist down upon the table. It shakes violently and his wife flinches from the sudden movement and noise. 'She went out too often, damn it. I always told you! I said time and time again that she was too young. She should have been here at home. Safe at home with us. These girls today, detective, they just want to be out, out, out. And I, stupid fool, should have said no. I should have put my foot down. I shouldn't have listened to *you*.' He twists his neck awkwardly to glare at his wife.

'Darling –' she says through a false smile, trying to cover up her embarrassment and failing.

'No, Margaret, it's not good enough to pretend. Not this time. I can't go on pretending. It was our decisions that meant she wasn't safe.'

'Sid, don't say that.'

'It's the truth. Stop kidding yourself. We were supposed to be her parents and we failed her.'

'Do you know what else she did on the day she died?' I interrupt, having observed enough.

They look flustered at my interruption. I do my best to maintain a neutral disposition.

'Yes,' Margaret says, 'she met a photographer. She'd had some pictures taken and was going to see them. She wanted to try a career in modelling, so she had some full-length images and headshots taken.'

'Do you know where?'

'Somewhere near Marble Arch, that's all she told me.'

'Do you know the name of the photographer?'

'Better than that,' she says. 'His card is still in her bedroom.'

7

'Detective Sergeant Davis,' Dean Wicks says, extending his hand.

As we shake hands, I notice how rough the skin of his fingers is. His hair is ruffled. He's unshaven, with ashen skin and bags under his eyes but, nonetheless, an incredibly handsome man. He's wearing a tailored T-shirt, which shows off his impressive physique, and a pair of faded jeans.

'Come in.' He steps back, pulling open the door to reveal a spacious one-bedroom apartment. I follow him in. 'Take a seat,' he says, pointing to the leather sofa. There are no armchairs. He pulls up a chair from the nearby dining table. 'I've been expecting a visit.'

That piques my interest. 'How so?'

'You're here about Fiona?'

'That's right.'

He gazes down at the floor. 'Well, it was only a matter of time, I thought. One of her friends posted about it online earlier this afternoon. Funny how quickly and easily gossip spreads online. Only this time it was true.'

'Tell me about her and how you came to know her.'

He shrugs, exhaling. 'Where to begin?' He paused. 'She was . . . magical. I photographed her a few weeks ago. She was a complete natural. She was amazing in front of the camera and the results were amazing too.'

'How did you meet her?'

'She emailed me. She'd seen some of my work online. I've photographed lots of models and they put their shots on Instagram. Some of them tag me. A lot of my business comes to me that way. Girls wanting to be like the other girls they look up to online, usually Instagram. You can get a hell of a following on there, you know. There's a lot of money to be made, careers to be had.'

'So I hear.'

'I'm a professional photographer and about sixty per cent of what I do now is exclusively for independent online clients. Not the models from big agencies like it used to be, magazines and adverts and the like. Now it's any good-looking girl who wants to give the online world a go. I used to shoot models exclusively for papers and magazines, but I went freelance when I saw how things were changing and now I mostly focus on models for their online profiles and other portfolio work. Fiona had seen examples of my work and was keen to meet me. So we met and she liked what I had to say. Money certainly wasn't a concern for her. I liked how she looked and I could see that I could make something special of the photos, so we set a date and she came and did the shoot.'

'Where did you take the photographs?'

'Here.'

'Here?' That was an odd comment. It seems like a typical bachelor pad, albeit in a very popular and expensive location.

He nods. 'I do tidy up when I have a client visiting, mind. There's no one booked in today or tomorrow. Bedroom's kitted out as my studio. It's a large space in there and the light's brilliant. That' – he indicates the sofa with a nod of his head – 'opens out into a bed and is where I sleep. I do well, but in this part of London property prices are extortionate and you can't get much space for your money.'

'When was the shoot exactly?'

'I don't remember the day. Two – maybe three – weeks ago.'

'Is that the only time you saw her?'

He lowers his head, seemingly ashamed, and places a hand over his face, rubbing his cheeks and jaw. 'No. I saw her yesterday.'

He's answered honestly; that's a good sign. I say, 'She wasn't here to collect her photos?'

He shakes his head, his eyes lowered.

'Tell me about it.'

When he lifts his eyes, he stares beyond me, at the wall. 'I feel so bad, detective. She was such a gorgeous girl. The perfect subject for a photographer. And she was so grateful when she saw her pictures.'

'When was that?'

'About a week ago. She said she adored them. I've never seen someone so excited. She jumped up and down, right here.'

'So, if she wasn't collecting her photos, what was yesterday for?'

'She was so happy. So, so happy.'

'You've said that already.' He's stalling.

He shakes his head slowly, closing his eyes. 'And so, so thankful.' He massages his temple. 'So young. Oh, God, what have I done?'

I lean forward. 'What have you done, Dean? Tell me.'

He finally makes eye contact. 'She was so attractive, detective. That figure she had.'

I cringe in repulsion and want to hit him. He's talking about a teenager, for Christ's sake. But I need his confidence, so I resist the urge to tell him how disgusting he is. 'I've seen her pictures. I know.'

'It could have happened to anyone.'

'*What* could have happened?'

He pulls a pitiful face. 'There aren't many men who could have said no. She was so thankful. Oh, but God, I wish I had.'

'You had sex with her?'

He nods.

'Yesterday?'

'Yes,' and he blubbers disgustingly, pathetically. I sit in silence, letting him absorb the dirtiness of what he's just admitted. I watch him and think: *This is the kind of man. The kind of man who takes what he wants from someone more vulnerable than him. A user. An abuser. A man like my father.*

After several moments, he composes himself and says, more calmly, 'I'm so scared, detective.'

'Why? What are you trying to tell me?'

'I –' He pauses a moment, then realises how it sounds. 'I didn't hurt her, detective. I meant . . . I've got myself into trouble, haven't I?'

'Ah, so you're scared for *yourself.*' I spit out the words. 'I see.'

'Yes. I mean –'

'And why would that be? Could it be because you took advantage of an impressionable young girl? She was a *girl*, Dean. Just sixteen.'

He's surprised by the sharpness of my tone and swallows. 'I know.' There's a slight pause. 'It's just –'

'Just what?' I say with raised voice.

'Look, she said she was on the pill. She told me not to bother with a condom.'

'You didn't use one because *she told you not to*,' I mock. 'A fucking kid.'

'Yes.'

Pre- or post-mortem? I wonder.

He shakes his head and a pained expression returns to his face. 'I know I shouldn't have. I took advantage of the situation. I'm sorry.'

How good a liar are you, Dean Wicks?

'She was young enough to be –'

'I know, I'm sorry!'

'How old are you?'

'Thirty-six.'

'She could have been your daughter. Imagine how you'd feel then. A sleazy photographer taking advantage of your sixteen-year-old child.'

He winces. 'Yes. I know. If only there were words I could say to make –'

'I think you're crying for the wrong reason, Mr Wicks,' I say, disdainfully. 'She was impressionable, and you were in a position of responsibility and authority. She looked up to you. *Men like you*.'

'Yes.'

'Was the sex forced in any way, or was it completely consensual?'

My question surprises him and he shifts uncomfortably. 'Absolutely consensual,' he says urgently. 'She leapt on me the first time we had sex.'

'So yesterday wasn't the first time?'

'No. The first time was when she came here to see the pictures. She was so thrilled with them. She jumped on me and I kissed her. I reacted, for fuck's sake. I'm only human.'

'No,' I sneer, 'you're a man. So why did you invite her back yesterday? For a nice cosy chat?' I ask sarcastically.

He speaks quietly. 'I wanted to have sex with her again.'

'How many times has she come here for sex, Dean? How many times have you invited her here?'

He squeezes his eyes shut. 'Yesterday was the third time.'

'Ever give her any money?'

His eyes flick open instantly and he says, 'No.'

He sits in silence for a time while I stare at him. I want to make him feel uncomfortable. I want him to feel pain, and this is the only kind I can inflict on him without getting into trouble.

Eventually, he starts speaking again. 'I know. I should have known better –'

'Did you kill her?' I ask directly, sick of listening to him whine and showing pity for only himself.

Now he looks really scared. And I'm pleased. 'Absolutely not. It was very friendly. Afterwards, she even hung around for a while. We had a few drinks. I gave her a couple of beers. I know I shouldn't have, but she came across as so much older than she was. Christ, *sixteen*. When I say that number, it seems so perverse. So unreal.'

'That's because it is perverse. And it most certainly is very real. She's dead.'

'I fucking know that!' He tries to take a number of steadying breaths. 'Listen, we talked. We did every time she came here. We watched a bit of TV. We sat where you are right now. It was nice. We had a nice time. I could tell she enjoyed my company. I liked her too. Yesterday, she was – fine, and she left fine.'

'And she left when?'

'Must have been about six. She said she needed to go. We –'

'Go on.'

'Look, as she was leaving, she asked if she could come and see me again. We made plans to meet. She was going to come over next Saturday.'

'To have sex again?'

He shrugs. 'I guess so. I know how it looks. But, you see, I couldn't have killed her. I was going to see her again. Which I know was wrong, but I was going to see her again.'

'Well, I'm glad you're clear on that much.'

'But, honestly, detective, believe me, however foolishly or badly I've behaved, I *did not* kill her.'

'You used her.'

'I couldn't have hurt her. I couldn't hurt anyone, as a matter of fact.'

'But you know how it looks?'

'Of course I do. Isn't that obvious? Look at me. I feel awful.' He pauses, drops his head and starts blubbing like a baby. 'I don't want to go to prison, detective,' he forces through his sobs. 'I was stupid, I know that, but I didn't hurt her. She left here happy. I was going to see her again.'

'You deserve everything you feel,' I say.

He doesn't look up.

'And you deserve everything you're going to get. Did you see anyone after Fiona Cunningham left here at six o'clock?'

'Yes.' He looks deflated.

'And who would that have been? Could be your alibi, Dean.'

'Her name is Hayley Turner.'

'Was it a job? Were you taking her photos too?'

He clears his throat. 'No, it wasn't a job.'

'Who is she, then?'

'My fiancée.'

'Ah,' I say on his behalf. 'Well, that's going to make things rather difficult for you, isn't it?'

'Look, detective, do you need to tell her? She was here. I promise you she was here.'

I manage to stifle a laugh but smirk. 'Oh, I'm afraid so, Dean. You see, a young girl's dead, and I need to make sure you didn't kill her.' I turn my notepad to a fresh page and hand it to him. 'Write down all her contact details. Mobile, home phone, email, address.'

He reluctantly takes it from me.

'Everything, Dean. And be accurate.'

He begins writing. The very act of putting pen to paper seems to cause him physical pain.

'Would you be willing to offer a DNA sample?'

'Okay,' he answers, still writing.

'Come to the station with me now, provide everything we ask for, and then we'll see if you're able to clear your name.'

'Okay.' He hands me the notepad.

As I read what he has written, I say, 'And, of course, we'll have to see what Hayley Turner says. Just to be sure.'

He doesn't answer.

'Do you know where Fiona Cunningham went after she was with you yesterday?'

'When she was putting on her shoes, she giggled to herself and said she bet her boyfriend would be pissed because she'd kept him waiting for so long.'

'Boyfriend?' I repeat, surprised. Her parents were certain she didn't have one.

'Yes. Then she joked that she might dump him. She said –' he looks me straight in the eye – 'she said she preferred older men. "More mature", she said. Me, more mature. Imagine that.'

'How long till you do with it, you know, what you need to do with it?' Dean Wicks asks me, having just given an officer a tissue sample.

'Could be an hour,' I say. When I see his face relax, I add, 'Of course, it could be several days or weeks. Who knows. We'll have to keep you on tenterhooks for a while. Depends on how things go.' He's not relaxed anymore.

'When are you, erm, going to speak to Hayley?'

'Oh, she's already being interviewed by a colleague,' I lie. I can imagine him running out of here when we're finished, straight to her to try to make things better, and in the process completely incriminating himself. I will speak to

Hayley Turner later myself, but I won't let him know that. He deserves to suffer in every way possible for what he's done, which at this point I don't necessarily believe means murder.

'I think you should have other pressing matters to worry about, Dean, not whether your girlfriend's going to find out what a lying pig you are. After all, your DNA is likely to be found on the victim. We'll have that matter to sort out first.'

'I was with Hayley. She'll be able to tell you.'

'She might be able to,' I say, but add tauntingly, 'although she might not *want to*. And who could blame her, if she doesn't want to help you? Did you sleep with her, after Fiona Cunningham had left?'

He looks away, which is as good as a clear answer.

'Don't stray too far from your phone, Dean. Don't you dare.'

I open the main door and watch him walk away.

When I return to the MIT, DCI Lange is waiting for me, lurking in the main workspace and looking over the shoulders of several members of the team at once. 'Davis,' he says, 'my office.'

'Sir?' I ask when I enter the office. I don't sit down.

'First DNA match on the sperm found in Fiona Cunningham came through.'

'That's quick.'

'From a fourteen-year-old cold case.' He sits down and leans back in his chair. 'This brings back fucking memories.'

'Was it one of yours, then?'

'I was involved, yes. The only one like this I've ever known. It was like – the killer just stopped and disappeared.

He was a ghost. He couldn't have been real. That was the only way we could all justify it. There's been no trace of him since. Until today. He's been a ghost all this time, but now he's human again.'

'What was the case?'

'A seventeen-year-old girl named Megan Goldman. She was killed in her bedroom in the house she shared with her mother. Middle of the day. Her face was smashed in, she was strangled and she was raped.'

'Is there a reason you put raped at the end of the list?'

He nods. 'It was post-mortem.' He breathes deeply. 'He's back, Amelie. This time we've got to stop him. The killer's crept out of the hole he's been hiding in all these years.'

8

'I called ahead,' I say to the receptionist, holding up my warrant card for her to see. 'Richard Sumner said I could have some time with Mike Freeman.'

'Oh, yes, he mentioned you'd be coming. Do you want to take a seat and I'll let Richard know you're here?'

I'm in the staff reception area in the John Lewis department store in Brent Cross Shopping Centre. As I sit on the deep leather chair, I pull out my mobile phone and call the number that Dean Wicks gave me for Hayley Turner.

She answers after the third ring.

'Hayley Turner?'

'Yes, who's calling?' Her voice sounds hard.

'This is Detective Sergeant Amelie Davis. Do you have a few moments to answer a couple of routine questions, or could I arrange a time to come and see you in the next couple of hours?'

'Now's fine. I'm on my break. Otherwise I'll be home about seven.'

'If you don't mind now, then that'd be great for me.'

'What's this about?'

'Dean Wicks.'

There's a slight intake of air on the other end of the line. 'Is he all right?'

'He's not hurt in any way. You don't have to worry about that. Could you confirm your relationship with him?'

'He's my fiancé.'

'How long have you been engaged?'

'A year last Christmas.'

'And how long have you been in a relationship with him?'

'Three years now. Why, what's the matter?'

'I'm afraid he's got himself mixed up in something rather serious. Has he not spoken to you today about it?'

'No, I haven't heard from him. I've been working and my phone's been off. I'm working overtime to save for our honeymoon.'

'Can I ask when you last saw Dean?'

'This morning.'

'Where?'

'At his place.' She gives me his address, though I know it already.

'Could you tell me what time you arrived at Dean's apartment?'

'Last night. Around seven. Yes, must have been seven.'

'And were you with him all the time, from seven last night till this morning?'

'That's right.'

'What time did you leave this morning?'

'Half ten. I had to be at work for eleven.'

'Where do you work?'

'Champney's. I'm a beautician.'

'Was there any time when you were staying with Dean, between seven p.m. last night and ten-thirty this morning when he could have left the apartment without your knowledge?'

'No, we were together the whole time. Except when one of us was in the bathroom. We were together all the time. Why, what's this about anyway? What are you suggesting he's done?'

'I'm not suggesting anything, Ms Turner. I'm trying to ascertain where he was.'

'And I've told you,' she says with a slightly raised voice, 'he was with me. He couldn't have gone anywhere else. You have my word.'

'In that case, I'm satisfied,' I say. 'Thank you.' I know I should end the call now. That would be the professional way to behave. But the thought of Dean Wicks getting away with what he's done and continuing to take advantage of a none-the-wiser fiancée makes me sick. He hasn't called her, so he clearly has no intention of owning up. Which means it's down to me to say something. I need to protect this woman, whom I've never even met.

'Do you trust your fiancé, Ms Turner?'

'Sorry, what?'

'Do you trust Dean Wicks?'

'Yes. Of course I do. Why?' A pause. 'Shouldn't I?'

'I think you should ask him some questions. You deserve to know the truth.'

'What truth?' She sounds agitated. 'What are you saying?'

'A young lady Dean Wicks had in his apartment before you arrived has been found dead. I needed to ascertain where he was. I'm satisfied that he was with you.'

'Wait, what girl? He told me he hadn't had any jobs yesterday.'

'Oh, yes, I know. He wasn't taking photographs of her. At least, that's what he told me.'

'What do you mean?'

'I think you'd better ask him, Ms Turner.'

Now she sounds in a rage. 'No, tell me now! I deserve to know! What do you mean?'

'He had the girl in his apartment and now she's dead. With his DNA on her.'

'He fucked her?'

I don't answer. Her breathing intensifies and then she says, 'He fucked her. But – but – we made . . . Afterwards, we – no.'

'I'm sorry,' I say simply.

'Fuck you,' she says and hangs up on me.

I had no choice. I didn't want her to be angry with me and in time I'm sure she'll direct that anger where it is deserved. I feel sorry for Hayley Turner, for how I've upset her, but I've no doubt that what I did was for the best. A man like Dean Wicks isn't a man any good woman should want to spend her life with. *I've done her a favour*, I tell myself.

Women should look out for one another. They don't exactly have many other people to do it for them.

A door opens and a man appears. He's got thick black hair, a beard and moustache. 'Detective, I'm Richard Sumner.' He holds out his hand as he approaches me. I stand and take it.

'Thank you for arranging this,' I say.

'This way, please.'

He leads me into a corridor on which there are framed pictures of employees of the month and posters containing handwritten numbers: targets, units and dates.

'Can I ask what this is about?' Richard Sumner says as he leads me up a staircase that's reminiscent of a lavish hotel.

'I'm afraid not,' I tell him, stepping through as he holds a door open for me. He points towards the end of another corridor, where the space opens up. We enter it. It's a canteen, empty of everyone except a young man who's sitting by a window and an old lady who's preparing some food.

'Well,' Richard Sumner says, 'if I can help in any other way please just call. Mike knows where my office is.'

'Thank you.'

The young man at the table nods to Richard Sumner who then departs.

'Thanks for seeing me, Mr Freeman.'

'Mike, please.'

'Mike.' I sit down opposite him.

He's a young-looking eighteen-year-old. In front of him is a bottle of mineral water and he fiddles with it nervously while he listens to me.

'I'm sorry about Fiona,' I say.

'Thank you,' he says. 'You know, it hasn't really sunk in yet. It's like I haven't been able to process what's happened.'

'How long have you known her?'

'Since she started secondary school. I was two years above her.'

'And how long have you been dating?'

'Just over a year. Not many of her friends would be able to tell you that, of course. The thing is, she wanted our relationship to be kept a secret. She told me her parents wouldn't approve of it. I wasn't really happy about that, but she was kind of in charge. I cared about her a lot, so I went along with it. At first, she said it would only be for a little while, but it went on and on and on, and eventually I understood she wanted it to be that way or no way at all.'

'A year and not a word to anyone?'

He shrugs his shoulders. 'Well, *I* never told anyone, even though I wanted to shout it from the rooftops. Her closest friends knew, obviously. But I guess she had me wrapped around her little finger, so none of my mates know. She was gorgeous and she meant too much to me for me to risk losing her.'

'What made you think you might lose her?'

'She told me once. She said I mustn't tell anyone or –' he pauses for a moment to compose himself – 'sounds stupid, I know, and I should probably have stood up for myself, but I didn't. I wanted to be with her so much.'

'Did she ever tell you she loved you?'

'Yes.'

'And did you believe her?'

'Absolutely. And I loved her very much.'

'Tell me about the night of her murder.'

'She was supposed to come to my house. She sent me a message to say she was running a bit late – something about some photographs – and that was the last I heard from her. She didn't turn up.'

'Why didn't you report her missing when she didn't arrive?'

'I saw her post on Instagram. She was getting ready to go to a nightclub. I thought she'd come and see me today instead.'

'Was that normal, then, for her to make plans and not do what she said?'

'Yeah, sometimes. She was busy and popular. And sometimes she was asked to post things online, sometimes by companies, so she had to be flexible. Sometimes she didn't turn up. Sometimes she was just late. I had to learn to be patient. I had to learn to accept it, I guess.'

'Why put up with that?'

'I put up with everything.'

'But why? It's not really a way of behaving that shows much respect for you.'

'You've seen her pictures, you know how gorgeous she is.' He bows his head for a moment. 'Was.' While I'm giving him a moment, I notice how covered with freckles his forehead is. 'Every time we went out, guys came on to her. She liked it. I could see, I wasn't blind. She even flirted back sometimes. I think she wanted to get a reaction out of me, but, most of the time, I stood there like a fool. Maybe I should have shown her I was jealous, but it was the only way I could be with her, so I put up with the games she liked to play. She liked being the centre of attention. It was just the same with her social media stuff.'

'Social media?' I decide to keep to myself what I already know.

'She was trying to make it as an influencer. You know, on Instagram and Twitter. YouTube too. She liked people looking at her. Wanting to be like her. She knew how she looked. And she loved getting free things, which is what people get all the time when they've got a good number of followers. Even though her family's minted and she doesn't need any of it, it's insane. You'd be surprised how much stuff – and I mean expensive stuff – they get. Packages every day, sometimes. The more followers you have and the more likes you get, the more free things they send you.'

'Would you have preferred her to have behaved differently? Would it have been better if the online world wasn't so important to her?'

'Of course,' he says simply. He peers at his hands. 'But when we were alone together, she was so different; you've got to understand that. She was so loving and caring. She was . . . just perfect. She made me feel so happy. And I know at those moments I made her happy too.'

'How did you find out about what happened to her?'

'Rebekah, one of Fiona's best friends, Snapchatted me. Then there was a lot of stuff on social media. When something happens, we find out really fast. Everyone does.'

'Did you ever get jealous of Fiona?' I ask.

'No. I mean, I wanted to be with her, and I didn't like it when she was flirting and when she cast me aside, so I suppose my reaction to those individual moments could have been called jealous, but no, I wasn't *jealous* . . .' He locks his sad eyes on mine. 'I can see where you're going with this. I didn't hurt her. There's no way.'

'It just sounds like she didn't treat you very well.'

'She didn't. I can acknowledge that now because saying it can't sacrifice my relationship with her. But at the time – oh, at the time I accepted anything because I wanted to be with her. It would never have been a reason to hurt her.'

'Will you submit to a DNA test?'

Mike Freeman sits upright. 'Why? What do you mean?'

'Were you having a sexual relationship with Fiona Cunningham?'

His eyes widen. Like he sees.

'Yes. But – it was . . . That's a normal part of a relationship. Surely you can't –?'

'Did you use protection?'

'We used – she was on the pill. She didn't like condoms. I often said we should, to be safe, you know, to be sure. But, like I said, we did what she wanted. And she didn't want to use them, so we didn't.'

'When was the last time you had sex with her?'

'The last time I saw her.' His voice has a lilt of panic in it. He recognises the implications of the situation and understands the danger he might have put himself in.

'When was that?'

'Two days before she died. But you've got to believe me, the sex we had was normal, it was part of our relationship, it was what we did. I didn't force myself on her. I didn't do anything wrong.'

'Who do you live with?'

'My mum.'

'Father?'

'I don't know him. He left before I was born.'

'What did your mother think of Fiona?'

'She loved her to bits.'

'What about the time of her murder? What were you doing last night?'

'I was at home, alone.'

'Where was your mother?'

'She was working. She works in a local supermarket. She got home about half ten.'

'Did she see you?'

'Yes, after she came home,' he says. Then he repeats, more firmly, 'Yes.'

'I want you to come to the station now and voluntarily give those samples.'

'Okay,' he says. 'I'll do whatever you say.'

9

'Do you think you know your husband, Amelie?'

What time is it?

I struggle to open my eyes. Squinting, I recognise a faint red light in the distance. It's the alarm clock that's on the chest of drawers at the end of the bed. I can't see anything else, not yet, not so quickly after being awoken by the shrill ringing of the phone. I'm groggy; I must have been in a deep sleep.

'Do you think you know your husband, Amelie?'

The voice, it isn't clear. There's a dull metallic lilt to it, something muffled, words forming a question. Yes, it's a question, but I don't register the meaning of the words immediately. It's only the sound I hear at first.

'Do you think you know your husband, Amelie?'

My name echoes around my head. That's what I hear most of all. My name. The voice, it's talking to *me.*

And the word *husband.*

A few deep breaths, then I manage to emerge from my swimming head, asking, 'Who is this?'

'Who I am doesn't matter. What matters is your husband, Amelie. Or rather *who* your husband is.'

I glance to my left, expecting to see Edward asleep next to me. My husband. But there's just crumpled duvet.

His side of the bed is empty.

What day is it? I'm not sure, I can't remember, my head isn't clear yet.

Oh yes, Birmingham. A business trip. But he was supposed to be back last night. Where is he?

The darkness remains an enveloping force, like a cape, suffocating and cluttering my mind, making me more uncertain, not less.

I lean to the right, reach out and switch on the bedside lamp. Perhaps the light will help to clear my head. The sudden brightness stings my eyes, so I squeeze them shut.

'*I* know who Edward is, Amelie. But you don't.'

The words echo.

You don't.

You don't.

You don't.

I feel hungover, but I'm certain I didn't drink last night. *Or maybe I did.* I've been drinking too often lately, and yesterday was a tough day. Yes, yesterday was really hard and I needed to relax after the things I saw and the things I heard about. So I drank. I remember glasses of whisky. Mixed with Coke. I drank too much.

Even though I don't understand what the voice is suggesting, its sinister tone makes me shudder. *And who can this be?* All I can tell is that the voice is female, dull and quiet – metallic also; some kind of deliberate distortion perhaps, like in films or ghost stories when someone tries to disguise their identity. The effect it has on me is chilling.

'What do you want?' I ask cautiously, afraid of the sound, not completely sure I want to hear an explanation.

'I want you to answer my question.' There is no change in its tone. Perhaps it's unable to change. 'Do you think you know your husband?'

I sit upright, my mind clearing, bracing myself. 'I know my husband,' I say deliberately, not sure why I'm allowing this conversation to continue. I should simply hang up without a second thought.

Put the phone down and be done with it. Don't listen to another crazy word.

But I don't. *Because I can't.* Only I don't know why I'm drawn to the metallic voice, drawn to it like a magnet. There's something hypnotic about it, or at least the situation I've awoken to.

'I know Edward,' I say, trying to sound even more confident, trying to speak with force. I might not be believable.

'No, you don't.'

I swallow deeply. 'Who are you? And how do you know my husband?'

'I'm the fount of all knowledge, Amelie. All knowledge Edward-related, that is. And it's knowledge I'm going to share with you. I'm desperate to say more, but that's for another time. All I want to say now is, think carefully, think on your husband. Do you know him, I mean *really know* him? I mean, where is he now? Do you know? What's he up to, and with whom? And where has he been all the other times? How many more times, Amelie?'

'How many more times what?' I ask, oblivious.

The voice ignores me. 'What was he like when he was thirteen, when he was eighteen, when he was twenty-three? Ask him, Amelie. *Ask him*. How many times? Think. And prepare.'

'Prepare for what?' I ask, despair creeping into my voice. I can't conceal it. 'And what do you mean, "how many"? How many what, for God's sake?'

'Have I got your attention yet?'

'What the hell do you mean?'

Louder now: 'Have I got your attention?'

Suddenly, loudly, because I am baffled, I reply, 'Yes. Yes.' Desperate to hear more. Yet urging myself to hang up.

'Soon, Amelie, soon. Can't have too much excitement in one night, can we?'

The line goes dead, leaving me staring at my mobile phone.

In the light of the room, I find I'm alone and in the dark.

Pitch-dark.

Once Upon a Time

The hulking silhouette has become a curled ball, much smaller, in her bed now, next to her. The heat that emanates from him is unbearable, as if the bed is on fire, yet somehow she's shivering, she's freezing.

A hand reaches across the darkness. She can't see it, but she can sense it coming for her.

It reaches over her body and comes to rest on the back of her wrist, which is prostrate on the bed by her side. The hard, calloused fingers circle for a moment, a sharp pain stirring within her, but she holds in the cry that is desperate to be unleashed. Then the fingers travel north, slowly up her arm, over the elbow joint and then on the shoulder blade where they linger, circling again.

She squeezes her eyes shut. She tries to think happy thoughts. Memories of times before this started happening.

There was one trip, she thinks, when she was perhaps five, it was at least ten years ago, when they went to the beach, she doesn't know which one, somewhere that was a long car journey from their home. She remembers playing on the sand, with a bucket, a couple of spades, cupping the sand in her hands, throwing it in the air, the grains drifting down and along in the light breeze, the joy of something so simple. How happy she was. She flung what remained of the grains in her palms as high into the air as she could, squealing, giggling in delight. How the grains, compressed together, felt against the soft soles of her feet, between her toes. A kind of tickle. A kind of itch. Comforting, she thinks, it was comforting, as she sank into the sand.

Surely comfort will help her to get through this.

There is another memory, this time when she arrived home one day, maybe when she was eight or nine, and found that her father had installed a swing and slide in the back garden. How her mother had guided her through the hallway and dining room and out of the back door with her hands covering her eyes in excited anticipation. And there was some kind of countdown. Ten, nine, eight. She knew what was coming was going to be special. Three, two, one.

Delighted, she would spin on that swing, twisting herself as she perched on the plastic seat, more and more until the ropes became so taut that she could turn no further, and then she let go and relaxed as she was propelled in the opposite direction, circular, circular, dizzying, dizzying.

Circling and dizzying now, his hands on her skin, her head in circles, as waves of nausea flooded over her. Her head spinning in the darkness.

And she screams.

Screams and screams.

10

I've spent the past three hours lying in bed. I dozed off for five minutes. I'd had a horrific dream. Since then, no more sleep.

Edward isn't here. Which means he didn't return last night as planned.

Much as I've wanted to, I haven't phoned him, haven't called out to him. I haven't even gone downstairs. I've been too worried, energised yet somehow without energy. I'm concerned about the phone call and what it was suggesting to me.

That voice. It said so much while revealing so little.

Something is wrong, that's the extent of what I understand from the voice's message.

Just after 8 a.m., I manage to drag myself out of bed. I head straight to the calendar in the kitchen and put my finger on today's date. The square is blank. And in yesterday's space it says *Edward home*.

This doesn't make sense. If he's delayed, he always lets me know.

I try to think about our last conversation. Whether he told me about a change in plan. Maybe he did. *Why can't I remember the last conversation I had with him?*

I've been so busy at work. Now with this investigation and the memories it has reawakened, I'm struggling to remember. And the drinking – I have been drinking too much. I wanted to forget last year, but now it's started screwing with my mind.

I peer into the kitchen cupboard and immediately spot several bottles of whisky and gin, half empty, or nearly empty. There's a glass next to the sink. I pick it up and sniff.

Whisky and Coke. Yes, I was drinking last night.

Grabbing the home phone from the kitchen table, I dial Edward's mobile.

He answers after three rings.

'Where are you?' I ask, ignoring his cheerful 'Hello'.

'I'm still in Birmingham. Didn't you get my text last night? I've been held up.'

I hesitate – I *have* been working hard, perhaps so hard that I haven't been able to concentrate on anything else, and I certainly haven't been able to sleep properly, I wonder how I'm functioning at all – and then I say, 'Oh, I don't know. I don't remember. I don't think so. I wasn't sure, just wanted to check, that's all. I'm just so tired. Work's difficult at the moment. And it's so hard here when you're not home. When are you coming back?'

'Tomorrow evening, I hope.' There's a deep breath his end, then he adds, 'It's not going all that well, if I'm honest, but listen, forget me. You sound stressed. Is everything all right?'

Who are you? I want to ask. *And why did a strange woman call me in the middle of the night? She said you're not who I think you are!*

But I can't force the words through my lips. What would I sound like anyway? Some unreasonable, paranoid wife who can barely remember what day it is, let alone whether her husband is on a business trip. And Edward is my life; I don't want him to think I'm being unreasonable, and I certainly don't want him to worry about me. There's been enough of that over the years.

God, I'm overworked. I need to rest properly.

'I'm okay,' I finally say. 'It's just hard. Same as every other day.' I sigh. 'I didn't sleep well, that's all. I woke up early and my head still hasn't cleared. I'll be fine. I'll feel better when I see you.'

'Me too. It won't be long. One more night.'

'I know,' I say. 'It won't be long. I need to get to work soon anyway.'

'If I get back around ten, will you be home?'

'I should be. Depends on how things pan out.'

'What's been happening at work?'

'A sixteen-year-old girl was murdered, found in Hampstead Heath.'

'Oh, darling, I'm so sorry. Are you okay?'

'Yes,' I say softly, lying.

'You'll figure it out, darling. It'll just take a little patience.'

'I know you're right,' I say. He usually is. 'I know.' But this time I'm not sure I believe him.

'Listen, I've got to get to a meeting, so I'd better make a move.'

'I understand,' I say. 'I hope it goes well.'

'Me too.'

'Have a good day,' I tell him, not knowing what else to say.

'Are you sure you're okay, darling?'

'Yes,' I lie. 'I'm fine.'

'Then I'll see you tomorrow.'

'Yes,' I say. 'See you tomorrow.'

And that quickly, he's gone.

What did she mean? That's what I wanted to say, what I wish I had said. *What was she suggesting when she said I don't know you? Who are you and what is going on?*

My head hurts. Interrupted sleep or hangover, I'm not sure. My days have become too similar and without light. I arrive home from work, which could be at any time of the evening or night, unable to clear my head of the things I've seen and the memories they spark off, unable to think about anything else. I turn to gin and tonic, or whisky and Coke. It's the same every time. *Only a weak one*, I tell myself. *One won't hurt.* The small dose of alcohol makes me feel different, it helps a little, but not so much that my thoughts are blocked, so I decide to have another.

And so the process repeats itself. With each drink, the shot of alcohol gets a little larger, and by the final glass I'm probably drinking a double.

How many did I have last night? Five or six? I don't know.

Perhaps it was the alcohol, then. Maybe there wasn't even a phone call from a woman with a strange voice. Maybe it was something I imagined or dreamt, some kind of drunken aural vision.

I head back upstairs and grab my mobile phone from the bedside table, a beech double-drawer cuboid. The phone's screen comes to life. I select the call history.

It's there. I see it instantly.

So I didn't imagine it. There it is: a phone call from a number I don't recognise, one that isn't part of my contacts list. It came in at 4.15 a.m.

It was real. A strange woman with a distorted voice did call me in the middle of the night.

Do you think you know your husband, Amelie?

'Yes,' I whisper to myself. 'I know my husband.' Then I linger, thinking, and stare at myself in the mirror that's on the exterior of the built-in wardrobe door. 'At least I think I do.'

It can't do any harm, I urge myself, so I press the icon next to the phone number to return the call. The phone thinks about what it's going to do for a long time. I put it against my ear. It offers nothing but silence, but then it starts ringing.

And ringing and ringing.

When the call automatically cuts off, I consider my options. Ignore the call or pursue it to try to better understand what the voice was suggesting.

My head tells me I should ignore it. It was probably a crank call. I've got far more important things to worry about at the moment. Work won't wait for me to catch up; every moment spent thinking about something else is another moment when a girl's killer is on the loose.

But my heart says I should pursue it. *I can't ignore this. I need to know what she meant. The call history proves the phone call was real.*

I redial, but the result is the same. Endless ringing followed by automatic cut-off.

I decide to send a text message to the number. I don't want to sound anxious or concerned, I want to sound neutral.

I need to talk to you, I write. *I need to understand what you meant about him. Please, call me.*

Before I press Send, I reread my words. *Please* sounds all wrong; there's a sense of pleading in it. I delete the word. And *need* – no, that makes the phone call sound important, like it's bothering me. I change *need* to *want*.

I want to talk to you.

I press Send, hoping it won't be ignored. I have one more trick up my sleeve to find out who called, but I don't want to use that option unless I have to. I could get into trouble if I'm discovered taking that route.

Startled from my thoughts by the phone coming to life, I glance at its screen, expecting, or perhaps hoping, to see the unfamiliar number returning my call.

But it isn't the unfamiliar number.

It's work.

'Davis,' I say, hoping my tone has the professional resonance I always aim for.

'It's Lange,' says the voice of my SIO, or senior investigating officer. 'Another young girl has been found.'

'Oh, no.' Something guttural escapes my mouth.

'Sounds similar to the last one. I think we might be facing the start of something.'

I close my eyes and shake my head as I hear details including the body's location.

'I need you there. Now. Not in ninety minutes. Now. Get there and get back to me.'

'Half an hour,' I tell him.

11

Hendon, London

I can see the police cordon at the far end of the field near where it's bordered by a large wood. I'm following a muddy path that leads from the field, through a gap in the trees and bushes, deeper into the woodland.

Scene investigators are combing through the area, kitted out in white coverall suits, as I head to the police cordon, which is guarded by two uniformed officers. I approach them with my warrant card in my hand and hold it out for inspection.

'DS Amelie Davis of the MIT,' I say. 'Has DC Ryan Hillier arrived yet?'

He nods. 'Head along the path and you'll find him somewhere in there. Not that far. The body's only about twenty metres in, just as the path veers off to the left.'

I thank him and make my way along the path, my eyes skirting both sides, the bushes and weeds that line it, which would have provided plenty of cover for whoever did what I'm about to see.

'Ryan,' I say, as soon as he comes into view. He's standing back, watching as Daniel Emerson works with his team, some on their knees, some on their feet, searching the area immediately around the body and the wider surroundings.

'How are you, Amelie?'

'I'd be better if we weren't doing this again.' I stand next to him. 'What have we got?'

'Female, no ID on her, teenager, seventeen, eighteen at a guess, long blonde hair, party dress lifted up.'

'Like Fiona Cunningham.'

He purses his lips. 'Yep. Except this time underwear wrapped round her neck.'

'Who found her?'

'Dog walker. Middle-aged man by the name of Larry Carter.'

'Where is he?'

'Uniforms have taken him home. He was quite shaken. They'll take a statement from him there.'

'What time was she found?'

'A little after six. Good job Larry Carter's an early riser. This path's used by hundreds of kids as a shortcut to the local secondary school. Two hours later and she could have been found by an eleven-year-old.'

'Jesus,' I say involuntarily. I don't want to reveal any of the thoughts that are swirling around my mind, but it's so hard to keep my personal feelings out of this. 'Anyone see anything?'

'Nothing so far.'

I peer around at the scene investigators to try to get a better view of the body. Seeing another young girl like this hits me hard. I want to close my eyes. I murmur, 'She looks just like Fiona Cunningham.'

And they both look like I did when I was their age.

'Yep.'

Daniel Emerson repositions himself and looks up. He catches sight of me and smiles. Due to his size, it's an effort for him to pull himself up, which he does slowly, and then he comes over to us.

'Amelie,' he says, his voice as friendly as always. 'I was hoping we wouldn't see each other again quite so soon.'

'You took the words right out of my mouth, Dan. How does it look?' I ask.

'Everything looks very similar to last time. Even what she's wearing. Black underwear around her neck. At a guess, I'd say she's been dead around eight hours. No obvious sign of a struggle. We'll search every inch of the area. We won't miss anything.'

'Prints?'

'Some on the body, as you'd expect. Lots of footprints around the body, too. We're going to test, measure and photograph every footprint within a twenty-metre perimeter and cross compare with yesterday's.'

'Nails?'

'Nothing under them that's obvious. And we'll run the toxicology reports as soon as we can move her and see if she was drugged like Fiona Cunningham was.'

'Semen?'

'On her clothes and on her skin. Traces inside, too.'

'Any clue, however little, I want to hear about it.'

'Absolutely,' he says.

I take a final look at the poor girl. *Jesus, she's another one who's so young.*

'Let me know when you've got her in the morgue and after you've run some tests. You know where to start.'

He nods. He knows exactly what I want to know. 'Will do.' He moves back to the corpse.

Turning away, maybe to myself or maybe to Hillier, I say, 'I want to find this bastard.'

'You and everyone else, Amelie.'

'What if Lange's right?' I sigh. 'What if this is only the beginning?'

X Marks the Spot

I was born a normal boy into a normal family. My family and I lived in an average-sized semi-detached house in the south-east of England. My sister was born two years prior to my arrival and we both went to the local primary school, then the nearest secondary. It was a completely unremarkable childhood; we went to family gatherings, our parents hosted parties, we visited friends' houses, just like everyone else we knew.

I was quite a lonely child, but I was never alone. That might sound like a contradiction, and perhaps it is, but although I was always surrounded by people, I was never truly satisfied with their company. I always felt like I could do better. Even at a young age, I saw the faults in people almost as soon as I met them. That meant I always wanted more from the people I met and it was inevitable that they always failed to satisfy me. I quickly drifted away into my own thoughts, into my own world, thinking about being elsewhere, no matter who was in front of me or where I was.

Our parents were sociable. There were often visitors in our home and we often went to the homes of others.

My parents' best friends had a son who was the same age as me. His name was Gregory. Our parents made us play together from a young age, even though Gregory did little for me. Gregory became my best friend by default, really. I certainly saw him more than anyone else.

Over time, we did most things together, and I grew to be fond of Gregory. He was a perfectly likeable and acceptable child, but I was always at my happiest when those times of play came to an end and I returned home to re-enter the sanctuary of my bedroom, alone.

I didn't understand why back then. I understand perfectly well now.

I did the usual things that a child does, and then when I was a teenager I did all the things the average teen does.

I remember clearly the day I discovered sex, or at least when my interest in it was piqued. I was fourteen years old. My sister was sixteen.

My sister.

The change was so sudden and completely unexpected. I caught sight of her entering the bathroom one day. She had a towel wrapped around her body, hooked under her arms. Her bare shoulders were on display. Prior to that moment, I'd never noticed how tanned and sleek her skin was. Her legs, too; she had sharp calf muscles and they were of a deep, dark brown colour. It was late summer; she had spent much of her time outdoors.

She shut the bathroom door and I heard the lock click into place. It happened automatically and even though I felt shame, I was drawn towards the bathroom like a dog on heat.

I pressed my ear against the white door. I still remember how cold it initially felt. But then how it warmed as the heat from the shower spread around the bathroom. I remained still the whole time, holding my breath until inhaling was absolutely necessary, listening to every one of her movements, trying to imagine what she was doing in there.

The suddenness of the shower being switched off made me jump back and I quickly hid behind my bedroom door, which was opposite the bathroom, my eye pressed firmly against the slit between the door and door frame, waiting for the moment when she would emerge.

She eventually came out, the towel wrapped under her arms in the same way as when she had entered, only this time her long blonde hair was up and dripping wet. She went into her bedroom and pulled the door to. She didn't fully close it.

Feeling like I was light and drifting through the air, I ended up at her bedroom door and applied a tiny amount of pressure to it with my index finger, just enough to edge the door forwards a touch. I acted so slowly that she couldn't possibly see the door move; just enough so that I could put my eye in position and watch everything.

Everything.

She was rubbing cream onto her toned thighs. The sight of her brought on a moan which I stifled with a fist in my mouth. I bit so hard that I drew blood.

Something animalistic had awoken within me.

I watched her. For the first time in my life, I watched.

And I knew I had found my path forwards. It was a picture I wanted to remain in my mind forever. She was perfection.

I would make sure this would happen again. Again and often, I'd find a way.

And one day, I determined right there, even at such a young age, I would have her, and others who looked like her.

12

Rachel Adams's mother, Karen Seymour, is sitting near two small children, a boy and a girl, who can't keep still. But I can see they're providing her with a much-needed and welcome distraction.

Until yesterday, sixteen-year-old Rachel Adams also lived here, in this cramped two-bedroom second-floor flat on the edge of Golders Green.

Karen Seymour is on the sofa, her elbows leaning awkwardly on her knees, the twins at her feet. She leans forward, wiping a mouth, moves a toy, tickles the other's chin and ruffles their hair while we speak. Her eyes are drawn, pain written on her face.

'So you think this could be connected to the poor girl the news mentioned yesterday? She was blonde and young and pretty.'

I cock my head. 'It's possible,' I tell her, even though I'm almost sure it is, even without Daniel Emerson's confirmation of the finer details on which I'm waiting. Now just isn't the time to make the connection official. 'I can't be certain –'

'But you think there's a strong possibility?' She eyes me cautiously.

I hesitate before I reply, studying her eyes. She hasn't had an easy life and now it's going to be even harder. I need to give her something. I slowly nod. 'Yes,' I say simply.

'Motherfucker,' she mouths.

'My sentiments exactly.'

'How can you sleep with a fucker like that out on the loose?'

'I can't,' I answer honestly. 'Believe me, Ms Seymour, I want him locked up as much as you do. I want him to be stopped. We're going to do all we can to find whoever has done this.'

She leans back in the sofa and shrinks. She looks away from me. 'I know,' she says, her voice fragile. 'I know. I guess it's natural to be angry when something so senseless happens. There's no rhyme or reason. My Rachel didn't need to die.' Her eyes well up. 'She didn't need to die.'

'You're absolutely right,' I say, 'which is why I'm here. I know you haven't had much time to process what happened, but if you could answer just a few questions, it might make all the difference.'

She looks at me quizzically. 'What else can I do?' Then she glances at the twins near her feet. 'Quite a lot, actually,' she mumbles. 'I've still got these two. Have to be strong for them.'

'Yes, that's very true.'

'What do you want to know?'

'Was there anyone,' I ask, 'who might have wanted to hurt Rachel?'

'She was harmless,' Karen Seymour says. 'Absolutely harmless.'

'No friends she was in dispute with? No boyfriends? Gangs?'

She shakes her head, then says, 'No, nothing like that. No.' She places a finger near her mouth and then starts chewing a nail. 'No one,' she adds.

'Have you ever heard the name Fiona Cunningham? Did Rachel ever mention her?'

She shakes her head.

'Did she have a boyfriend?' I ask.

'No, I don't think so.'

'You don't think so, but you couldn't be certain?'

'I don't think so,' she says. 'Of course I can't be certain. I can't keep track of her twenty-four-seven. Not with these two.' She nods towards the twins.

'They look lovely,' I say.

'They are,' she says. 'Rachel thought so too.' She bows her head and begins crying.

I give her time.

After a time, Karen Seymour says, 'If only her bastard father hadn't left us, maybe things would have been different.'

'How so?' I ask.

'A man, you know. Protection. A father figure. It makes a difference. I know it does.'

'Sometimes,' I comment, but inside I disagree. Personal experience tells me otherwise.

'It does make a difference,' she says, stronger now and looking at me directly. 'Men, for all they're worth, and they're not worth much, help to keep kids on the straight and narrow. A single mum, one with a younger kid, much less two like me, she struggles. It's hard to keep track of what the older one is doing when you're trying to stop two little ones from throttling one another or jumping out of a window. I don't know, but much as I hated the bastard, I've always thought things would have been better if her father had hung around and helped me.'

'Her father left you when?'

'When Rachel was six.' She spits a look of disgust. 'Men.' Then she pauses. 'You know, when she was fourteen, I met another man, the first in all that time, and look at what he did to me.' She nods towards the children. 'Wouldn't change it for the world, of course. Look at them, they're gorgeous. But when he found out I was pregnant, he buggered off too, just like Rachel's dad did all those years ago. It was déjà vu.'

'Did Rachel's father keep in contact with her?'

'No, but about a year ago she started to act a bit strange, secretive like, and she eventually told me why. Took a lot of rows to get her to open up, but she did. We were close, see, and she didn't usually keep secrets, so I knew something was up. One day, she said he'd been in touch with her and she felt guilty because she'd kept quiet about it for so long. She understood how badly he'd treated me all those years ago and thought she was betraying me by the desire she had to see him. I told her it was all right, see him if you like, it's no skin off my nose. So she did. She started seeing him. She saw him only a couple of weeks ago, in fact.'

'Did you ever see him?'

She shakes her head. 'No. He never even tried. Knew better, I suppose. Knew I'd have given him a piece of my mind. They always met somewhere outside, not here.'

'Why did Rachel's father leave you, if you don't mind me asking?'

'Another woman.' She sniggers to herself. 'Isn't it always the way? But not before he roughed me up a bit a good few times. He wasn't a nice man then. Rachel said he's nice now.'

'He beat you?'

She nods solemnly, then quickly adds, 'But he never laid a hand on Rachel. Never. He loved her too much. Me, I guess not so much. She told me he was a changed man, said he promised he'd changed the moment he left us. I never wanted to see him again personally to find out whether that was true or not. Never really cared, but he must have been doing something right this last year – she was always so happy after she saw him, that much I could see clear as day.'

'You weren't worried about her being with him?'

'No, never. Like I said, it was only me he ever took his anger out on, and it was only a few times at that. We were together seven years.'

'Do you have contact details for him?'

'Jimmy?'

She smiles but sighs. 'Yeah, but only because I have Rachel's phone now that she's –' Her head drops. Then one of the children knocks into her knee and she lights up again, stroking his mousy-brown hair. 'Go on with you,' she says, forcing a smile. She turns back to me. 'Yeah, it's just over here.' She stands up and retrieves from the dining table the phone that, until recently, had belonged to her daughter. 'Here,' she says, handing it over. 'Password's twelve-oh-eight. Her birthday.' Then her shoulders shudder as the emotion overwhelms her and she collapses onto the settee. 'Oh, it shouldn't have happened, you know. Life's so bloody cruel. How could she have been taken from me?'

'I'm sorry,' I say. I know there aren't any words that can help her. Dealing with grief takes time. Time is all there is. 'It's not fair. I know it's not. I'm going to do everything I can to find him and bring him to justice.'

'I know, love, I know. Only it's just . . . it's shitty. It's not on. I fear for these two, you know. Bringing them into a world like this. It's so dangerous out there. What was I thinking? Everywhere you go, it's dangerous. I've always thought that, and now I have proof I was right.'

'If there's anything you can think of—'

'I keep thinking of her. Helpless. I know she would have called out for me. *Mum*, she would have called. *Help me, Mum.*' She closes her eyes. 'And the hard part? I'll always know I wasn't there for her. I'll never get over that, you know. There wasn't a damned thing I could do to help my little girl when she needed me the most.'

I lean forward and place a hand on her shaking knee. 'You weren't to know, Karen. There's nothing you could have done. You mustn't blame yourself. This is the fault of one person and one person only. Sick people like that, they can operate in society and remain hidden. It's only after they do something like this that they stick their head above the water, and that's when we have to pluck them out. We will, I promise, do everything we can to make sure we pluck him out. Or better still, drown him.'

'Make him suffer.'

'Nothing would give me greater pleasure,' I say. 'Tell me, was there anyone in Rachel's life you can think of whom you weren't so sure about? Anyone who stood out for perhaps the wrong reason?'

'No boyfriends,' her mother says. 'We were close, like I said. She would have told me if she had a boyfriend, and she never did. I never saw her interested in boys. Not in school either. She liked being here with me, with them.' She indicates the twins. 'We're a close family. We haven't got much, just each other. She loved her little brother and sister. She was like a second mum to them. Only when her dad came back into her life, about a year ago, like I said, did she start to go out more. She was usually cooped up in here, with us. That phone of hers was her main contact with the outside world. She didn't ask for much more. Us and her phone were all she was interested in. Family and that social media stuff. You know, who follows who, who likes you. She used to tell me all about that. Went right over my head, it did. Couldn't really follow what she was talking about, but I knew it made her happy, so I listened and just smiled and nodded, and she talked and talked and talked like we were sisters. Those were good times. Everything was so simple. In a way, I guess we were like sisters. I certainly didn't feel like a mum.' She is silent for a moment while she thinks, then adds, 'God, I miss her. I don't know how I'm going to carry on without her. She was my rock.'

'You've got these two little ones to focus on. How old are they?'

'Two.'

'You'll find a way. You're a strong woman,' I say, 'and I have no doubt that you'll get through this. You'll be a good mum to them like you were a good mum to Rachel.'

She cocks her head and glares at me. 'She died, though, didn't she?'

I shake my head. 'Not your fault, remember. Promise me one thing, if you remember anything from our conversation today, remember that one short message: not your fault. Never. Never, ever your fault.'

13

I reached Jimmy Adams not long after leaving Karen Seymour and her two young children. I called him as soon as I got to the car and he agreed to delay his lunch break so that we could meet.

I'm at the Burroughs Hotel in Camden where he works in the kitchen. 'Sous chef at the moment,' he told me when we greeted one another, hands extended, 'but I hope I'll make head chef in a few years. I wasted a long time as a young man and now I'm playing catch-up. It's not been easy, but I'm determined to succeed. Or at least I'm going to do my best trying.'

We're sitting at a window table in the quiet hotel bar, each with a glass of orange juice. It's a nice bar, well-stocked, lots of shiny dark wood and mirrors.

'I'm sorry about Rachel,' I say.

He shakes his head slowly, his body deflated. His face is heavily lined and he has thick, curly black hair. 'There's nothing else to say, is there? I got to show her this place, what, only a few months ago, and she was so proud of me. I could see it in her eyes. She was so happy, so impressed.

I'm glad I got to do that at least. Show her I wasn't a loser like she'd grown up thinking. Rightly, I might add.'

'When was the last time you saw her or heard from her?'

'We spoke yesterday morning.'

'And what did you talk about?'

'I was about to head off to work, so it was just a quick call,' he says, his eyes moistening. 'She let me know what time she was coming over today. She was supposed to visit me this evening. She was going to come to my flat for a meal and then we'd planned to go to the cinema. I had a gift for her, see. A sweater. I saw her looking at it on her phone one day, you know, on one of those, erm, social media things – you know, where they scroll through pictures of people posing.'

'Instagram?'

'Yeah, that's the one. She was always looking at photos on it; I was amazed it never made her go blind. We were sitting together having a meal one day and I saw her stop, kind of pause, staring at the phone. Her eyes lit up. She looked so happy. I asked, "What's that?" and she just shrugged and twisted the phone round. She didn't ask for it, but I could tell she was really keen on it. So I got it for her. Wanted to surprise her.' More solemnly, he says, 'Now she'll never know. I'll keep it forever, though. I'll never throw it away.'

'Like all memories, Jimmy. You'll never lose any of them, even though it's only been a year. They'll stay with you forever.'

'Too right,' he says. 'I'll cherish each and every one. I'll never forget her.'

'Karen told me about the break-up. When did you get in touch with Rachel again?'

'I can remember precisely. It was a day that meant so much to me. I'll never forget it. The twelfth of September last year. I found her on Facebook and sent her a message. Wasn't brave enough to call my ex, even though I'd had her number for what must have been three years. Got it from a former mutual friend, but I was too much of a coward.' He sniggers mockingly. 'Afraid of being rejected, I guess. I waited three years to do it, and I finally convinced myself to bite the bullet last September. I can't tell you how glad I am I did. Imagine if I hadn't.'

'What did you say when you made contact?'

'There wasn't much I could say, was there, just that I was sorry, that I had changed, and that I hoped she'd give me a chance to show her the real me – at least meet with me or something, just say a brief hello. Maybe, if I was lucky, have a drink with me and see if she might want to see me again.'

'Where did you meet?'

He sighs. 'McDonald's in Leicester Square. I know, I know, not very impressive, but I wanted her to be somewhere she felt comfortable, so I asked her where, said anywhere would work for me, and that's what she suggested. I'd told her I worked in a fancy restaurant, so I reckon it was her way to play a little joke on me. I don't know. I can tell you, it was weird sitting there with so many people coming and going, having that kind of conversation, saying words that were more emotional than any words I've ever said in my life, trying to reconnect with her, but we did it and I'm so glad we did because we ended up seeing each other a lot over the last year.'

'How often did you meet?'

'Sometimes weekly, every couple of weeks if not. Depended on my job. It's shift work, so the hours can be difficult, but she was patient with me. Had waited so many years, what was a couple more days, I suppose. We spoke quite a lot on the phone too, or sent messages on Facebook. We had a lot of catching up to do.' He winces and then squeezes his eyes shut for a moment. 'God, I wish I'd done it sooner. Had more time with her, you know, and really done everything I could to show her how sorry I was about not being around while she grew up – and to show her how much I loved her. I did try. I hope she at least saw that.' He pauses for a moment and smiles. 'Oh, we had some good times this last year; I'll always be grateful for that, as much as I'll always be sad.'

'Did she ever mention anyone to you, perhaps a boyfriend? Did she ever seem upset or worried about anything?'

He shakes his head. 'Nothing more than your average teen, no.'

'What did you talk about?'

'We generally avoided talking about the past. Instead, we did a lot of talking about the future. We wanted to travel together. We planned to go to Spain next summer. Tenerife. We thought a week away, our first proper holiday as a sort-of family.' He sighs again. 'Now that can never happen. She was so keen, so excited. I was too, if I'm honest. When she said yes, it made me feel like she'd properly accepted me back into her life. She was such a good girl, such a sweet girl; I couldn't have asked for more. Apart from more time, of course.'

'What were her plans for the future? Did she tell you? Did she have any ambitions?'

'She wanted to model, clothes and all that. Or something in fashion. She loved clothes. Not an easy thing when your family's got no money. Every time she came to see me, she stopped off in a shop on her way. Nothing expensive, mind you, she knew how to find a bargain, and she knew how to make it look good. She and her mum haven't had it easy, and I know I'm to blame for that, but she'd always manage to find something that looked stunning on her. She'd show me. On her phone. She showed me lots of pictures. She's a beautiful – was a beautiful girl.'

We sit in silence for a moment.

'I tried to make it up to her, you know, by giving her a bit of money when I could, not that I have a lot; some vouchers too, for some shops I knew she wouldn't normally go in because the clothes were too expensive. I knew things like that made her happy. I just wanted her to be happy.'

'Where were you yesterday?'

He offers a wry smile. 'I've been waiting for that one.' Then he leans towards me. 'Did Karen put you up to that one?'

'Not at all, Jimmy. It's standard procedure, that's all.'

'I know, I know. I'm sorry. I was here, working. Finished gone two in the morning.'

'Is there a supervisor who can verify that?'

'I'll introduce you before you leave.'

*

After I've finished speaking with Rachel Adams's father, I call DCI Lange. He answers quickly. 'What news?'

'I've identified an immediate connection. It might be tenuous at the moment, but I think it's something worth looking into: social media. They were both trying to make it as influencers. It sounds like Fiona Cunningham was more advanced, but they were trying to achieve the same thing.'

'Aren't all girls on that crap and constantly taking pictures of themselves pouting?' he asks dryly.

'It's possible, but beyond the crime-scene similarities it's all I've got so far. Might be nothing.'

'Worth checking out, I suppose,' he says. 'I'll ask Micah Ainsley to start looking into all things online, then. Lucky her.'

Once Upon a Time

First a silhouette, then a curled ball, then the hand tracing circles on her skin.

He checks that both her arms are by her sides, that she won't resist, and he climbs on top of her. Fear has paralysed her.

That's the thing about fear: you cannot react.

The swing and slide had made her so happy when she was nine. For years afterwards, he kept reminding her about how grateful she should be. Because he cared for her. Because he loved her so much. But he was only preparing her for what would come years later, for this. What he was doing – what they were doing – was therefore only natural, he told her.

For two years, he slid in bed beside her. For two years, he did with her as he pleased.

She's sixteen. She understands perfectly well now. He's lying on top of her.

She screams.

14

It's windy and raining. I'm walking, but I can't feel the ground because I'm gliding. My shoes float above the pavement, then above the grass. Then I come down. The grass is moist, I can hear the squelching, and there's a sinking sensation every couple of seconds, but I can't feel the earth. The wind is piercingly cold; it's hitting my face from the right, pushing hard against my whole body, rocking me.

And it's getting stronger, more intense. I push through, persevering, looking ahead to where I want to go. I'm not going to let the weather stop me. I wince, my eyes watering, and my body doubles over, as if I'm being repeatedly punched in the stomach, but I press on. Over the field, heading for the muddy path.

When I reach it, dripping wet, the rain even more intense, my feet scrape along it, but I still have no sensation of touch. I have a weightlessness and I glide along the unsteady path.

There's a mound on the floor only metres away. A white sheet over it, feet protruding from one end. Black high heels. Tanned legs, slim. A gust strikes and the sheet lifts upwards, first revealing a knee, and then another gust, so now the sheet's higher up, thighs, again and higher still, no underwear. Then the largest gust and the sheet flies into the air, tangling in the dead tree branches, and the sheet's quickly soaked through, and I look down at her naked body lying there, leggy, slim, blonde hair, blue eyes.

Dead eyes.

And then another gust, this one the largest but from behind me. It pushes my body forwards and I plummet towards her, falling down, down, my body stopping only centimetres from her, and I'm suspended over her, as if lying on an invisible flat plank, face down and she's face up. We're face to face, as in the morgue. I'm looking into her eyes when another gust hits, but this time I don't move, I'm firmly fixed, even though I'm struggling to get free and to escape from here. An invisible force is keeping me here, and her eyes spring wide open and her shocked expression gouges at mine, at the sight of me or something else, I can't tell, and then her eyes tell me to help her, please, *help me, save me, find him*, and I want to help, I want to place my arms around her and tell her it'll be okay, but my arms won't move, they're straightjacketed, because the truth is it won't be okay, it'll never be okay again, and I know that better than most people. And suddenly she starts to sink into the ground, her panicking eyes pleading with me, deeper, deeper, deeper, mud covering her body, blood erupting from her eyes, and I try to call out to her but I have no voice. Her arms reach up until all that's left is a hand stretching out from beneath the earth, and within seconds, as if a drain has been emptied, she becomes part of the earth and is gone.

My voice returns and I call out her name – *Fiona! Fiona!* – but the sound is quickly drowned out by the wind, which picks up in pace and volume, an approaching train, a locomotive colliding with the platform, and all the screams that go with people being run over, men, women, children, couples, defenceless, falling, unable to get out of the way, crushed, mixing into a cacophony of fear and chaos and destruction. And death.

All dead.

And that's when another body appears, again blonde and slim and pretty, this one with underwear wrapped around her neck. As I scream her name, my eyes spring open. 'Rachel!'

15

It's morning and I'm in the kitchen, thinking about the nightmare, struggling to shake it off, when I hear the front door opening.

It's Edward.

'You're late,' I say. 'You said you'd be back last night.'

'Didn't you get my message?' he asks, concerned. His brow creases. 'That's twice now. You really must have your phone checked. My flight was cancelled. There was a terrible storm last night. Gale force winds. I had to wait till the first flight this morning. Had to get up at the crack of dawn. I'm shattered.'

'What message?' I ask, confused.

'Your phone. I sent you a text message.'

'Oh,' I say, 'I don't know.' My phone is plugged into the wall socket on the other side of the room. I don't remember leaving it there. I was so tired last night. It was such a draining day. I don't even remember going to sleep.

I stumble over to my mobile and peer at its screen.

I sigh when I see it. 'Oh, sorry, I didn't see it.'

'Don't worry,' he says from the kitchen doorway. 'You must have been really tired.'

'I was,' I concede. 'It's this new investigation Ryan and I have been working on.'

For a moment, it looks like he's about to groan, but then he exaggerates a yawn and says, 'Long trip.' He drops his bag and moves towards me, reaching out. He's a handsome man, tall with tidy brown hair, dark eyes and a friendly face, and the sight of him still has the power to calm me. He hugs me and leans his head forward to kiss me, but, awkwardly, I turn my head and his lips land on my cheek.

'How was Birmingham?' I ask, embarrassed by my reaction.

'Good, thanks, in the end,' he says, ignoring the awkwardness. 'What about you? How are you feeling now?'

'It's not been easy,' I say, but offer no more details.

'Well, I'm glad to be home,' he says, holding me more tightly and kissing my forehead. The touch of his lips is warming. 'Glad to be back with you. Oh, I've missed you.' He places his nose in my hair, breathes in deeply, and squeezes me in another hug.

I cling onto him, not because I feel safe and secure right now, I don't, but because there's something familiar about him at a time when my life is filled with nothing but uncertainty and the unfamiliar. His hair and eyes. His shape, the broadness of his shoulders. The mint of his breath.

'What's up?' he says, recognising that something's wrong, knowing me like no one else does.

'There was another,' I tell him. 'Another sixteen year old.'

'Oh, no,' he sighs, and he rubs my shoulders. 'I'm sorry.' He takes a deep breath, then adds, 'It'll be okay. It'll be okay.'

'I don't believe that anymore,' I mumble. And then I bring my mouth up to his and kiss him, deeply.

'Does that mean you missed me too?' he asks when I stop, a cheeky grin on his face.

'I missed you,' I say. And I kiss him again. My whole body tingles.

He scoops me up in his arms and carries me upstairs and into our bedroom, where I hope I'll be able to forget . . .

Where I do forget, for just a short while.

X Marks the Spot

I repeated the same thing day after day. She was home, I was home, and I would wait for her to go to the bathroom and I would wait for her to come out of it, always dripping wet, always with towel wraparound in place. And I would position myself behind her bedroom door and see it all.

As my confidence increased, so too did the courage I felt in being there. Sometimes I stood on the other side of her door completely naked. So it wasn't long before confidence and courage convinced me that I could enter her room. Wait for her to be applying the cream and just appear and take hold of her.

I was in the grip of a fever, and that fever was a sweltering, unrelenting desire.

It had been long enough. I put my hand against the door and edged forwards, but something stopped my body from stepping any further, and I hated myself for that.

I hated my hesitation. It was my greatest disappointment, but right then I realised she couldn't be my first. The situation prevented me from getting what I wanted. There was simply no way to make it happen safely.

I couldn't let her go completely, however. I still felt confident and brave. I just had to be covert.

At nights, I started to enter her bedroom and stand over her as she slept. Sometimes she would be facing away from me, towards the wall, and I would gently stroke the skin of her lower back, the curve of her hips. Sometimes she lay facing me and I would crouch down and lean so close to her face that her breath tickled my cheek.

Her features hypnotised me: she had long blonde hair and, under her shut lids, deep blue eyes.

Oh yes, desire lay thick on me, like tar.

One night, I crouched down as usual and stroked the curve of her hip. She stirred, and then she rolled onto her back, and then she opened her eyes.

Her blonde hair. Her wide-open blue eyes.

And she screamed.

16

I'm awoken by the sound of my phone ringing and vibrating. Through the sleep in my eyes, I see it's now 9.30 a.m. Edward and I must have fallen asleep after making love. I grab the phone. It's a mobile number, one I don't recognise, and for a few moments I stare at the screen.

Have I got your attention?

Even though I don't know for certain, I know. She has my sleep-addled attention.

Edward's voice startles me. 'Who can be calling this time of the morning?'

'It's half nine,' I groan, pulling the phone towards my chest in an attempt to stifle the sound. 'Work,' I lie. 'I'd better answer it.' I shuffle out of bed and pull the door to behind me as I leave the bedroom.

I answer the call as I'm making my way down the stairs. 'Yes,' I whisper. There's something covert about receiving this call.

'Didn't think you were going to answer,' she says. It's the same voice. Female, something tinny.

'Why are you calling me again?' I say, walking into the kitchen.

'I promised I would. Besides, you didn't answer my question last time.'

'Yes,' I say forcefully, 'I did. I know my husband. Clearly, you don't.'

'Okay, then you didn't answer it satisfactorily. I'm going to give you a little helping hand.'

She wants me to say more, but I don't; I resist the temptation.

Eventually, she continues. 'Nice and snug, were you?'

'What do you mean?'

'Did I disturb your sleep? Nice and snug in bed – with your *husband*?' She spits out the final word; there's venom in her voice. '*Husband*,' she – it – whispers.

I swallow. *How does she know he's back, and that we were in bed?* I feel like we are being watched.

'I bet you were nice and snug and comfy.' She laughs to herself. It's a sinister sound. Something glottal.

'What do you want?'

'I want to help you, seeing as you're living a life so much in the dark.'

'Like I told you—'

'You know nothing,' she snaps, her voice suddenly sharp. And now slowly, she says, 'You know absolutely nothing. Now, get a pen before I change my mind about helping you.'

I should tell her to go to hell, but there's something bizarre about the whole situation, and there are questions about how she knows the details she knows, so something instinctive makes me obey. I need to know more. I want to know who the hell she is. So I grab a pen and pad of paper from the sideboard.

'Are you ready?' she asks.

I swallow. 'Yes.'

'Write down these numbers. Make sure you don't mix up the order.'

'Go ahead.'

'Ten, six, ten, twelve, ten, thirteen.'

I write down the numbers carefully, in large letters.

'Do you have that?'

'Yes.'

'Are you sure?'

'Yes,' I repeat, more loudly. 'But what do they mean?'

'The answer to your question is in the numbers, Amelie.'

'And what exactly does that mean when anyone's home?' I ask, exasperated and confused.

'Understand the numbers and you'll understand your husband.' She adds in a whisper, 'Then you'll know *everything*.'

'Edward is—'

'*Edward*.' His name echoes and gets louder, so loud I have to pull the phone away from my ear. Then there's some kind of static on the line, a muffled voice and, after a moment, the words regain clarity. 'Work out the numbers, Amelie, and you'll know *everything*. You'll know who Edward really is. You'll finally know your husband. But be careful, Amelie. This isn't going to be easy. *Be careful*.'

The line goes dead.

I don't move, just stare at the phone's blank screen.

'Is everything all right?'

Edward's voice startles me and I jump. 'Oh God,' I gasp, pressing the phone against my chest. 'You scared me!'

'It's just me,' he says, smiling. 'Your husband.'

I try to produce an artificial laugh. 'I know. You surprised me, that's all.'

He nods at the phone. 'Is everything all right?'

I look down at it. 'Oh yes, it was nothing. Just some details about the investigation, some things I'm going to have to look into. It was just Ryan.'

He suddenly looks angry. Then he steps back and immediately looks like normal Edward again. 'And they called you at this time to tell you that?' I try to look deep into his eyes, but he's moved partly into shadow. 'I've got to get in. There's lots we have to do.'

I'm not sure I trust my husband. The man I love. The man who saved me from . . . from myself.

From memories of him.

Although now he has returned. But what about the girls?

Who are you, Edward? There's something about the call and the woman's voice. I can't shake it. It's like she reached inside of me.

Somehow, she knows me.

As Edward places his lips on mine, my mobile phone rings again.

I wince, because I fear it could be her again.

Seeing my face, Edward asks, 'You all right?'

I don't want to hear that voice again.

'I'm fine,' I lie, placing the phone to my ear, expecting the voice, dreading its arrival.

The dread blocks out the first words.

'. . . another,' I hear but don't understand.

'What?' I ask, and I pull the mobile from my ear to glance at the screen.

It's DCI Lange.

I should be relieved, but instead I feel sick.

'There's another body. Same as Cunningham and Adams. This is out of control, Amelie. Off you go.'

Once Upon a Time

She's spent three years at university. Far away from home. Leaving was the only way it would stop.

As far away as she could get, in fact.

She's rented a small flat on her own. She hasn't made many friends. Just one or two girls she speaks with between lectures and seminars. She's studying criminology and psychology.

She wants to understand her own mind, and she wants to understand her father's. Then she wants to spend the rest of her life stopping people like him.

She fills each day in more or less the same way. There's always a lecture and there's always a seminar. In between them, she sometimes sits with the two girls – Claire and Lorraine – at a corner table in the busy canteen. They're her first new friends in a long time. The only other friend she'd had in recent years was Amelie, a girl she met during the summer holiday before starting university. Amelie was visiting from France and was only in the UK for two months. They had fun together. She returned home and they both promised to keep in touch.

They didn't.

She never forgot Amelie.

She doesn't say much when she's with Claire and Lorraine, spends most of the time listening to their gossip. They're nice girls and, for reasons she can't really fathom, they seem to like her. When they aren't together during the day, she spends the hollow in-between time at a corner booth in the university library. Reading, always reading, wanting to find out more, wanting to understand.

Often left wanting. More questions, not enough answers.

The rest of the time she spends in her flat, reading books, watching television, crime programmes, real-life and fictional, series after series following detectives who are trying to make right the wrongs of others. And in the evenings, she works in the local supermarket, sitting menially behind a till, scanning item after item, her mind going numb, the only time it can truly switch off and forget, the conveyor belt of goods becoming a blur, and she's barely able to make sense of the words muttered at her by the strangers whose shopping she's handling.

She went home for the first Christmas break, three months after starting the three-year university course, when he tried one more time. She left the next day, which was before Christmas Day, so Christmas was spent alone. She doesn't know her parents anymore. She never called again after that day and she stopped answering their calls. They've been dead to her for years.

Her father, because he –

Her mother, because she didn't pay enough attention. Or maybe she looked the other way; maybe she ignored what he was doing.

She doesn't believe in forgiveness or reconciliation. She refuses to believe in rehabilitation. She only believes in moving on and forgetting as much as she can. And she believes in punishment.

She's alone now and is used to living her life this way. It's only three weeks till the start of her final exams. A sense of impending doom – the end, and the choices she will be forced to make thereafter – is making it hard for her to focus. She's in the library, her head buried in a book, a pen in her hand, notepaper strewn across the desk. Her mind is clouded, she's unable to concentrate.

But she doesn't give up. She doesn't know how to give up. She's always been a fighter; her father saw to that. She continues forcing her eyes to scan the words, squeezing her forehead. She fights each word, phrase and sentence, and she puts pen to paper, the tip of her biro pressing harder and harder, indenting sheet after sheet, scoring the paper until the letter shapes are indecipherable.

Several hours later, her bladder full, her head aching, her ears blocked to the outside world, she pushes her chair back and stands. She doesn't hear the approaching footsteps, so the chair blocks the path of someone walking by. His feet trip over its legs, and he stumbles onto the floor, his arms outstretched to break the fall.

In just an instant, the block and muffle are broken and she's alert, completely aware of what's happened. Instinctively, she reaches out to where the stranger is crouching.

She asks him if he's okay and takes him by the arm, helping him up. She apologises profusely, is embarrassed beyond compare.

Getting up, he says he's fine, that it's nothing to worry about, and he turns to face her. At that moment, she stares into kind, sincere-looking brown eyes, perhaps the first male eyes of that kind she's ever seen. His face is nicely tanned, his dark hair wavy. He's older than her, perhaps five or six years older, a mature student technically, probably studying for an MA or a PhD, but he gives off a sense of radiant youth.

He extends a hand and introduces himself. She takes it and says her name, the one she started using when she joined the university, the one she legally adopted almost three years ago.

The person she has become.

'Edward,' he says.

'Amelie,' she says.

Seeing that she's still embarrassed by what's happened, he reassures her that everything is fine and places a hand on her arm. Her pre-programmed switch tells her to flinch, but the touch is so light and delicate, masculine yet friendly, an alien thing, that she doesn't pull away.

He smiles as he reassures her, revealing a straight line of neat-looking teeth, his cheeks ballooning softly, and then she laughs and says something silly, and he laughs and they laugh.

They laugh.

That night, she's sleeping when the silhouette appears. Like it still does every night. It lingers in the doorway, as always, and she understands its intent, as every night.

It's going to come towards her. It's preparing itself.

Her father is ready.

But this time it doesn't come any closer.

Instead, the silhouette remains in the doorway, a wide expanse between them. But whether out of fear or because of habit, she screams anyway.

17

I need to know who the mystery caller is. As much as I need to understand what her words actually mean, I also need to know her name. I have to put a face to that voice.

There's no other option. Being a police officer puts me in the unique position of being able to check whose name a phone number is registered under. This isn't for a police enquiry, but it's my only option.

As soon as Lange hung up, I dressed and left the house. No breakfast. Hillier and I returned from the crime scene in East Finchley a short while ago and I haven't been able to eat, even though I bought a sandwich from Pret on the way to the station. Images of another poor girl remain wracking my mind. Eating just isn't possible.

Hillier and I are sitting side by side in the conference room, a small team amid a much bigger team, members of which are busy in the MIT workspace just metres from us. We're sifting through paperwork, trying to make sense of the three murders we're investigating and trying to identify any connections between them. So far, they look like carbon copies of one another, but we're struggling to find any solid clues.

He picks up the conference-room phone when it rings. 'Hi, Kate,' he says and listens. 'Thanks.'

Putting down the phone, he says to me, 'Positive ID. Niamh O'Flanagan, seventeen. Originally from County Armagh. Living in London since she was fifteen. Her father works for the MOD.'

Having a name only makes it more difficult to deal with the situation. Putting a name to a dead person humanises them, makes them even more real, strengthens the connection I feel to them. Makes me more determined to help them and their families.

After a while, Hillier offers to make me a coffee so that we can have a break. Seeing an opportunity for a few minutes alone, I say I'd love one. When he's gone, I bring the desktop computer to life, typing in my password, and I reanimate my mobile phone, selecting the call log. I type the first phone number into the computer system and click search.

Just as I suspected and feared: not registered, so it must be a pay-as-you-go number, essentially a burner phone, one that someone buys from any number of retailers without a contract. A separately bought SIM card is placed inside it, making it completely untraceable and easily disposable.

I type in the newer number from last night. As the search loads, I go over what the voice told me. And the sequence of numbers she read out to me. I pull the piece of paper on which I've written it out from my pocket and stare at it.

I lift my eyes back to the computer screen. Search results: the same as the first. Another untraceable phone.

If she calls again, I suspect any future searches will yield the same result.

If.

I look back from the screen to the piece of paper.

10, 6, 10, 12, 10, 13.

I try to decipher some kind of sequence. Gaps between numbers, adding and subtracting. Repetition of the number ten.

Take away four, add four, add two, take away two, add three. There doesn't seem to be a discernible pattern.

'What's that?' Hillier's voice surprises me and I scoop up the piece of paper, stuffing it into my jacket pocket.

'Nothing,' I say, 'just picking my lottery numbers for the week.' He places a mug of coffee on my desk. I reach for it. 'Thanks.' He looks at me a bit oddly, so I ask, 'Do you play the lottery?' trying to distract him from any suspicion my behaviour might have aroused.

'No, I don't,' he says.

I nod. 'Maybe smart. Probably a waste of money, but I can't help myself.'

He sits heavily in his chair and leans back. 'Speaking of odds, what odds do you give us catching this guy?'

My face falls sour. I shake my head, deflated. 'More chance of winning the bloody lottery at the moment. He's a shadow, Ryan, nothing more. So what are the odds? I don't know, but whatever they are, they're not in our favour. We need something more.' I pause for a moment, thinking. Then, more to myself, I say, 'He's got to slip up somehow. We need a little luck on our side.'

18

'Tell me you've found something else, Dan,' I say, entering his base at Charing Cross Station. 'We need a bit of luck.'

'I've found lots,' he says from a kneeling position, looking up and over Niamh O'Flanagan's body, which has been placed on the investigation bench in the centre of the room. 'But everything I've found is the same as with the other two.'

'Shit,' I say.

'Semen, pre- and post-mortem, inside and out. Ketamine used to incapacitate.'

'It's scary how fast he's managing to act.'

'Three in three days. I see the mainstream news has started to speculate.'

'Speculate as in figure it out,' I say. 'As in cause a scare fest.'

'Well, they are good at that, I suppose.'

'Does the DNA match across all three?'

'Perfectly.'

'Dean Wicks?'

'Only in the first. And that was pre-mortem. I don't think it was him.'

'No,' I say, 'neither do I. Does the semen match the cold case again?'

'A perfect match. Yes.'

19

Ciaran and Loretta O'Flanagan live in an exclusive side street in St John's Wood. I pull up at the gated entrance and press the buzzer. After introducing myself, the automatic gate opens and I drive in. I park behind an Audi A6 and a Tesla.

As I get out of my car, from the front door of the house emerges a tall, slim man who walks down the steps with his hand outstretched. His chest is broad and his arms remain by his sides as he moves. He has a soldier's posture, carrying himself with dignity. 'Detective,' he says, speaking with a thick Irish accent, 'I'm Ciaran O'Flanagan. So glad you could come.'

'Thank you for agreeing to see me. I know you're busy.' I looked him up and learnt that O'Flanagan works in an undisclosed role at the Ministry of Defence.

When I get close, I notice how shaky he is. He appears to be much older than his forty-five years of age. 'I don't know how we're going to move on with normal life. Niamh was our everything.'

'You have my sincerest condolences.'

'Thank you.' He realises where we are. 'Ah, look at me and my manners, keeping you out here. Please, do come in.'

We enter the largest foyer area of any home I've ever seen. A corridor veers off to the right and there's a stately set of stairs at the far end. There's a closed door on the near right.

'Do come through.' He leads me along the corridor and into the lounge. The room is large and ornate. The furniture is antique-looking, but it's offset with all the mod-cons that can be expected from the rich: a huge flat-screen television on the wall, a music player in the corner, a large iPad lying on the sofa.

A lady is sitting next to it, staring out of the window.

'Darling,' Ciaran O'Flanagan says.

She stirs. 'Oh, goodness. Forgive me.' She stands up and shakes my hand, but her puffy eyes remain glazed over.

'My wife, Loretta.'

'Hello.'

'Pleased to meet you,' I say. 'As I've just said to your husband, I'm very sorry it's under these circumstances that we're meeting.'

'We appreciate that,' he says, after his wife fails to respond.

'Please, have a seat,' Ciaran O'Flanagan says. 'Can I get you anything?'

'No, I'm fine, thank you,' I say, sitting in an armchair. 'This is a lovely home,' I add.

'Comes with the job,' he says matter-of-factly.

'I find it . . . cold,' his wife says, her eyes still vacant. 'Or at least I do now, now that it's only us.' She stares into the empty air.

'My wife is understandably upset,' Ciaran O'Flanagan says. 'As am I.' He drops into an armchair on the opposite side of a large coffee table. 'I don't think either of us know how we're going to go on.'

'It's all so cruel,' his wife mutters to herself. 'Snatching her from us like this.'

'I'd like to try to establish whether we can identify any links between the girls. I want to try to find any connections between the victims in the hope they might lead us in one particular direction,' I say.

'How's it going so far?' Ciaran O'Flanagan says. Seeing that I'm about to resist, he adds, 'I know you're not supposed to discuss details of an investigation, but I can assure you, in my line of work, I deal with the most sensitive information in this country. I just want to know if you're close to finding the son of a bitch, that's all.'

I look him in the eye and understand. It will help him as grieving father if I reveal a little. 'No, sir, not at the moment. We think the same person is responsible for two other murders –'

'Fiona Cunningham and Rachel Adams?'

I pause. Fiona Cunningham's name has been released through the press, but Rachel Adams's name hasn't been made public yet. I wonder how he knows. But then the answer is obvious: in his line of work, he can probably find out anything.

'That's right,' I say, 'and I'm afraid because of the pace at which he's been killing he's managing to keep one step ahead of us.'

'Makes you wonder, doesn't it, how long it's going to last. Three poor girls and two other families destroyed like ours. I don't know how we're going to carry on without her.'

'I understand, and I haven't come here professing to have any answers yet, but for what it's worth, I'm so exceptionally sorry and I'm not going to rest until I have him in handcuffs.'

'I know,' he says. 'I know. But sorry is an empty word, detective. I want to hear the word *caught*. I want to know that monster's behind bars and unable do anything like this again. It won't make us feel any better that we've lost our daughter, but it will give us peace of mind at least to know that he can't hurt anyone else.'

'We are trying.'

'I can tell you what a dictator is doing right now in the Far East. I can pinpoint his precise location from my study upstairs. I can track him anywhere he chooses to go. Yet he's thousands of miles away. This man you're looking for, he's right here, under our noses. He's probably within a ten-mile radius. So there can be no excuses. He has to be caught. Promise me, detective, promise me you'll do whatever it takes to make the arrest and ensure the bastard goes down for what he's done.'

I swallow hard under the unwavering glare of a powerful man who, for the first time in his life, feels powerless and helpless. 'You have my word,' I say. 'I promise. I won't stop.'

'Now,' he says, 'what would you like to know?'

'You were assigned to your role here only a few years ago, is that right?'

'I was sent over here three years ago. Loretta and Niamh moved here two years ago, when Niamh was fifteen.'

'That's a difficult age to make such a big change.'

'She was used to it. I've been moved five times since she was born. She's lived in four countries. But she liked London, so that made the prospect a bit easier. Although she wasn't happy saying goodbye to her friends, I can't deny that. Fifteen is a challenging age.'

'Did she settle in easily?'

He turns to his wife, who remains silent. 'She liked London, but she hated the school we chose for her. I'm ashamed to say she truanted regularly. I can't tell you how frequently her school had to contact us to say she either hadn't shown up or she'd disappeared during the day, but it was a lot. She found friends easily enough, but they weren't all good influences. Some of them led her astray.'

'How so?'

'They didn't go to the same school. Niamh was being privately educated. They went to the comp down the road. Or, rather, they were enrolled there but rarely attended. Somehow, on the bloody Internet, I suspect, she met them and got waylaid. She wasn't like that back in Ireland, or in the other countries either. We never had a problem with her there. Here, somehow, she ended up with those girls most of the time, God knows where. We did our best to keep track of her and we tried to stop it from happening, but you know kids these days, they're so damned wilful and bloody stubborn. She was simply unstoppable at times.'

'So truancy was a real problem.' No connection there: Rachel Adams and Fiona Cunningham were both regular attenders to school. 'Is there anything else important about her that you think I should know?'

'I found dope in her room a couple of times.' He speaks the words in a way that comes across as uncomfortably matter of fact. 'They were bad influences on her, as I said. I forbade her from going out with them. We grounded her, but she snuck out. It was an ongoing battle. We didn't give in, but neither did she. She wasn't like this anywhere else. It was this Godforsaken city that did it to her.' He's angry, his fists are clenched. 'I fought and fought and didn't get anywhere. And now she's gone and I'll never be able to fight again. I'll never be able to make a difference –' He stretches his shoulders and twists his neck. 'You know, detective, when you have children, no one ever tells you how difficult it's going to be. And they never tell you how to handle things the day your grown-up child says *no* and means it.'

After a substantial pause, during which he appears to be reflecting on his words, Ciaran O'Flanagan adds, 'I was at work. My wife was here. It was too much for her to deal with on her own. She did her best. I did all I could, often from afar, but it wasn't enough.' He inhales deeply. 'We failed, detective. We tried and we failed, absolutely.'

'Do you know if she was trying to make a name for herself on social media? YouTube, Instagram and Twitter – did she have a presence on them?'

'Not a clue,' he says. 'Darling?'

Loretta O'Flanagan shakes her head. 'I don't know.'

'Can you tell me the names of any of the girls she was hanging around with?'

'Not personally, no, but there were five of them. They were picked up at night several times by the police, up to no good, so there'll be records you can access. I can't tell you the shame we felt the first time officers brought her home. By the third time, that shame simply disappeared and turned into despair. Do you know what it feels like to live in absolute despair, detective?'

Yes, I think. *Yes, I most certainly do.*

I steady myself and turn towards Loretta O'Flanagan who has completely retreated into herself, then say to her husband while looking at her, simply and clearly, 'Yes, Mr O'Flanagan. Yes, I do. More than you could ever know.'

20

The first four girls didn't answer my phone calls. DC Anders is going to keep on trying to make contact with them. The fifth, however, did answer my call. Her name is Laetitia Samson, a seventeen-year-old from Swiss Cottage. She has long black dreadlocked hair. Her initial reaction was *no, fuck off*, but I persisted, appealing to the side of her that wanted retribution for someone she considered to be a good friend. Revenge, I said, would only be possible if we got all the information we could to help with our investigation. Maybe she, Laetitia, would be able to help us find the person responsible.

She isn't stupid; she didn't believe she could do something vengeful herself, she didn't share the kind of delusional belief that so many others her age swear by.

She doesn't carry a knife.

'Guys, you see,' she says, sitting on the couch in the flat where she lives with her mother and younger sister, 'they think they can do what the fuck they like with you. But we stick together. That's why I decided to talk to you. Niamh was always there for me and I'll always be there for her. She deserves that.'

'Do you think your friends will talk to me? I haven't been able to get hold of them.'

She shakes her head definitively. 'Where we're from, the police don't do you no favours, you know what I mean. We don't snake. But I ain't snaking. I'm just helping you out for Niamh.'

'I need to know her. I need to know Niamh *as you knew her.* Her parents wouldn't have known her the way you did. Maybe in knowing her like you knew her, I'll be able to find an important clue. You might know something important without even realising it.'

'She was solid, was Niamh. You could always rely on her. She'd be here helping me in a heartbeat if I ever got stuck looking after my little sis. Wouldn't want me to be on my own.'

'How old is your sister?'

'Three. My mum works two jobs. Things ain't been easy for her. So things ain't easy for me. Sometimes the second job is nights. I only knew Niamh for a year and a half but I can't tell you how many times she stayed here keeping me company when the others just carried on doing what they usually do. Don't get me wrong, we're all tight, they're fun and all, but they wouldn't put themselves out for me. In this place, taking care of number one's everyone's priority. Niamh, though, she was different, so that's why I call her a *real* mate.'

'Do you know if she was worried about anything? At home, at school, anything to do with a boyfriend?'

'Nah, didn't have a boyfriend. Home, well, her parents were always bothering her, her dad especially, he wouldn't give her any space to breathe. Was paranoid as fuck when most of the time she was just sitting here quietly with me.

The worst we'd do is share a bottle of cider. But those times the police got us, that really freaked her parents out. Her dad literally went loopy.'

'Did you truant school a lot together?'

'Yeah, we bunked. Don't have time for that place, you know. But a lot of it was so I could be here to look after my little sis, so I'm not all bad. Mum can't afford childcare, so it's me a lot of the time. Not exactly what you'd call a choice, not that I'd want to be in that dump every day anyway. That place ain't gonna do me no favours.'

'Don't you have any family that can help?'

'A couple of aunts, but they're in the same position. They have young kids themselves, have to work too. No men to help them, it's all down to them. No one wants to steal to eat. And we don't like handouts, despite what people think and what those shitty newspapers write. My mum would rather work two jobs than live on benefits. I won't be taking none neither, let me tell you.'

'How often was Niamh here?'

'All the time. Too many times, I couldn't count.'

'When was the last time you were picked up by the police?' I know the answer already, but I want to hear it from Laetitia to test if she's being honest with me.

The seventeen-year-old thinks for a moment. 'Probably around a year ago.'

Test passed then. The other four girls have continued to be picked up regularly since then, but not Laetitia.

'What about Niamh?'

'There was one time, I think, when she was smoking weed with the other girls somewhere at night and they got caught.

After I stopped being out so much. Must have been about five, six months ago. But she backed off the other girls after that. Her dad sort of got through to her, and I had a word too. Don't believe in taking none of that shit. I don't get it. So she spent most of her time here with me. Or if we bunked, we went to the cinema or shopping centre. I don't have much money, but it's nice to look around. We'd try clothes on. You can fill hours just trying clothes on. They always looked so much better on her, though. Sometimes she'd treat me, if she'd managed to sneak a few quid out of the house without her parents knowing.'

'You're a pretty girl,' I say.

'Thanks, but it's the likes that count, and she always got so much more.'

'The likes?'

'Yeah, on Instagram, you know.'

'She was on Instagram?' Of course, I already know this – I've seen Niamh O'Flanagan's account – but I want to get Laetitia talking.

'Duh, who isn't? She was trying to make it. Everyone is.'

Instagram. Social media. I know that's got to be the connection between the girls. There's something about it . . . I just don't know what yet.

'I'm not,' I say self-deprecatingly.

Laetitia laughs. 'Old people aren't.'

'Oh,' I say through a smile, 'but I never really thought of myself as old.'

'Well,' Laetitia says with a cheeky grin, 'you could be younger.'

X Marks the Spot

I was surprised by how convincing I was, and also by how quickly she believed me. I jumped – the fright after she screamed was genuine – and then I screamed myself, quickly mumbling, petrified that I would be kicked out of the house – and she mistook that genuine fear as a sign of my confusion. She leapt onto her knees and shook me by the shoulders, trying to wake me, then speaking to me and encouraging me to wake up. Realising that she thought I'd been sleepwalking, I groaned something about where was I, what was going on?

Oh, sorry, was I sleepwalking?

The incident made me even more cautious, but I knew I wouldn't be able to go into her room again. I had to keep away from her, had to find the necessary self-control, and it was a struggle.

She moved out as soon as she was eighteen, had found a boyfriend and, much to our parents' disapproval, as he was three years older than her, she moved into his flat.

It didn't last; she moved out a year later, saying he'd hit her once too often, but by then I was gone, away at university, and home wasn't a place I wanted to visit often. To make doubly sure, I chose a university as far away as possible; I wanted to give family as little reason to visit me as possible, and I wanted to have a convincing excuse for rarely coming to visit them.

I had what I would term fairly normal experiences at university. I met a lot of girls, and I slept with a large number. I knew what I'd been doing at home was abnormal, so I thought that maybe having relationships with girls at university would dull those odd senses. Maybe sex would make me normal.

And, to an extent, that was true. I tried out my luck with as many different types of women as I could. I was a reasonably good-looking guy, quite athletic with a nice, trim physique, so attracting them was fairly straightforward, and in the end it became quite routine. In fact, while the sex was always enjoyable, the whole thing became rather dull after a while. They were too easy. There was no challenge.

I needed more. They weren't similar enough to my sister. They weren't young enough. They had to be exactly like she had been.

21

'Instagram again?' DCI Lange asks.

'Yes, sir, like I've said before.'

'So Ainsley's got to pick things up, then. She'll need a couple more to help her work on their online accounts. Pick a couple of the cretins and tell them to sit next to her, would you?'

'Cretins or colleagues?' I ask.

He peers up from behind his desk and gives me a sardonic look. 'Same thing,' he says and nods towards the door.

I've learnt not to bother.

After helping Micah Ainsley choose a couple of colleagues to build a small team to explore the online side of the investigation, I return to my desk. As I sit down, I see the light on my mobile phone is flashing. I'd left it on my desk before going to see Lange.

What time will you be finishing tonight?

Edward's text message surprises me. He doesn't usually ask.

I answer: *Seven. I hope.*

His response arrives five minutes later: *Table booked for eight. Will pick you up from station. Let's switch off, go out for dinner.*

This is unexpected. Edward doesn't usually act spontaneously.

Much of the day, while I'm focusing on my work, I think expectantly and keenly about the evening ahead, looking forward to whatever dinner plans Edward has arranged for us.

'Here you go,' says Ryan Hillier, entering the office in his usual good mood.

'What's that?'

'The list of Fiona Cunningham's close friends from her mother.'

I look up from the computer screen. 'Took her long enough,' I say, extending my hand to take the piece of paper.

'She's a busy person, don't you know,' he says, pulling an amusing face. 'You know, where to lunch today, where to lunch tomorrow. She has difficult decisions to make, things that take time.'

I smile as I place the paper on my desk and look down at it. 'Long list,' I say.

'Uh-huh.' He nods exaggeratedly. 'In order of preference, she told me.'

'Preference?'

'Best friends starred at the top.'

'Oh, right. Well, I'll take the top two, you take the next two, and then distribute the rest to some of the others out there, will you?' I jot down the names, addresses and phone numbers, then hand him back the paper. 'And make me a copy of that, will you, in case I need it later?'

'Already done,' he says. 'On the whiteboard.'

I'm impressed. 'Very good,' I say, getting up and heading to the door.

DCI Lange appears and cuts off my exit. 'Fucking circus out there,' he says.

'What is?'

'TV, newspapers, every god damned website that pretends to be a newscaster. They won't leave me alone. We've got to announce what we think we've got.'

'Which is?'

'I think you damn well know.'

I know.

'I want you to head a press conference, confirm what we know for sure. I've just scheduled one for four p.m.'

'Okay,' I say. I don't like going on camera, but if we warn enough people, then maybe we can save a life. And if we alert the right people, then maybe there'll be someone out there who knows something that can help us find the man we're looking for.

'Usual place,' Lange says, then walks away.

I step out of the office door into the busy MIT open space. People are dashing left and right, conversations at desks, conversations on phones.

'Sir,' I call after Lange.

'What is it, Davis?'

'Regarding what we have. What language are you happy for me to use exactly?'

He gives me a grim look. 'Say what you have to say.'

I nod.

Serial.

22

Rebekah Taylor is tall and slim, as Fiona Cunningham had been, equally blonde and equally pretty. She's my second appointment; the first, a girl named Steph Rowells, spoke almost as much as a hollow tube, revealing nothing of use whatsoever.

Rebekah Taylor sits opposite me in the coffee shop of the House of Fraser store where she works part-time. Nursing a glass bottle of Coke with a straw, she says, 'I still can't believe it, you know. It's like I think I'm going to wake up from a dream some time soon and it won't have been real.'

'When was the last time you saw her?'

'The day before it happened. But that's not all, we were Snapchatting until what must have been an hour or so before . . . it happened. She sounded so happy.'

'Do you know where she'd been that day?'

'She went to see a photographer. She said she loved her photos. I'd just had some taken too. We both want – wanted – the same thing.'

'What's that?'

'To be online models. Social media influencers. Instagram stars. We've been building our profiles for about the same length of time. We were talking about it one day, then we just sort of started doing it. We have a similar number of followers as well.'

'Did you use the same photographer?'

'No, mine was a bit cheaper. My parents don't have as much money as Fiona's and I only work here at the weekend usually. Fiona's parents have got shedloads, so she went for one of the most expensive. Although, if I'm honest, I think the colouring on his work could be better. You want it to be bright, see. Everything shows up that way.'

'Do you know when she left the photographer?'

'Oh, I don't remember, but she sent me a message saying she'd left and that he was cute.'

'Can you not check what time that message arrived?'

'Snapchat messages disappear. It's not like texting or using Messenger.'

'Oh.'

'From what she said, I think she may have slept with him.'

'What makes you say that?'

'She said she was tired, that she'd just had a good workout or something like that, and she sent some wink emojis.'

'Forgive the way this might sound, I don't mean it to be disrespectful, but has Fiona slept with a lot of guys?'

'A few.' She shrugs. 'I wouldn't call her easy. But if the opportunity with a good-looking older guy came along, and if it could benefit her in some way, she'd be up for it, sure. Most girls would be nowadays. Depends what's in it for us, you know?'

I nod but I don't understand such a way of thinking. 'Her parents are under the impression that she wasn't interested in boys.'

'She wasn't. But her parents are wrong. She was only interested in *men*. Boys our age have so little experience and they have so little they can offer us.' She leans forward. 'Look, you mustn't tell her parents, they'd be crushed, but all girls our age go for men with nice cars and their own money, guys who can give us something in return.'

'By men, you mean . . .?'

'Could be twenty-one, could be thirty-one. Anything, just not a kid from school. Look, if she shagged – sorry, I don't mean to sound like a bitch, but it's the right word – if she'd got with the photographer, I could understand why. He might give her pics to her for free or he might take some for free in the future or use her pics or her for some of his work.'

'Didn't she have a regular boyfriend?'

She nods and speaks quietly, as if we're being watched. 'She did. But it wasn't exactly official. He was only eighteen, which is way too young for public knowledge, and – how can I put this without sounding like a complete spoilt bitch –'

'Oh, don't worry about *sounding* like a spoilt bitch,' I say. She doesn't recognise the sarcasm.

'He was like her soulmate. She sort of loved him, you know. Had real feelings for him. But he couldn't offer her anything, see. He can't do for the likes of us what he needs to, like I told you earlier. So she saw him but saw him quietly so that people wouldn't know, and she saw the others on the side. You know, the ones who had something more to offer her. Last time we all went out, he got quite angry actually.'

'Angry in what way?'

'Oh, a bit of pushing and shoving, you know. She slapped him at the end of it all. That embarrassed him.'

'Who slapped him?'

'Fiona.'

'When was this?'

'Last Saturday. You know, I thought he was going to punch her. Looked like he could have kill –' She thinks for a moment. 'Sorry, I shouldn't have said that.' She pauses, then adds, 'I miss her, you know.'

'I know,' I say.

Looked like he could have killed her.

'I know,' I repeat.

X Marks the Spot

I almost got married when I was twenty-one. I came out of university and moved into a flat in the same area. I couldn't bring myself to go back home.

I continued having one-night stands, seeking nothing but self-pleasure, but I had changed. I still longed for girls like she had been. I wondered whether a real relationship would quell what was forever stirring within me, maybe it would offer me something more, maybe it would fulfil me and help me be normal, so I sought out a nice girl, one I thought was the right kind to play home with. And she was really nice, so much so that I started to believe in the kind of life we were sharing. Working in the day, spending time with her in the evenings and at the weekends. Over time, I even started to miss her when we weren't together, and I found myself smiling involuntarily when she appeared or when I thought about her.

One day, after we'd had a walk in the park and dinner in a restaurant, we were lying on the sofa, her head on my chest, and the words came out of my mouth quite unexpectedly.

Let's get married.

It wasn't what I wanted; it was more a feeling, or a sense. It made no sense.

She was lovely about it, but she was also sensible and practical, and she told me no. She hugged me tighter and expressed all kinds of feelings for me, but no, we shouldn't get married now, she told me, we should wait.

I felt so small as I lay there, though, and helpless, because I couldn't get up with her lying on me. I was trapped. In truth, I wanted nothing more than to fling her off me and walk out of the flat forever. Her rejection had enraged me, but it had also awakened my senses. *What the hell was I doing there?*

The next day, while she was at work, I packed up my things and left that place for good. Left that entire life behind me, work included. I never wanted to see her again. Something made me think I might kill her if I did.

23

'Tell me about last Saturday night. The fifth of October.'

'I don't know what you mean,' Mike Freeman says.

We've brought him in for questioning and he sits opposite Ryan Hillier and me in an interview room.

'I think you know what I mean,' I say. 'There's no use pretending, Mike. Fiona's friend, Rebekah Taylor, has told us what happened.'

'I didn't do anything to her,' he suddenly snaps. 'She was the one who hit me.'

'Why?' Hillier asks.

'Because I'd got sick of her flirting with every guy who looked at her and said something nice about the way she looked, that's why. She was supposed to be at the party with me.' He pauses a moment and leans back in the plastic chair. 'Slapped me, she did. Said I'd embarrassed her – after she'd spent month after month embarrassing *me*. I simply told her to stop. Shaking her arse in front of them, she was, dancing like a tease, so I told her to stop. I said it loudly after she didn't react and carried on as if I wasn't there, and said if we were going to be together, then she needed to act like we were together. I wasn't a prop, you know. I wasn't something she could use to try to make others jealous and then play us off against one another.' He looks me in the eyes. 'That's what it was like with Fiona, see. That's who she was. Or who she became, at least. Since she started to get a following. You know, since she started to try to be a personality. Wasn't much of a personality – less like a person, really. It was all better till she started that online crap.'

I lean forward, elbows on the table that separates us. 'Did you kill her, Mike?'

He winces as if in pain. 'No. No, I loved her.'

'Even though she treated you that badly?'

'Yes.' He looks thoughtfully at me. 'Yes, even then. I just wanted her to treat me properly. I just – I wanted to feel like her boyfriend.'

24

The lectern has been placed outside the station and there's a group of press huddled awkwardly in front of it. I peer out of the window, looking down on the group as I ready myself to go outside and speak words that have the potential to stoke even more fear into the residents of North London. It's not something I want to do, but I understand the risk involved in press conferences such as this one. There's a fine line between saying enough to make people cautious and scaring the wits out of everyone so that a community lives in fear.

'Ready,' Lange says. It's not a question, rather an instruction to get moving.

'Yes,' I say, for my own benefit.

I make my way out of the conference room, clipboard in hand. On it is my speech; I intend to stick to a script, although I know I'll have to speak freely when answering questions at the end.

Lange is ahead of me as we make our way down the stairs. 'Limit press questions to five,' he instructs. 'And,' he adds, pausing at the bottom of the stairs, turning back towards me, 'don't fucking scare anyone. That's the last thing I need. The mayor has already started chasing my tail about how this could possibly be happening so fast while we haven't a clue; I don't want him to have another reason to take another bite. That leftist scumbag is always on the lookout to chew at me, so don't give him any more reasons to do so. Use the word serial, fine, urge caution, yes, and stick to the script.'

'Of course,' I say, nodding.

He turns, opens the door and walks into the foyer. I follow, catching the door to let myself out of the stairwell.

He walks out of the station and takes the steps to the right. The press huddle and lectern are straight ahead. He's going to watch from the sidelines, I can see.

I brace myself and then step towards the double doors. I'm not sure where he has appeared from, but suddenly Hillier is by my side and opening the door for me. 'Bit of moral support,' he whispers as he holds the door. 'Or doorman's duties, as he's not going to do it for sure.' He nods over to Lange. 'Good luck.'

'Thanks,' I say.

Hillier hangs back and to the side, out of camera view, as I step down towards the lectern.

'Good afternoon,' I say as I arrive at the microphone. I adjust it so that it's closer to my mouth. 'Thank you for coming. I have a brief statement to make and then I'll have time to take only a few questions. We're at an important stage in our investigation and I know there are a lot of rumours circulating online and in the press, so I wanted to come here today to address some of the speculation that we've seen today and yesterday.'

I open the folder and follow the words. *Eye contact*, I tell myself. *Read, but keep lifting your eyes and look at the cameras. Try to appear personable but serious, someone the public can trust. If they trust you, they are more inclined to listen to you, and they may be more inclined to help you if they have suspicions about someone.*

'On Saturday the twelfth of October, the body of a sixteen-year-old female was found in Hampstead Heath. She had been drugged, sexually assaulted and strangled to death. We believe she was abducted in the late evening of Friday the eleventh October while on her way to a nightclub, where she was due to meet her friends, and she was killed sometime after midnight on the twelfth. On Sunday the thirteenth of October, the body of another sixteen-year-old female was discovered, this time in Hendon. She had also been drugged, sexually assaulted and strangled to death. We believe she was abducted in the late hours of the night before, Saturday the twelfth of October, and killed very early on the morning of the thirteenth. And this morning, Monday the fourteenth of October, the body of a seventeen-year-old female was discovered in East Finchley. She too had been drugged, sexually assaulted and strangled to death, and we believe the time of death to have been late last night, Sunday the thirteenth of October. Each victim was discovered in a wooded area, parkland that in the daytime is popular with families and teenagers, but deep enough in areas of vegetation to make concealment of the bodies possible. DNA has been taken from each scene and, at this point, this, along with other evidence and similarities between each crime, suggests that they are all connected and are the doing of one individual.'

I pause for a moment to let the details of what I've said sink in.

'We are alarmed by the speed at which this individual, who we believe to be a male in his thirties or forties, has been able to commit these crimes. The speed has, until now, played to his advantage, but now that the crimes have been linked, we have been able to identify patterns in his actions. This means that we will be able to tailor our police resources – first, to more effectively deter him from committing any more crimes and second, and most importantly, to discover his identity, arrest him and make sure he is unable to hurt anyone else. We urge caution and especially ask teenage girls to avoid going out on their own at night. If you must go out, keep together in groups, and it is important to avoid dark and secluded places. All activity seems to be in North London at this point. We would also warn against going into parks or woodland at night time.

'At this point, I'd request everyone to respect the privacy of the victims' families. They are naturally going through a very difficult experience, and disturbance by the press, or unhelpful speculation or commentary on social media, could potentially do more harm than good.

'Anyone who thinks they have information that might be pertinent to our investigation should contact Crimestoppers – the number should appear on screen in a moment – or your local police station. Using nine, nine, nine should be reserved for emergencies only, but if anyone is in danger, if you believe anyone's life is at imminent risk, then please do not hesitate and dial nine, nine, nine. I'll now take questions.'

An instant buzz from the crowd of press surges forward and I'm momentarily overwhelmed by the voices calling out to me. Unable to hear a distinct question, I raise a hand. 'One at a time, please.' Then I point to a reporter near the front and say, 'Yes?'

As per Lange's instructions, I answer only five questions – they turn out to be the usual kind: things I either can't say or have already said and need to repeat.

'Thank you for being here today and for your help in raising awareness about these heinous crimes. With your help and with caution from members of the public, I am sure we will be able to identify the suspect.'

Relieved it's over, and pleased with my performance, for that's what it truly must be when a person, even a trained police officer, has to stand in front of strangers and reveal such upsetting information, I head back into the station.

Hillier is there to hold the door open for me. 'Well done,' he whispers as I pass him. 'You did really well.'

'Thanks, Ryan,' I say. 'Thanks.'

25

I always keep a change of clothes in my locker, although nothing fancy. I tie up my hair as elegantly as I can.

When I emerge from the station later than expected, at 7.45 p.m., Edward is standing next to his Mercedes CLA. I pause at the top of the steps and smile at him as our eyes meet. I come down the steps quickly, eagerly, like a schoolgirl going out on a date. *This is exactly what I need.* Hopefully, it'll be a welcome distraction from everything that's been on my mind lately.

I cross the road and we embrace. I hold him close, even though I'm slightly wary of him because of the phone calls. *Because of a faceless voice*, I remind myself. *A stranger, someone who could be nothing but a hoax.*

Edward is my husband; I know him like no one else does, and he's here in my arms and it feels so right. I know the love he has for me knows no bounds, like mine for him.

'Surprise,' he says. His smile beams at me.

'This is a surprise,' I say.

'I thought maybe this would cheer you up.'

'It has,' I say. 'It has definitely done that.'

'And well done. I saw you on TV today and you were brilliant.'

I smile.

He takes me by the hand and leads me to the passenger side of the car, holding the door open for me. 'Madame,' he says, with exaggerated grandeur in his voice.

'Thank you, monsieur,' I respond cheerfully. 'My car?' I ask before he closes the door.

When he's in and sitting by my side, he says, 'I'll order a car to bring you to work in the morning.'

'Where are we going?'

'It's a surprise,' he sings before accelerating down the road.

We arrive at François's, a fancy French restaurant in Soho. Its décor is beautiful and the food divine. Edward relaxes me, making me forget about the troubles that await me at work and in sleep, troubles that seem a long way from being resolved: these dead girls whom I can't bring back, a killer whose identity I'm clueless about, the nightmares that take me back, the night-time phone calls and what they suggested about my husband. The man whose hand I'm holding right now. It's a familiar hand, I know the skin intimately, but since the phone calls, something in his touch feels different somehow.

There are moments when he speaks to me that remind me of why I married Edward. He makes me laugh and puts me at ease. It's all so natural for him. The charm, the personality.

After a delightful three-course meal and a glass of champagne each, followed by several glasses of wine, we have a cup of black coffee, and then Edward pays the bill and we start to leave. We walk arm in arm. Even though we've drunk the same amount, Edward props me up; he can take it more than I can. The coffee has helped, and I feel more clear-headed than I did ten minutes ago, but without him I'm not sure I'd make it very far.

As we step out of the restaurant onto the pavement, it's drizzling lightly. Edward pulls up the collar of his jacket and I do the same. His car is parked on the opposite side of the road. We walk towards it, crossing the road. After only a few steps, I hear the screech of tyres and I stumble to my right, pulling out of Edward's grasp. A car, without headlights on, is heading towards us at speed. Edward is talking, he's not paying attention – I don't know what he's saying – while the car careers towards us. He's completely unaware of what's happening, lost in his words. He notices too late that I've broken free, but I manage to straighten up and grab him by his jacket. I push him backwards with all my might. He stumbles, tripping on the kerb and falling onto the pavement. The car is only a metre or so away from me, angling towards the kerb, so I know I can't jump back in time. Instead, I leap forwards, one step, two steps, then I dive further into the road, avoiding the car by mere centimetres. It speeds past. As I come to a crashing halt on the asphalt, my eyes align with the direction of the car. I see its red brake lights as it screeches to a halt and then its white reverse lights come on.

The car starts speeding back towards me. I'm tired, drunk and hurt from the fall. I know I'm going to be hit. With what feels like only seconds to spare, I feel Edward's hands under my arms. He pulls me up and drags me towards the pavement. The car – it looks like a Mondeo – skids to a stop. I stare at the back of it. There isn't a number plate and it's too dark to see inside. All I can make out is the outline of a person. Then, suddenly, it speeds off into the distance, disappearing around the next corner, and Edward and I are left gasping for breath, holding onto each other as if for dear life.

26

After we arrive home, I take a long hot shower. I need to wash away whatever it is I'm covered in. I'm not sure there's a word for it.

As the water runs down my body, I stare at my arms and legs. A few grazes, a couple of bruises, but nothing serious, thank God, but I'm shaking. It could have been so much worse. *So why is my body reacting this way?*

Edward was at first speechless. He immediately assumed it was something to do with my work, perhaps today's press conference. I came so close to speaking up and telling him what I was thinking. *It might be connected to the phone calls,* I wanted to say. *To that voice.* But I didn't say anything.

Once I'm out of the shower and dry, I wrap the towel around myself and go into the bedroom, pulling from my jacket pocket the piece of paper that contains a sequence of numbers that makes no sense to me. Staring at it, I urge it to mean something, but all I see is ink and a sheet of crinkled paper.

What are the numbers about? And what have they got to do with Edward?

Or perhaps this is a joke, a cruel hoax being played on me by someone obsessed with Edward, or maybe it's someone I've put away in the past who's seeking revenge. Maybe it is because of my work.

I shake the piece of paper in frustration.

Then a hand reaches round my body, takes the sheet from me and releases it, letting it drift to the floor, a leaf falling from a tree in the autumn. My eyes watch as it appears to fall in slow motion. I fear that he may see the numbers and know precisely what they mean.

Edward releases my towel with his other hand. He runs his fingers over my skin and with his right hand turns my head and brings my mouth to his. After a long, deep kiss, he says, 'Are you sure you don't mind me going away tomorrow?'

'That's come around fast.'

'I could try to cancel.'

Yes, I want to tell him, *cancel it.*

'No,' I say, 'I know it's important. I'll be fine.'

'Are you sure?' he whispers.

'I'm sure.'

He kisses me and leads me to bed. He places me on top of the duvet, and slowly gets on top of me.

Our lovemaking is deep, passionate. I get lost in his body.

My Edward. The man who the caller suggested is someone else, not my Edward.

My Edward. The man to whom I owe everything. He saved me; until him, I couldn't trust men. Until him, I never thought I'd be able to. I never thought I could move beyond what happened to me.

For a short while, I forget about the thousand thoughts floating around my head.

Soon afterwards, lying in his arms, they return and I think about the crumpled piece of paper on the floor.

They can't just be random numbers. They have to mean something.

'Why don't you ever talk about your childhood?' I ask.

I feel his body stiffen. 'Well . . .' he says, but he doesn't finish the sentence.

I slowly sit up and face him. 'And the years before we met. You've always said so little about them.'

'Well,' he repeats and lifts himself into a sitting position. He leans against the headboard. 'I don't talk about my past, Amelie, because – well, because I don't want to.'

He can see I'm about to interrupt, so he holds up a hand.

'You know better than most people how events from your past can shape a person. How they can affect you and dictate your life every single day. Some people open up and talk and seek help to deal with those things. Other people close up and are able to compartmentalise and carry on with life. I don't talk about my past, Amelie, because I don't want to. I don't want to remember. I have compartmentalised. You opened up to me and I know how important that was to you and I know how special it is that you trusted me enough to do that. I am so pleased it was me. But you opened up because you needed to. You couldn't escape your father's shadow. I'm so glad I was able to help you escape. But I've escaped my shadows. I don't need any help. That's why I don't talk about them.' He puts out a hand and touches my knee. 'You always seemed to understand that. I hope you still understand now.' He looks me deep in the eyes, searching.

I smile at him. 'I understand,' I say. I did, I really did, but I'm not sure I do anymore.

Once Upon a Time

She said *no* time after time after time. He came to the library every day. Sometimes twice a day. He asked her to go out for a coffee, a milk shake, a light lunch, a meal. No, she said. She always said no. Yet he persisted, with each rejection his humour seeming to improve even more. And with each reaction to rejection, he made her laugh more and more.

On the day of her final exam, knowing she might never see him again, she said yes. She had never been spontaneous before, but today, with a sense of finality upon her, she decided to be. A coffee. Just a coffee. But coffee became coffee and cake, and that led to a salad, and that led to a walk on the pier, and that led to more time together.

She has learnt to trust him. It's taken her a long time to reach the point when she can speak openly to him, but he makes her feel relaxed and they're getting to know one another quickly. No one has ever known her like this.

It's on their second anniversary that she decides to tell him. Words she's never said aloud to anyone before. Something she never thought she'd be able to say to a man. She realises she won't ever tell him everything, but she will say enough.

She pours them a glass of wine each and they sit on the sofa facing one another. She wants to look into his eyes while she says the words. She needs to see him to feel the comfort that is always offered by his loving eyes. She needs that comfort now more than ever.

Somehow, she manages to force the first words out. They start to flow, as she tightly clutches her wine glass, half conscious that it might shatter under the force of her grip. And she doesn't hear what she says, not really, but the words are continuous, which hopefully means they are coherent, and he's nodding his head, which hopefully means she's making sense. And when she stops, he puts his glass on the coffee table and reaches around her, pulling her close to him. He offers a comforting squeeze, his voice a vibration that soothes, and she knows she's made the right choice, that this is the only man who can help her heal.

She hears the question clearly. He pulls back and he's smiling. And she smiles back at him. And she says yes, she'll be his wife.

That night, as she sleeps, the silhouette appears in the doorway, as it still always does. It takes a step forwards, but this time the step is tentative. Then, after a pause, it backs up. It disappears.

She opens her mouth to scream.

Only this time without success.

27

'Are you sure everything's all right?' Hillier asks me.

'Fine.' It's a lie. I know it's a lie. But I don't want to talk about what happened last night. I feel exposed enough already. I want to deal with it myself.

I've sent some uniformed officers to the restaurant and the surrounding buildings to try to obtain any CCTV footage from last night that might show the car as it tried to run us down.

It was a dark car, I told them. *It looked like a Mondeo. That's all I could tell from what I saw. Its headlights were off. No number plates that I could see, I think they'd been removed. I couldn't see inside. Just a silhouette. It looked like there was one person inside. That's all.*

'It must have been horrible,' Hillier says, concerned. 'Thank God you're unharmed.'

'I'm just – more tired than anything.' I lean my elbows on my desk.

'I understand. You've been pushing yourself really hard for months now. There are lots of us here, you know. You're not doing this alone. You should get some rest. That's what normal people do.'

'I guess I'm not that normal, then.' I try to laugh, but it hurts. The side of my hip and knee are sore.

He smiles.

'No, there's too much to do here. Too much to figure out.'

He shrugs softly. 'It feels like we've hit a dead end. Everything we learn doesn't seem to lead us anywhere significant.'

'Okay, then being here makes me feel like that's not the case. That we might get somewhere. It takes away the time I could have to think about how badly this is all going. I guess I'm living in a fantasyland.' I pause and think awhile, but I can't get my mind off what happened to Edward and me last night. *Who could it have been? And why?* I wonder whether that car last night, somehow, could have been related to this case. 'There's danger all around, Ryan,' I say. 'Be aware and make sure you take care of yourself. You never know.'

He looks slightly surprised and then shrugs. 'I'll be fine, Amelie. Don't worry about me. I'm always careful. Some might even say I'm paranoid. Comes with the territory.'

I sniff. 'I know. I thought I was too, but after last night I'm not so sure anymore.' *I was centimetres from being run over last night and it was only because of Edward that I wasn't.*

'I've got a couple of house calls to make,' Hillier says. 'Should be back in a couple of hours. Will you be all right till then? Maybe have a longer lunch break. Just get a break – of any kind. Promise me you'll do that.'

'Go on with you,' I say, swiping a hand melodramatically in the air. 'I'll be fine.'

After Hillier has gone, I retrieve from my bag the piece of paper with numbers on it. I smooth it out on my desk. Looking at it, I'm taken back to last night in our bedroom. Before Edward and I made love. I hope he didn't see this piece of paper, or at least what's on it.

Yet the numbers would likely mean nothing to him – how could such an odd sequence of numbers mean anything to anyone? – so I don't know why I'm worried about whether he saw it or not.

I don't even know if the numbers have anything to do with him, or whether they're just from a crank who's winding me up. The voice on the phone might have been lying. She hasn't called me since.

I look again at the numbers. *10, 6, 10, 12, 10, 13.*

Some kind of code. It must be. Surely they must mean something. Could each number represent a letter, perhaps? I'm not good at puzzles like this – this whole situation feels like one big puzzle, or a mind game – but I decide to give it a try. Grabbing a pencil and a pad of paper, I try to give each number a letter value. 10 is repeated. Perhaps 10 represents a vowel, which I remember hearing somewhere are the most common letters. I scribble down some vowels – *a* first, then *e* – then cross them out and scribble some more.

All I achieve is a mess on the sheet of paper. It's hopeless. I have no idea. I tear it off, scrunch it into a ball and drop it in the bin.

The phone rings.

'Davis.'

'It's Trevor,' the voice says, the phone line crackling. I can barely hear him, but I catch the gist. 'There are four recordings . . . moment of what happened . . . restaurant. They can bring . . . do you want to come here?'

'Yes,' I say without hesitation. 'I'll be there as soon as I've made a couple of urgent calls. Can you wait?'

'Yes.'

Before I leave, I do what I realise I should have done yesterday. I quickly photocopy and scan the numbers, send the scan to my private email address and place the photocopy in my desk drawer, locking it. I put the original back in my bag.

I'm not going to lose those numbers. Even though I don't understand their significance.

But something tells me they *are* significant. Important.

Deadly so.

X Marks the Spot

Months passed and I avoided relationships, remaining both embarrassed and angry that I had exposed myself to another person.

I was struggling to find work, so I decided to return to university to study for a Masters. I knew that'd give me two years of opportunity to once again enjoy myself.

To focus only on me and my pleasure.

The thought of younger girls instantly brought on the right level of rush inside me and I realised I'd been wasting my time. I would stick to the eighteen-year-olds, even though what I wanted was girls who were sixteen. They would have to be blonde. Blue eyes. I needed them to remind me of her.

I was what I was, and I understood that now. Oh, and I felt revived.

The day I arrived, I noticed how different things were. I was only five years older than the youngest students, but to them those five years made me ancient in comparison.

The first time one of them rejected me was a strange experience. Then it happened again. By the third time, my confidence was in tatters and then, after two more rejections, I decided enough was enough.

The first time I did it, I didn't plan to. It just happened. It was like fate.

I had parked in front of a fast-food restaurant. As I emerged with my takeaway drink, I opened my car door and was about to sit inside when the most gorgeous blonde walked past me. She looked like my sister did when I was fourteen. She must have been sixteen or seventeen, just the right age. My eyes trailed behind her and instantly I knew what had to be done. There was an autopilot inside me that was switched on by her. It was all her.

She was wearing some kind of green sports trousers and a sweatshirt. The trousers hugged her like a shell. And there was a pair of sunglasses perched on her forehead, even though there was no sun in sight.

She went into the shop two buildings down and I sat in the car, waiting for her, occasionally sipping my drink.

When she reappeared, I watched as she strolled past me and got into a small car. It was being driven by a male who looked a few years older. As they headed to the exit, I found myself putting my car into reverse and following the short distance to what I determined was her house. I stopped across the road as they pulled in to a parking area. They got out of the car and she rummaged around in the boot while he lit a cigarette and smoked it.

I knew at that moment that I had found the one.

28

Officer Trevor is waiting for me outside François's restaurant when I arrive. I stop in the same place where Edward parked his car last night.

'What do we have?' I ask.

Trevor says, 'Camera on the restaurant doors shows you leaving. The one next door catches you pushing your husband to the ground. A camera outside an off licence several buildings down there caught the car racing towards you. And there's a petrol station at the end of the road with CCTV that caught the whole thing, but it's an old system and filmed from quite a distance, so isn't at all clear.'

He leads me into the restaurant where I was dining only a matter of hours ago. It's surprisingly eerie now that it's empty, except for a cleaner who's mopping the floor in the far corner and someone else who's crouching behind the bar, loading beer and wine bottles into a fridge.

'Mr Lafayette?' Trevor calls. He repeats the name, louder, after no one responds.

Presently, a diminutive man with patches of black hair on an otherwise bald head comes through a door on the left.

'We're ready now,' Trevor says.

'This way,' Lafayette responds, his French accent fairly mild.

He takes us along a narrow corridor and through a set of heavy wooden doors. We enter what might be called an office, but in reality it's just a messy room: boxes piled up, bottles and papers everywhere. Yet amid the chaos, there's a desk with a computer and a printer on it.

'Here,' Trevor says, pulling a chair to the desk for me and another for himself.

He clicks the mouse and up pops a video screen. 'The feed from the CCTV recording last night,' he says. The date and time start ticking away in the bottom-right corner of the screen.

'The quality's not that good,' I say.

'It's not HD,' he tells me. 'It's an old system.'

He moves the cursor to the right and the video footage winds forward. Then he releases it and the footage plays at a normal speed.

Edward and I exit the restaurant. Edward holds the door open for me and I step out before him. He follows me out onto the pavement. And then we're gone.

'That's it?' I ask.

'That's it,' he says.

'Okay, then how do we see the others?'

'Follow me.'

As we're leaving the restaurant, I glance up to my left, where the security camera is. I stand still for a moment. Then I re-live the journey Edward and I took, the one I've just watched, stepping through the door that Officer

Trevor holds open for me, and onto the pavement. I stop, replaying the moment in my mind. Visualising. The car coming from the right. Edward and me walking towards the road, then stepping onto it. He's on my right and I catch sight of the car coming towards us. Edward's back is partly to the car. I manage to push him out of the way. He falls onto the pavement.

Something feels strange.

'Okay,' I say, 'where next?'

The building next door is a solicitor's office. We're taken to a back room by an efficient-looking secretary and she plays the recording for us, handling the computer herself.

Edward and I step onto the road. At the top-right of the screen, two tyres appear. I twist awkwardly and press against Edward's body. He falls back onto the pavement, his legs in the air for a moment, almost comically.

The off licence, which is a few doors further down the road, has a recording that shows the lower half of the car. *It suddenly erupts forwards, skimming along the top of the frame. It disappears from view as quickly as it appeared.*

And, finally, the petrol station. The manager, a skinny man with a nervous expression and shaky hands, introduces himself as James Bower. We stand in his office, which is a small alcove behind where the tills are. A camera positioned to record the forecourt catches the road outside the restaurant in the background of the frame. It's at least one hundred yards away.

Two tiny blurry figures emerge from a building on the right. They are but dark shadows. They head towards the road. Behind them, even further away, a blotchy shadow approaches them. As they step onto the road, they disappear as the shadow behind them consumes them and there remains just one black mass until a small figure falls back onto the pavement and another figure, me, falls onto the road on the left side. The bigger black mass stops and starts moving backwards. Then Edward takes me out of the road. Then the car speeds off, towards the petrol station, and turns left into a side road, ahead of the main road on which the petrol station is situated.

The outline of the car is a little clearer when it makes the turn.

'It does have the shape of a Mondeo,' Trevor says. 'Like you said.'

'Maybe,' I say. 'It was that kind of shape for sure.'

We thank James Bower and walk back up the road to the restaurant, my eyes fixed on the area where the car was, and where it careered towards us. Arriving at the point where Edward fell, my eyes fix on the spot.

I lift my head and look back towards where the car was. Then I look at the restaurant door.

'You were lurking there,' I say. 'But—'

'What's up?' Trevor asks.

'Hang on.' I jog to the restaurant door and place my back to it. The car was to my right, out of sight and about twenty metres away. I lean against the door and it opens. I stand again under the eye of the camera and twist my neck so that I can see it above me on the left. Then to the right, where the car was out of view. I pull the door open and step through it. I look to the right.

To the right.

'Did you?' I say to myself.

'What's the matter?' Trevor asks, jogging over to me.

'I want to see the recording again.'

He looks confused. 'Which one?'

'This one.' And with a sense of urgency I add, 'Right now.'

'What, of you walking out?'

'Yes, of us walking out. Quick, show me.'

Back in front of the computer, Trevor replays the footage for me. *Edward comes into view. He pulls open the door. He holds it open for me. I step out. He steps out. Then we're gone.*

'Again,' I say.

Edward comes into view. Pulls open the door. Holds it open for me. I step out. He steps out. Then we're gone.

'One more time,' I snap, leaning as close to the screen as I can, 'and now, get ready to pause.'

Edward comes into view. Pulls open the door. Holds it open for me. I step out. He steps –

'Pause.'

I put my hand on the monitor and squint. *No . . . Surely not . . .*

But that's it. That's what happened. I can see it.

As he holds the door open, Edward looks outside – to the right. As he steps out, he's still looking to the right. As he disappears from the shot, he's still looking to the right.

Edward is looking in the direction where the car was.

He's looking at the car.

That means he knew it was there.

He's signalling it.

Once Upon a Time

Their wedding celebration is small.

Just a few of their friends. They were his friends, but now they're hers as well.

None of his family, but he didn't want to talk about them. None of hers either, so why should she be surprised?

It's a simple service. A registry office followed by a meal in a fancy restaurant. She couldn't be happier.

After being waved off by their guests, they leave for their honeymoon. A beach hotel in the Bahamas. There, one drunken night, he mentions children. It's early in their relationship, but he wonders what might be in the future.

She says no, maybe not ever.

He looks crushed but says he understands. She needs time, he thinks. He won't bring it up again. When she's ready.

And two weeks later, they return to the UK to start their new life together. She's working on the beat, on the streets, and when the opportunity to apply for detective branch presents itself, she grabs it. She doesn't get in the first time and is devastated by the rejection – it's all she's ever wanted – but Edward comforts her, and it soothes her the way it always does.

The time will come, he tells her. You just need to be patient.

And because it's Edward who says the words to her, Amelie believes him. She believes every single thing he says. Because she loves him and knows he'll do anything for her. Because he's the only man she's ever trusted.

The one who helped her escape the memories of her father. By showing her that men could be human, could be compassionate, could make her feel warm, not fearful.

Edward is right. There's no rush. The time will come.

When she sleeps now, the silhouette isn't ever there. She doesn't scream anymore.

29

My eyes spring open. I'm in my car. Instantly, I think about what the CCTV revealed and I spend much of the rest of the afternoon and early evening in a daze. I didn't dare mention to Officer Trevor, or Hillier when he called to ask how I'd got on, what I had learnt.

Edward? Did he really know the car was there? Could that be possible? And if he did, what does that mean?

I'm baffled, more confused than when the first anonymous phone call came, more confused than I am by the numbers I heard during the second call, more confused than ever.

Does Edward want to hurt me?

But the way he fell, how I spotted the car just in time and pushed him out of harm's way and saved him, it seemed so genuine. *Could it all have been a performance, an act?*

I've no idea how I came to be asleep in the car. My body feels sore, like I've been here for some time. My neck is stiff. I glance at the dashboard clock: *18.38.*

Surely I can't have been here all afternoon.

I need to stretch. Opening the door and moving my legs, I kick something. I peer down and pick up a scrunched-up can. Jack Daniel's and Coke. Looking deeper into the foot-well, I spot two more.

I've been drinking.

I look around and realise I'm parked in a playground car park. There's a bin not far from me, so I grab the three cans and deposit them deeply into it.

I think about the time. How I've lost track of it again. And I think about my time at François's today.

I saw it, I scream in my head. *I saw Edward watching the car as we left the restaurant. He knew it was there. He was expecting it. Did he plan for it to be there, for me? Did Edward . . .?* I pause. Even allowing it to be a thought makes me feel guilty, but I can't shut it off. *Did Edward try to kill me?*

I don't remember getting in the car again, but I know I'm moving. A long way, and then I park and walk. I don't know where I am. I drift around, places I don't recognise, walk and walk.

A couple of calls awake my mobile phone and me, but I don't answer them. I don't even check who's calling. I can't speak to anyone. My mind's too full. I don't have the words, I've lost my voice.

I seem to be losing all sense of reality.

And now it's dark and I'm outside my home, sitting in my car. Unable to move. I've parked on the road. Edward's car's in the driveway. He must have taken a taxi to the airport this morning.

I want to call him. I want to tell him I've seen the footage and I want to ask him why he was looking where the car was when we left the restaurant. I want him to speak, to tell me the fucking truth. I want to know if he's somehow involved in what happened last night, or whether I'm just imagining it. Is my mind playing tricks on me? Am I getting carried away?

If it's me . . .

Or him.

I'm shivering. I'm very, very cold. I need a bath, or a hot shower. I fear I'm becoming ill. I need to calm my body, clear my head, find a way to get my senses back.

Get some perspective. Think more clearly.

I manage to pull myself out of the car. I enter the house but I'm still aimless and drifting, lost. I kick off my shoes and drop my jacket on the stairs, staggering to the upper level. I'm struggling to walk. I feel like I've had more than three drinks. *Is that possible?* I don't remember. Maybe. I turn to it too easily nowadays. I know that.

I start undressing as I'm walking, peeling off my blouse as I draw myself along the corridor, and then I push open the bedroom door.

Dropping my blouse on the bedroom floor, I unzip my trousers and let them fall next to the blouse. My ears are muffled and I can't hear anything. Then I unclip my bra and open the en suite bathroom door.

The room is steamy, the shower's on, but I can't hear it. And in the mist, there's a figure. I want to scream, but I can't. I blink hard. I'm seeing things.

No, it's Edward, my vision clear. He's standing in the shower, scrubbing his ankles. Streaks of mud are dripping from his skin, the pool of water in which he's standing is dirty.

I don't hear myself saying his name, but I must have said it.

Because he whips around. 'Amelie,' I see him mouth, his face full of surprise. There's still no sound.

He moves his mouth some more. I still can't hear and I can't read his lips. I need to lie down.

What are you doing here? I try to ask, but I don't know if anything of volume comes out of my moving mouth. *You're supposed to be . . .*

Edward quickly brushes off the remaining mud from his ankles, shakes the water from his legs and jumps out of the shower. He approaches me, naked, dripping wet, his arms outstretched, his mouth still moving. Everything's jumbled.

My husband is here.

He starts rubbing the sides of my arms, pushing the hair from my face. He grabs a towel, scoops up my hair, and wraps it up.

It's only after he's put another towel around my body and is using it to dry off the stream of dripping water that's falling from me, rubbing my body to warm me, that I realise I'm also soaking wet and my body is shaking uncontrollably.

Finally, there's sound. It peaks at the end of each sentence. He's asking me questions. After a time, they start to become more coherent.

'What were you doing in the rain?' he asks.

But I was in the car.

'Why are you soaking wet? How long have you been out there? My God, you're shaking. You're going to catch pneumonia.'

But I was in the car.

'Amelie, are you okay? Speak to me, Amelie, please.'

But . . .

'Darling? What's happening?'

Driving?

'Why –' My jaw chatters. 'Why – are you here?' I can feel him but can't see him clearly. My eyes are misting up as if I'm in the shower cubicle.

'I cancelled the trip. I decided I didn't want to leave you on your own for two days, not after what happened last night.'

'But – the mud?'

'I went for a jog and it started to piss down. I got soaked.' He tries to chuckle. 'Just like you, I see.'

'You went for a jog? This – time of night?'

'Yes. But forget me. What happened to you? I mean, where have you been? It's almost midnight. How did you get so caught up in it? I can see your car outside. Why are you so wet if you were driving?'

'But you don't . . .'

'What?'

'Job – I was—'

'Amelie?'

'I was – I thought I was – in it. I don't know.'

What is happening to me?

The CCTV footage. The restaurant. The car.

Edward.

'Amelie?'

But you don't jog.

30

I'm in a deep sleep, and feeling better, dreaming of a beach and sunshine, relaxation and happiness. Somewhere different. Somewhere away from all these worries.

Someone is by my side. I can't see him, but I assume it's Edward. Who else could it be? He's always there for me and with me.

The waves are lapping back and forth. The sun is bright and warm, as is the sand. There aren't many people around. In fact, now that I look, it's just me and my husband along with the peace and tranquillity of this beautiful place. And it's all for us.

The sound of the waves drifting towards us and then retreating comes and goes, comes and goes, regular as a heartbeat, but then it changes and becomes more of a studded sound, like the waves hitting a wall, or a cliff edge, and suddenly it's jarring and I'm stirring and there's tension, not relaxation, and my body stiffens and the beach disappears, leaving me lying on a layer of hot steaming tarmac and there's a car speeding away from me.

I'm brought out of my dream by the sound of my phone

ringing. I can see through the curtains that daylight has started to appear, but it must be early.

By the time I find my phone in my jacket pocket, the ringing has stopped. Looking at the screen, I see I've missed four calls. Three from the station and one, the most recent, from Ryan Hillier's mobile.

Momentarily, I breathe a sigh of relief that it wasn't the anonymous woman calling again.

I call Hillier's mobile.

He picks up instantly. I'm out of breath and before I can fill my lungs, before I can say anything, he tells me, 'Lange's been trying to get hold of you, Amelie. Now he's told me to be the messenger. Another girl's been found.'

31

Willesden Green, London

'Same MO,' Hillier says as I arrive, 'except one key difference. Dan?'

Daniel Emerson stands up. 'She had ID on her. It was in a bush just over there. Must have dropped it when he scrambled out of here. Laura Randall, sixteen-years-old. Time of death, I'd say, was around ten p.m. last night. Everything else initially looks the same, but take a close look at the earth around the body.'

We're standing in an area of woodland that borders a park and backs onto a row of local shops. The corpse is in a large bed of nettles. The earth in front of and to the side of it has been disturbed.

'It's been really kicked up,' Emerson says. 'Linking the time to this mess of earth around the body, I reckon he was caught up unexpectedly in the storm last night. So he was here with her when the heavens opened. Absolute downpour. There was thunder and lightning here too. I checked with the shopkeepers. They confirmed that it suddenly started to pelt down with rain. So, as he's preparing the body in its discovery position, he's interrupted and the ground quickly becomes soaked. Notice the trees aren't that thick here up top, not enough to shield him properly from the rain, anyway. He panics, rushes, realises he's left a shitload of footprints, and essentially kicks up the earth to try to cover his tracks. As he's doing so, he drops the wallet with her ID in it. And, of course, the earth is drenched all the way out of here, which means we'll pick up his prints; some of them will have survived. We'll get a piece of him from here for sure, hopefully something that will match what we found in the other locations. He must have been filthy; he won't have been able to hide everything.'

I freeze.

Filthy?

Mud.

Hillier traces the most obvious route out with his eyes, cocking his head to the left. 'That is, if he left along the path.'

'Would have stung the shit out of himself if he didn't,' Emerson says. 'There's no other easy way out. We'll have to hope that in trying to escape the storm so quickly he tried to get the hell out as fast as he could.'

'Okay, can you rush the comparisons?' Hillier asks.

'Already happening.'

'Shall I do next of kin?' Hillier says.

'Mmm?' I realise he's talking to me.

'Next of kin?' he repeats.

'Yeah, you do it,' I say, still preoccupied.

The storm.

Not just rain, Emerson said, but absolutely pouring. And thunder and lightning. Rain and mud.

Could it be . . .?

Rain and mud everywhere.

Mud.

Edward.

'Just let me know if you learn anything unexpected,' I say and I drift away.

Do you really know your husband, Amelie?

X Marks the Spot

I followed her for three weeks. Every day. I was dedicated; I had purpose in my life again.

It was a Monday morning, a day I knew she'd be going to the local college, so I parked my car down the road from her house. My movements that morning were automatic, and they continued to be so after she came out of the house and got into her boyfriend's car, which had arrived moments before, as usual.

From my time watching her, it was clear that there was no father in her life, and every day her mother left the house about half an hour after the girl departed. I waited till the neighbours in the closest houses were also gone before I got out of my car. I hurried to the gate by the side of the house. I knew it wasn't locked – I saw them use it regularly and they were careless – so I dashed through. I found myself in an attractive garden, freshly cut green grass, flower beds along the three fences, a patio, a swing, a shed in the far corner. I liked how it looked; my own would be similar one day.

Keeping low, I moved to the back of the house where I found that the back door was locked. I spotted a window that was slightly ajar, pulled it out as far as I could and crawled in. The squeeze was tight, but I made it. I landed on a bookcase in a dining area, a small room that bordered the kitchen. I picked up the books that I'd disturbed and checked each of the downstairs rooms. There was no one in the house, as I'd expected.

I headed upstairs and found her bedroom. It was easy to spot. The carpet was pink and there were purple and white sheets on the bed. She hadn't made up the covers; they were still in a crumpled mess. Without hesitating, I lay on them, letting myself sink into the place she rested every night. Her pyjamas were there, so I picked them up and placed them over my face, inhaling. I could smell her. Her scent was sweet, hypnotising.

Elsewhere in the room was a white dressing table with a mirror on top of it and a tall wardrobe that also had a mirror on one of its two doors. Drawing the pyjamas from my face, I stared into both mirrors. She would have been sitting there, eyeing herself, only an hour earlier. She would be here looking at herself later on.

When I was finished, I left the house, unlocking the back door and walking out with a pair of her black knickers stuffed into my jeans pocket. I thought leaving the door open might be fun, it might let me play with them a bit – both mother and daughter would wonder whether the other had done it, and then they might start questioning themselves. They'd be unsure. They'd feel unsettled, uneasy, overcome with uncertainty. So I left it open, got back in my car and drove away.

I had discovered something new and it was something I planned to repeat many times. It would give me the chance to find out all about her. I would feel closer to her than I'd felt to anyone else before, at least since the bitch who'd embarrassed me, and one day, I didn't know when or how, but I knew for certain that it would happen, I'd find a way to take her, to make her mine.

I'd find a way to have her.

32

I can't trust Edward, but then again, I'm not sure I can trust myself.

I don't know what to do, but all I know is that I have to do something. I'm staying at home today; I've told Hillier I'll be out making enquiries till it's time to see Laura Randall's family. He's going to let me know when the formal ID has taken place.

I wonder whether at home I can find some answers. I think: *Where in the house might there be clues?* But clues to what exactly? Clues about killing? Such a thought sounds ridiculous.

I need to think about this carefully, with a cool head.

Edward was in the shower, covered in mud. That's as clear as can be. Can it have been a coincidence? There's already something that indicates the mud wasn't just a coincidence: Edward isn't a jogger. He's never jogged in the whole time I've known him. And the car that tried to run us over, or run me over – I need to know whether he knew it was there, and how that might be connected.

Could he have killed Laura Randall, and the others? Could Edward be the murderer I've been searching for? He was away when each girl was killed. Unexpectedly delayed when the first two murders took place, and yesterday he was unexpectedly back when he said he was going away. And the phone calls, could they somehow be connected to the investigation? Were they a sign of some kind? But if so, a sign from whom? And a sign of what? Who could know what Edward has been up to, if not me? I'm the person who's closest to him.

He was washing mud off his legs when I returned home last night. Yes, he was. He said he'd been for a jog and was caught in a downpour. Why did he lie? Edward isn't a jogger; I've never known him to run. He was looking towards the car when we left the restaurant. The voice asked me if I know my husband. Because of these things, I'm starting to think perhaps I don't know him as I believed I did.

I circle the kitchen, trying to come up with answers in the labyrinth of questions that consume my mind. I decide to move through each room, slowly looking around, hoping that something I haven't noticed before might catch my attention.

After about ten minutes of walking around and searching, I arrive at the last room in the house: Edward's office. It's usually locked. That might seem strange, and at first I found it odd, but it's the way Edward has always been. Guarded about his work, that's my husband. I try the handle, hoping that today he might have forgotten to lock the door.

Which, of course, he hasn't. Even though it's what I was expecting, I'm disappointed and I'm beginning to fill with frustration. I press my shoulder against it, then again, harder this time, but the door won't budge.

I have to figure out a way to get the door open. I don't have a key, so I turn the handle and give it a slightly harder nudge. It remains resistant to my efforts. I get on my knees and peer under the gap between the bottom of the door and the parquet floor.

I can see the base of Edward's desk on the far side of the room. The bottom of some bookcases too. I straighten up and try to identify what kind of lock is holding the door fast shut. But I'm none the wiser. With the ornate handle, it looks old-fashioned.

There's a bag of spare keys that Edward keeps in a cupboard in the kitchen. They're mostly keys that are used for things outside, so I've never paid much attention to them; the garden is Edward's domain. When I get the bag, I see that there are various keys in it that look like garden shed keys, but there are also the kinds of key that look as though they could fit Edward's office door.

Returning to the office, I pull a key out of the bag and try the lock. It's not the right key. I work my way through each of the keys – there are seven in total – but none of them works. The other keys don't look like the right type, so I don't even bother trying them.

Despondent, I return the full bag to the kitchen cupboard. I don't have another answer. The room seems impenetrable.

It's stuffy in the kitchen, so I open the window. It overlooks the back garden. I can see that the grass has become overgrown and needs to be tended to. I'll tell Edward when he comes home.

I look closely at the window and draw my hand along one of the inner frames. *I wonder.* It's a warm day. Perhaps the house was stuffy before Edward left this morning. Perhaps he left a window open.

Quickly, I put on a pair of trainers and head out of the back door. I turn right and go to the office window. I feel an overwhelming sense of relief when I spot that there is a gap, but it's only open a fraction. I try to slide my hand in to release the catch so that the window will open fully. It's a tight squeeze and I have to twist my body. My arm scrapes against something metal and sharp and I know I've drawn blood. I wince, but I won't give up; I push against the glass, trying to force as much of my arm through as possible.

Holding my breath, squirming from the pain, I manage to catch the latch and flick it up. The window opens fully.

I'm out of breath, but I grab a garden chair, climb up and enter Edward's office through the window. The drop to the floor isn't far, but as I jump down my leg knocks into a picture frame and it falls. I try to catch it but I miss. There's a smashing noise as it hits the floor, which makes me shudder. 'Shit,' I say, swiftly picking it up. The glass in the frame has shattered.

I look around and think about what I should do. How can a broken frame be explained? The window was partly open. A gust of wind, perhaps. It could have happened that way. I decide to leave the frame and broken glass on the floor under the window. Hopefully, Edward will think it fell because of the wind. I might even tell him I heard a noise but couldn't get into the room to check what had happened. Maybe I could throw in a comment about what a windy afternoon it has been as well.

No, that would be too obvious. Too much. *A noise*, I'll tell him, just that I heard a noise. It sounded like something smashing. *Whatever could it have been?*

I feel strange being in here, like I don't belong, even though this is my house as much as it's his. Thinking about it, I've hardly been in this office over the years. We have a cleaner who comes to the house once a week, so cleaning it has never been a reason to enter.

First, I circle the room. There's a chill in the air – I shiver, even though it's a pleasantly warm morning – so I pull the window in.

Hugging my arms, I move towards the set of three large bookcases that cover the side wall. Row upon row of books, lots of IT and business titles, and several shots of Edward and me, in various places, with smiles on our faces.

Look at us, we're happy, I tell myself. *We are in love.*

At least, that's the way it looks, and looks can be deceiving.

Okay: I'm happy in them.

I scan the photos. There's one of us standing outside the Eiffel Tower – we went there to celebrate our first anniversary – and another of us on the top of the Chrysler Building in New York. Stunning views; it was a beautiful blue-sky day. On the South Bank next to the River Thames, with Parliament in the background. Posing in front of the Golden Gate Bridge, and then an amusing one of Edward sitting on the loo in a solitary confinement cell in Alcatraz. He's leaning back, his hand covering his face, miming despair. It was a funny moment. But it mirrors what I'm feeling now.

Abject despair.

At the bottom of each bookcase are three cubby holes. In them are some large felt-backed books. I pull one out and open it. A photo album. I flick through a few pages of our memories. Yes, we seem so happy in all these photos.

So many pictures of us in so many places. I've seen many wonderful things. I've been lucky. Edward brought me out of my depression and took me to all these places. They were all possible, thanks to Edward's job. It's his own company. He started it shortly after we met – an IT consultancy and sales firm – and it's gone from strength to strength.

Realising I'm wasting time by reminiscing, I put back the album I'm holding.

There are a few shelves in the room. I take a look at what's on them. Lever-arch files. I pull one down. It's filled with indecipherable paperwork. Mostly invoices and letters, all business related. Technical and business language I don't understand. I put it straight back.

Which leaves Edward's desk. Standing behind it, I gaze down at its mighty walnut surface. It's an impressive desk, both in size and appearance; you can see your reflection in its shine.

There's very little on the desk. A blotting pad, a tray of fountain pens, all high-end brands which he collects, a tray on the left containing neatly stacked paperwork, and a photo frame. In it, there's a picture of Edward and me in Milan, shopping bags billowing from our hands. He bought me the most gorgeous pair of shoes on that trip. And, finally, a small computer – an old netbook, in fact – that Edward never takes with him when he leaves the house. There's a wire coming out of the side, which disappears into a small hole in the desk. I trace it and see it's plugged into a ground socket beneath the desk. When I first saw the little computer, I asked Edward why he didn't just get a proper desktop machine. *Surely that would be faster and more reliable*, I said. He told me he'd had the netbook made super-duper by a tech specialist he knows. He said nothing could rival it, that it was now faster and more efficient than any new computer he could buy, despite its small size. He knows all sorts of people in the IT world. So many clever minds; *problem solvers*, he calls them.

I lift its lid and press the power switch. The computer's motor or fans or whatever powers it comes to life and within seconds the log-on screen appears. Edward was right; it's faster than any computer I've ever used before.

His username is saved in the sign-in box: *E*. I click into the password box and quickly see that the password isn't saved in its memory. I think for a moment: his birthday, our wedding day.

I try his birthdate as six digits.

Incorrect password. 1 attempt remaining. Computer will lock.

I step backwards. I've never seen a lockout warning after only one incorrect password entry. I wouldn't even know how to change a computer's settings to increase the security to a level like that. Edward has always been cautious of the dangers associated with computers and being online; as an IT expert, he says it's part of his day-to-day work. He's urged me many times to come up with far more elaborate passwords to protect myself.

Numbers, I think suddenly. *The numbers*.

I rummage in my pockets and find what I'm looking for.

The piece of paper. I stare at the numbers on it.

10, 6, 10, 12, 10, 13.

There's a sense of urgency and excitement in me, but in only a moment it changes to reluctance and concern. It doesn't make sense that these numbers could be the password to Edward's computer – *how could that genuinely be possible?* – but then not much else makes sense to me at the moment. So much of what's happening doesn't seem real, I suppose anything's possible.

But what if the numbers aren't the password and the computer locks? There'll be no explanation for that – a broken frame is quite different from a computer that's locked because of two failed log-on attempts. One more incorrect attempt and Edward will know I've been up to something.

I'm tempted, but no, it'll have to wait. There's no shutdown tab or option I can see, so my only option is to hold down the power button. After a few moments, the screen goes blank and, gently, I press down the lid. I feel strangely dirty. Snooping around Edward's office and trying to log on to his computer, I've invaded his privacy and done something I shouldn't have.

I lean back and sigh; I realise I'm risking everything by being in this room. But I have to search. I have to check. I may be betraying Edward's trust, but what if . . .?

On the right-hand side of the desk are three drawers. The top two are smaller, the same size, and the bottom one is larger, about three times deeper than the ones above. I try them from top to bottom. Like the door, they won't budge. I scan the room, wondering if Edward keeps a spare key for them somewhere.

Of course not; that would be daft.

And I don't have one.

My mobile phone rings. I breathe deeply and answer when I see who's calling. 'What news?' I say.

'Laura Randall's ID has been confirmed and welfare officers have just left her parents,' DCI Lange says. 'They're ready to see you. Where are you? I came by your office but Hillier said you were making enquiries.'

'Researching a few things I learnt from Fiona Cunningham's friends. I can be with the Randalls within the hour.'

'Okay,' he sighs, 'but don't keep them waiting any longer than that.'

As I glance at my watch, he hangs up. I return my focus to the drawers. I need to find a way to see inside them. Running my hands around their edges, I check to see if there's any way to get in.

There doesn't appear to be.

I desperately want to see inside the drawers. I know there's only one way I'll be able to do that. I have to get to the Randalls, but I'll be able to return before Edward arrives home. I know what to do when I get back. It'll be risky, but if I'm home when he returns, I might have a chance.

I straighten up and take a final look around, making sure nothing but the broken frame is out of place. Everything appears to be fine, so I make my way to the window, understanding what I'll have to do later.

I have no choice.

With the greatest of care, I climb back out of the office through the window. I stumble as I land on the concrete, dropping to my knee. It grazes, drawing a little blood. First my arm, now my leg. I put my hand to it. Then, standing,

I push the window to the position in which I found it, give one final glance around the office and make my way back to the kitchen.

33

Philip and Brenda Randall are understandably in pieces when I meet them. They're sitting opposite me at the kitchen table in their three-bed semi in East Finchley.

'Had her behaviour changed in any way in recent weeks?' I ask.

'No,' her mother says, clutching a soaked tissue in her hand. Every so often, she brings it to her nose and eyes.

'She was a wonderful daughter,' Philip Randall adds. 'Everything a parent could ever wish for. No trouble at all, ever.'

'She had her whole life ahead of her,' his wife says, and repeats 'her whole life ahead of her.'

'She had so much going for her, and so much to look forward to.'

'Such as, if I may ask?' I lean forward.

'She was an ambitious young woman and she had the looks to make it and she was on her way.'

'On her way?'

'Shall we show her?' he asks his wife.

She nods.

They lead me upstairs. At a closed door, they pause, it looks like they're saying a silent prayer before entering, and I can see that Brenda Randall, who's at the front of the line, braces herself by moving her shoulders in a circular motion. 'This way, detective,' she says after a few moments and taking a deep breath.

They enter a bedroom. It is painstakingly decorated, with everything matching, walls, carpet and bedding. There's an oval mirror on the wall at the head of the bed, a heavily laden dressing table. It's all so stylish. On the wall above the dressing table, are the words: *Dream big and achieve.*

Rows of framed photographs line the walls on all sides. I move to one, look at it, and then move along the wall, studying each picture. All posed, all professional.

'This is Laura's room,' Brenda Randall explains.

'She wanted to be a model?' I ask.

'Yes, and she also wanted to be a social—'

'A social media influencer,' I finish for her, turning to face Laura Randall's parents.

'That's right. How did you know?'

Because that's what they all wanted to be. Yes, social media is a connection, and that's been obvious from the start, but it's more than that; the connection is what they were trying to achieve on social media. They were building their profiles. Micah Ainsley, the DC who's in charge of a small team exploring the social media profiles of the girls, really has to step things up a gear with her search.

'I've been hearing a lot about social media lately.'

'Do you think this is connected with the murders of the other three girls?' Brenda Randall asks.

'It's still too early to say, but naturally it's something we're looking at.'

'I *know* it's connected,' Brenda Randall says and she leans forward.

'How can you be so sure?'

'Fiona Cunningham,' she says, pointing to a picture on the wall before taking her husband's hand.

34

'Laura Randall met Fiona Cunningham,' I tell DCI Lange when I manage to get into his office. 'I've got a picture of them together. Here.' I hand it to him.

He scoffs and drops it on his desk. 'Well, how the fuck was that one missed?' he barks. 'What the fuck is Ainsley doing? She's supposed to be searching properly.'

'We only verified Laura Randall's identity today. She can only work so fast. She probably hasn't even got to her accounts yet. But all four girls certainly had an online presence, either a big presence like Fiona Cunningham or one that was up and coming. They were popular girls.'

'But we need a specific link. Everyone has *Snapchat* nowadays. I can't tell the mayor to go fuck himself with something as vague as that. Bastard's already been on to me again. I need to understand the relevance of all this.'

'That's what we're trying to figure out. And, look, the mayor's concerned like the rest of us. Give the guy a break.'

'Give him a break?' he says incredulously. 'Give him a break? He's trying to cut me a new behind, Davis. You know, that's the problem with these left-wing nut—'

'Yes,' I tell him. 'Yes, you've already said. Left-wing lunatic, I get it. Look, this is what Brenda Randall, Laura Randall's mother, told me. Laura Randall was trying to establish a following on social media, in particular on Instagram. She'd read some posts from her friends about a local girl, Fiona Cunningham, who had achieved a big following and was starting to make money online. So she sought out Fiona Cunningham and managed to meet her at a party a few months ago. That's where they had the picture taken. The reason her mother remembers is because she said she'd never seen her daughter so excited about having met someone before. It was like she'd met a Hollywood star, she said. She showed her mum the photo and it's been in a frame on her wall ever since.'

'Good, a concrete connection. Speak to Ainsley. Give her the photo.' I take it from his desk. 'Give her everything you've already got.'

'I have. I spoke to her before I came in here and gave her copies of everything.'

'Well, that's just great. Why is it that I find out everything after everyone else?'

And with that he picks up his phone and starts barking orders at someone else.

35

Back at my desk, I open Instagram on my mobile after I see lots of its functionality is disabled on a desktop. Altogether, the girls have many thousands of followers. 'Like finding a needle in a haystack,' I say to myself. I don't even know where to start, so now I see why Ainsley has been struggling so much.

I open an earlier email from Ainsley that gives the girls' online accounts, including many links that make it easier to land directly on the correct pages. Facebook, Instagram, Twitter and Snapchat.

Each Twitter account has between one and four thousand followers. The numbers are even higher on Instagram. From hundreds to thousands, lots of friends on Facebook too.

All their profiles were public, except Rachel Adams's Facebook page, which was set to private so that only her friends could view her posts.

Of the four, Fiona Cunningham was by far the most popular, with over six thousand followers on Instagram alone. After one look at the page containing her photos, I see that it's really obvious why this was the case. She was a gorgeous girl, with a long, slim but curvy figure, and she didn't have a complex about showing it off; her Instagram page is filled with pictures of her clad in bikinis and bras.

I think about how I might possibly work through such large numbers of followers and how I might be able to organise them into lists. I open a blank Excel document and select Laura Randall's follower list on Twitter. Under each follower's name, there's also a profile. When I highlight the followers, I end up highlighting every word and image on the screen. It doesn't look promising. I copy and paste into Excel and, as I feared, I'm met with a huge amount of unfilterable text rather than only the usernames which is all I wanted. I don't have an Instagram account but I imagine the results will look similar. Facebook also doesn't transfer into a simple list of friends that I can cross compare by using Excel.

I spend some time sifting through the comments. A lot of loving and supportive comments from friends, and some sexually offensive comments from those who appear to be strangers, mostly much older men. The girls all interacted with their followers, those who made admiring comments; sometimes just emojis or love hearts, but sometimes comments in return and, sometimes, what read like conversations. They smartly ignored the negative or inappropriate comments.

Pretty girls encourage a lot of followers – or friends, if you can call them that. *And plenty of nutcases, too.*

I don't understand the obsession that youngsters today have with posting pictures of themselves in a near-naked state online; all it does is highlight their naivety. Pictures online with no filter, for friends *and* strangers to see. Friends *and* foes, or those who might become foes. Those who can do you harm. Someone who may very well have done harm to these four girls.

This kind of easiness online is something I encounter all too often, and my greatest fear is that we're not learning any lessons from it all. No one: not the young people themselves, nor their parents, their schools, our government.

Where I spot obscene comments, I click through to see the profile of the people who posted them. I make a note of their names, whether they're real or just online pseudonyms I don't know, but their profiles suggest that a lot of them live abroad. If true, that would rule them out as suspects.

On the Instagram pages of Rachel Adams, Fiona Cunningham, Niamh O'Flanagan and Laura Randall, which is where they presented the vast majority of their pictures, there isn't a single picture showing a school or college, or an identifiable logo, which might suggest where they attended, and would make them easier to find in person. It doesn't make sense to me; I was sure I'd find something to suggest the name of their school or college, thereby providing the killer with access into their real lives.

Perhaps a reference to school or college is in the comments somewhere and I'm missing it; there are thousands of comments across the four profiles and I don't have the time to read them all. Hopefully Ainsley and her team will eventually find something.

I turn to Twitter and then Facebook, again hoping to find some revealing pictures but failing. I don't know Facebook well – I opened an account years ago when it was the thing but have remained largely inactive on it and don't remember much about how to use it. As I'm about to give up and close the site, I spot a section called *About* and recall that it asks for personal details when creating an account. Some of that information can be made public.

I wonder.

So I click on the *About* section of Laura Randall's page. It contains very little information. Just some names of television shows and musicians, things she likes, small pictures next to the names.

I continue working backwards, typing Niamh O'Flanagan into the search box. I click on *About*. There's a little more this time, including a date of birth and the name of a sibling. Still no school or college.

Then I try Rachel Adams's page. Nothing on that one at all.

Finally, Fiona Cunningham. *Bingo*. Under *Education* is the name of her school, along with a link to its Facebook page. I click and am taken to the school's website.

So the killer could have found out the name of Fiona Cunningham's school using Facebook but not anything education-related about the other three girls. He could have followed her as she left school one day and discovered where she lived that way. But not the other girls, or, if he found out the information, I can't see how he managed it.

Finding any overlapping followers is an impossible task for one person alone, and even Ainsley with her small team is struggling. I'd envisioned sitting down with a pen and paper and simply making a few lists. It's too complicated, with the number of this generation's followers.

A text message arrives, grabbing my attention. It's from Edward. *Home by 7*, it says.

I snatch a glance at my watch. I need to hurry home if I'm to be ready for when Edward arrives. I am apprehensive, knowing what I'm going to do at home this evening.

Shortly after seven, I'm in the kitchen, nursing a mug of tea, when I hear the front door opening. I glance at my watch.

'Hi, darling,' Edward calls from the hallway.

'In here,' I respond, putting the mug to my lips and sipping slowly. It's hot.

He enters, removing his suit jacket and loosening his tie. 'Feeling better?' he asks, coming over to me and kissing the top of my head.

'Yes,' I say. 'Thanks.' This morning, I told him I had stomach cramps so I would work from home for much of the day.

He rubs my shoulders. 'Smells good,' he says. 'What is it?'

'Roast chicken. It's resting. The veg still needs another half hour.' I bought a ready-cooked chicken from the counter in Tesco, so I've put it under silver foil on the cutting board.

'Perfect,' he says, and kisses me again. 'Enough time for a quick shower, then.'

I straighten up a bit. That's exactly what I was hoping he'd say. 'No need to rush. There's plenty of time.'

He gives my shoulders one more gentle squeeze before leaving the kitchen. I hear him arriving at his office door, the key turning in the lock and the door opening. I can hear him moving around in there for a while; there's a lot of shuffling and some clanking sounds.

Presently, I hear him coming back towards the kitchen. I haven't heard him close his office door. That's good, just what I need. I listen for the sound of his footsteps on the staircase. When I hear him walking along the upstairs landing, I go to the bottom of the staircase, listening for the shower. It comes on. I keep listening for the shower door. It opens on a metal rail, which rattles as it's pulled shut. I hear it closing with a thud.

Instantly, I turn on my heel and move towards Edward's office. The door is open, as I'd hoped. I glance quickly in the direction of the staircase. All clear.

I enter. Edward's briefcase is on his desk chair. There's a duffel bag on the floor behind the desk. A few carrier bags are perched in the nearest corner of the room. On the desk is a leather-bound book, I assume his diary.

Moving behind the desk, I unzip the duffel bag. Some spare clothes. A toiletries bag. Nothing else.

The netbook is on and the log-in screen is ready for a password to be entered. I need Edward to have logged on before I try again, just in case the numbers I enter are wrong and the computer thinks it's the second attempt to log in. I'll have to get in here again if I'm to try the numbers.

I stand up and try to open Edward's briefcase. Its combination lock is secure. I try our wedding date first and, after that fails, his date of birth to see if I can work out the correct combination to unlock it. The four-digit birthday selection also fails.

I dash over to the carrier bags. Some new whisky glasses in one, some paperwork folders in the other.

I listen carefully, keeping absolutely still, trying to hear whether the water is still running in the bathroom upstairs.

It's difficult to hear the sound of running water from here, but I think I can make out a faint trickling sound.

I return to the leather-bound book on the desk. It's got the year and Edward's initials on the front cover. Yes, it is his diary.

I stand over it – it's made of luxurious brown leather – and open it. Today's date is marked by a strap of deep red linen, which acts as a bookmark. On the page are several names next to times. Meetings, no doubt.

I start flicking through the pages, scanning, not taking in much, seeing a blur of names, dates and phone numbers.

Then I stop. Something strange catches my eye. Something that makes no sense.

On 6 October, no names, no phone numbers, no times. Just a symbol, a bold '**X**'.

I flick back another couple of pages and come to another one. Yes, another bold '**X**'.

Moving through the pages with more urgency now, even though I don't understand why, I find another and another. Several of them.

What do they mean?

I scramble for a piece of paper, but there isn't anything on the desk. I pull at the top drawer to see if I can find a sheet, but it's still locked. 'Shit,' I mumble, unsure of what to do but certain, for some reason, that these markings are important.

With little other choice and time running out, I grab a fountain pen and attempt to write the dates of the '**X**' markings on my hand. Then I flick back to where I started. I turn the page and see two more crosses. My body fills with a chill as I stare at them.

12 October – the date of Fiona Cunningham's murder and when her body was found. Marked with an '**X**'.

13 October – the date of Rachel Adams's murder and when her body was found. Marked with an '**X**'.

My mind starts racing. The dates of the murders of Fiona Cunningham and Rachel Adams have been marked with a cross in Edward's diary.

Just as I'm about to turn the page to see if any other dates have been marked, I'm startled by what sounds like footsteps coming along the corridor towards the office.

I can't remember whether the diary was open or closed when I got in here and don't have time to think, so I shut it quickly, put the pen back in the pot and edge myself around the desk.

As I reach the door, Edward appears, now wearing a pair of jeans and a cream jumper. I shudder to a stop.

'Oh,' he says, looking surprised to see me in here.

'I – I thought you might be in here. Came to say dinner's ready.'

I dread to think what this must look like, what he's thinking. I hope my face doesn't give away too much.

He eyes me curiously. 'But –' Then he glances behind me.

'Thought I heard you coming down,' I add, desperate to convince him.

'Sure,' he says, smiling again, and he takes me by the hands and brings his lips towards mine. He kisses me softly. When he pulls back, he releases my hands. There's a moment of hesitation as I fear he's seen the ink on them. *The numbers.* I move my hands to my sides as quickly as I can while trying to act nonchalant.

'I'll just set the table.'

'I won't be long,' he says, and he grins as he steps out of my way.

I walk past, unable to look him in the eye, my heart pounding.

I hope I've made it. I'm not sure I have.

'You know,' he says, stopping me in my tracks as I'm in the doorway, 'there was a smashed frame on the floor in here when I got back from work.'

'Oh, that,' I say, my pitch unintentionally higher. 'So that's what it was, then,' I feign faint recognition. 'I heard a noise earlier. Came to check what it was but the door was locked. Must have been that. It's been such a windy day.'

He eyes me carefully. 'Yes,' he says eventually, 'it has been, hasn't it? Such a windy day.'

'Thought the house might come down at one point,' I say, my eyes widening, fearing my words sound ridiculous.

'I bet,' he says simply.

I smile and turn around.

'Oh, and Amelie?' he says.

I stop and slowly turn back to him.

He's walking towards me and, just before he reaches me, he leans down and removes from one of the carrier bags a box containing whisky glasses. 'Why not pour us one each and use these. Picked them up today at lunch. Aren't they beautiful?'

I don't look at them. 'Very,' I say, and then I realise he can't know I've already seen them, so I look admiringly at the box and what's inside.

'Yes,' he says, and stares at me.

I stare back.

Has he been using X to mark the dates of the murders in his diary? If he has, that can mean only one thing. Edward is a killer.

He is the *killer.*

And the car at the restaurant. Edward knew about it. That means he sent it after me. That means he wants to kill me too. He wants to kill me like he killed the girls.

Then he nods towards the kitchen. 'I think you said the food's ready.'

And, forcing a smile, I say, 'Oh, yes,' and leave to set the table and serve our meal.

36

'Thank you,' Edward says as I put a plate on the table in front of him. 'Smells great,' he adds, leaning over the plate and inhaling through his nose. It's a habit he has before a meal.

I don't answer. I'm too preoccupied.

I linger for too long by the side unit and Edward asks, chewing, 'Aren't you going to come and eat?'

I try to shake off the distraction. 'Yes,' I say. 'Just pouring us a drink.' I fill the new whisky glasses and pick up my plate, taking them to the table. I sit opposite him. 'Such beautiful glasses,' I say.

'I knew you'd like them.' He holds up the glass and eyes it in the shine of the ceiling light. Then he holds it out and adds, 'To us.'

I flinch and pick up my glass. Slowly, I bring it to his. 'Yes,' I say, 'to us.'

We each take a mouthful.

He closes his eyes in pleasure. 'Hits the spot,' he says.

After we've started eating, I ask, 'Tell me about your day,' knowing that while Edward talks I'll gain some time to try to disconnect and think.

As he speaks, I don't absorb any meaning from his words. Instead, I try to work out how I can get away from him for a few moments.

I don't know how long I zone out for – I hope my face hasn't glazed over – but when I come to and it sounds like he's reached the end of a sentence, I rub my stomach and say, 'Sorry, got to use the loo.'

I get up, without waiting for him to say anything. As I start moving past him, he catches hold of my wrist. *Oh God, no,* I think, *he's going to turn my hand over, or he's seen the ink already. He knows something's wrong.*

I brace myself, waiting for it to happen, waiting to react, ready to incapacitate him if I need to.

I can't believe things have reached this point.

'Aren't you feeling any better?' His face shows concern. 'Something's not right.'

'I'll be okay,' I pretend.

He lets go of my wrist and says, 'You know, I'm worried about you.'

'I'll be all right,' I say, clutching my stomach. 'Have to dash.'

He nods and I quickly leave the kitchen, breathing heavily, and heading upstairs.

From my bag in our bedroom, I grab my work notebook and pen and quickly jot down the dates from my hand, the whole time listening for the sound of Edward's cutlery connecting with his dinner plate. I'm sweating, such is my concern that he'll walk in on me, and what explanation would I have if he found me in here? He thinks I'm in the bathroom, for Christ's sake.

I hear a dining chair scrape against the kitchen floor. I've copied the dates from my hand to my notebook, so I thrust it and the pen back into my bag and move as quickly and quietly as I can towards the bathroom, on tiptoes, praying that the landing floor won't creak.

Fortunately, it doesn't. I reach the bathroom and gently close the door as I hear Edward making his way up the stairs. I pull down my jeans and sit on the toilet, listening carefully for any sound outside. Suddenly, I'm worried he might go into the bedroom. *Will he look in my bag and find my notebook? And when I come out, will he check my hands?* I glance down at them. I've got to get rid of this ink.

There's a moment when the light from the hallway, which I can see under the doorway, is blocked. I can't hear anything, but the light being blocked means Edward must be standing on the other side of the door. *Is he trying to listen to me?* Instinctively, I hold my breath, expecting him to knock, as he knows something's the matter, but then the shadow moves away from the door and I exhale, relieved.

I stand up, flush the toilet and soak my hands in the sink. Tap on, I scrub until most of the ink has faded.

As I leave the bathroom and walk past our bedroom door, an arm reaches out and catches hold of me, pulling me into the bedroom. I gasp and find myself in Edward's arms. Suddenly, the smell of whisky on his breath is rancid.

'Are you feeling better now?' he asks.

'Yes, thanks,' I say, our faces exceptionally close together. Uncomfortably close. I try to edge my neck back without making it too obvious. I don't want to be this close to him right now.

Slowly, he lowers his hands to my hips and then round onto my backside. I try to pull away again as subtly as I can, but his tense arms, as if he knows what I'm trying to do, have formed a pincer grip around me.

I stare into his eyes.

'You look – strange.'

I can't tell whether he's joking or being serious, but then he smiles.

'I'm just not feeling well. I don't feel well, I told you. I – I can't.'

He brings his head even closer, so that our noses are only centimetres apart. The scent of whisky turns my stomach. 'Thought you said you were feeling better.' His smile broadens, his straight white teeth exposed. 'Maybe this would make you feel even better.'

'I don't want to – I'm sorry.'

He rubs his nose against mine, Eskimo-like. At any other time in our relationship, it would be a sign of affection; now it seems like an act of hostility, and then he presses his lips to my neck. 'Give it a try, you never know.' He nuzzles my neck. I lean my head back, partly to get away from him, but he takes the movement as a sign of pleasure, so his nuzzling becomes more intense, to the point of biting, and he grips me tighter, squeezing my body so much that I fear I won't be able to breathe. Then he lifts his head up and plants his lips on mine, pushing hard at me, as if he wants to open up my face.

I try to speak, but he keeps his lips affixed to mine and starts moving me backwards. Presently, the back of my legs press against the bed, but before falling I manage to swivel around and Edward drops onto the bed alone.

'I can't,' I say. 'I just can't.'

Relaxed, he lies back, propping himself up on an elbow. Casually, he says, 'Whatever you say.' He prises at something in his teeth with a fingernail. 'You're the boss.'

I step out and go back downstairs, but instead of finishing my meal, I think about the man I married, the man I trusted, the man I dedicated my life to. I don't want it to be so. I don't know, if push came to shove, whether I could do what I would need to do to Edward. My eyes glaze over as I picture him, initially my handsome husband smiling at me on our wedding day, but then he becomes a shadow, and suddenly I feel a level of fear that's never been connected with Edward before, because it's the fear I felt for my father, and that's who the shadow is, my father.

I open my mouth to scream. A sound starts to come out, but I manage to stifle it. I can't let him know how rattled I am. Instead, I grab my glass and fill it with whisky to the halfway point, then I start drinking it, as quickly as I can. I want to be numb. I want to be somewhere else.

X Marks the Spot

I spent many days in her home, in her bedroom. I searched the space, high and low. I wanted to know all about her. And I found lots of answers. She became part of my life and for over six weeks I was fixated on her. She became my obsession.

I developed a sort of ritual in her home. I spent around half an hour looking around. I went from room to room. I went from drawer to drawer, from cupboard to cupboard. And then I spent about half an hour in her room, my final moments there always spent lying on her bed. I felt like I was becoming part of her. I could almost feel her skin on mine, and when I closed my eyes, that was what I imagined.

Her name was Megan Goldman. She was sixteen years old when I started. She was seventeen when I finished. Tall, slim, with long blonde hair, beautiful blue eyes.

A pang of regret hit me. I could never be that age again, yet I longed to be, and I could never share with her in the way I wanted to. I wanted to be able to meet her, to do with her what sixteen-year-old couples do.

I knew there was only one way I could ever get close. I didn't want to hurt her, even though I craved her.

The only real time I met her was on a Saturday. I followed her to the local town centre. She went into a clothes shop and spent a long time browsing. I entered and pretended to browse. Casually, I sifted through a clothes rack near where she was standing. Then I stepped towards her, the whole time touching the clothes that were hanging on the racks behind her, getting closer and closer, until I was standing right behind her. Removing an item of clothing from the rack, I turned around. The back of her head and body were only inches from me. I inhaled deeply, taking in her beautiful sweetness. How I longed to take those flowing locks into my hands and run my fingers through them. How I longed to massage her shoulders and run my hands down the small of her back.

Somehow, I managed to restrain myself and continued moving, passing her.

I lingered near the exit and, when I saw her approaching to leave, I moved towards her. As if by accident, an act of confusion, a stranger not paying attention, I stepped in front of her. Then as she tried to side-step me, I moved in the same direction. The same the other side. I smiled and shrugged. 'Sorry,' I said. She also smiled, revealing small pearl-white teeth, and sniggered. It was a childish sound and it made me want her there and then. No problem, she said, in a tone that was music to my ears. She was bright and smiling as I stepped aside, allowing her to pass, and I watched her as she disappeared around a corner.

It was a meeting I would never forget.

37

I'm lying in bed, staring at the ceiling. I can't sleep.

When eventually I stumbled up to bed, Edward was fast asleep. I stood over him and watched as he slept so peacefully. He looked so calm, so pleasant. *How is it possible I don't know you?* I thought.

I contemplated waking him, trying to explain or trying to question him. But I didn't know what to say and even though I willed myself to speak, no words came out of my mouth.

Now, he's lying next to me, on his side, facing away. He's in a deep slumber, breathing heavily, occasionally snoring.

I turn on my side and see the back of his head. Perhaps it's the head of a stranger. Perhaps, if I stare long enough, I won't recognise him at all.

I almost expect him to blend into the figure of someone else. My father, perhaps.

I shouldn't have had more alcohol. I have to be clear-headed. I have to think through everything, there's so much to process.

The answer must be somewhere online and I need time to support Micah Ainsley on that angle, but I also need to work out why that car tried to hit me and how Edward knew it was coming. How the hell Edward is involved in everything. The car, yes, and also the mud in the shower the night that Laura Randall was murdered. The odd symbols in his diary. And I need to find out who the woman who made the phone calls is.

But something isn't right. I'm certain of it. I know Edward – or I thought I did – and something feels off when I'm around him. He's . . . different somehow. The man I sat down with for a meal this evening wasn't the Edward I know. Or maybe his odd behaviour is a reaction to my behaviour, which to him probably seems odd. I'm trying to conceal my unease but likely failing.

I need to find out more. There's only one way for me to do that. Edward is planning to go to his office in London in the morning, so when we wake up I will remain unwell. I think after my performance this evening, Edward won't take much convincing to believe I'm not well. *I need to stay home*, I'll tell him. *I'll be all right, I just need some more rest.*

And I'm sorry, of course I'm sorry, I don't know why I behaved the way I did.

It's imperative that he goes to work without any suspicions. He also mustn't worry about me. Ideally, he won't even think of me. For if I'm to be successful in what I plan to do, I must not be on his mind.

I will get some answers. I won't relent until I find out what's going on. That is, if anything actually *is* going on.

I will follow my husband.

38

'I'm sorry,' I say as soon as I wake up.

Edward is near the wardrobe getting dressed. He turns and stares at me. He doesn't say anything for a short while, which feels much longer than it likely is, and then he walks around the bed to where I am. He perches on its edge beside me, tracing the side of my face with the tips of his fingers, but he doesn't make eye contact. It feels like he could strike me at any moment. For the second time in two days, I brace myself to counterattack. 'It's fine,' he says, monotone. 'It's fine.'

I don't believe him.

He bends down, closing his eyes, and kisses me on the forehead. Then, finally, he looks into my eyes.

Instinctively, I clutch the back of his neck and pull his lips to mine. I kiss him and he draws back.

'I am sorry,' I repeat.

'It's okay,' he says. 'Rest well.' And he squeezes my hand before departing.

Edward's office is located near Covent Garden in London. Drury Lane. That's where I'm going to lie in wait. As soon as I hear his car pulling away, I jump out of bed and dress with haste. I choose some clothes that are casual and inconspicuous – a hoodie and dark jeans. After tying my hair in a ponytail, I find a baseball cap and search for an old pair of sunglasses. I don't want Edward to see me and I also don't want to be recognised by any police officers I know who might be in the area.

I ring for a taxi to take me to the train station, arriving there around fifteen minutes later, and then it's a journey of a little over twenty minutes to reach London Euston. From there, I take the underground to Covent Garden station and, when I emerge, walk the five or so minutes to Drury Lane.

There's a coffee shop on the other side of the road and a little way down the street from the office block. After ordering a latte and a muffin, I grab one of the complimentary newspapers and sit at the table nearest the window. From here, because of the signage on the floor-to-ceiling window, I can just about make out the entrance to the office block. I place the paper on the table, pretending to read it, occasionally sipping the hot coffee, and I stare hard through the window. My focus on the door to the office block is intense. I'm not sure I blink. The streets are busy, people keep blocking my view, but I'm confident I'll see him if he comes out. And when that happens, I'll follow him.

I never thought I'd be the suspicious wife, lurking, waiting to catch her husband doing who knows what, almost willing there to be something to actually catch.

For if there's nothing, if my mind has created problems out of nothing, what does that mean is happening to me?

What have I become? And how could such a change in me even be possible? I know I'm strong – I spent years fighting against the horrors of my childhood and I managed to find a way through. If I could beat that . . .

It's just – these girls and the memory of my father that have affected me so much. I see them and their beautiful long blonde hair when I close my eyes, and then I see him again, appearing out of the shadows. How they remind me so much of myself when I was their age, of when my father was doing unspeakable things to me. Things I will never be able to forget, but that I have managed to suppress through my dedication to my job and my marriage.

I try to think of my wedding day, of the vows Edward and I shared, of what we promised one another in those words, and I know instantly that I'm breaking everything I vowed when I looked into his eyes and said *I promise.*

Were they just empty words, empty promises?

And what about him and his vows? Was every word he said a lie?

I hope to God I'm wrong, that Edward has done nothing wrong, that the woman on the phone was a liar or a drunk, but there's something deep within me that tells me she was speaking some kind of truth and that she very much meant what she said. I fear Edward has done something terribly wrong.

My bladder is full and I desperately want to use the loo, but I worry about missing Edward if he leaves the office, so I remain where I am, squeezing my legs together, telling myself that it surely can't be much longer. *Just hold on a little more.*

I'm just about to succumb to the stirring within me when the main door of the office block opens and Edward comes out. His secretary is with him and they stop on the pavement and speak. After a few moments, she nods and heads off in one direction while Edward turns and walks the opposite way.

I get to my feet and step outside, ignoring my bladder's ache for attention. Now, I have to be very, very careful.

39

Edward is crossing Charing Cross Road and entering Leicester Square. I keep my distance. He's walking with his attention directly ahead; he isn't glancing into windows as he passes shops and other buildings, and he isn't paying attention to any of the people he walks by.

There's a sudden throng of people in my way as I approach the far side of Leicester Square. Momentarily, I lose sight of him. Skirting around some tourists who are milling about trying to take photos, I pick up my pace, but he isn't anywhere. I scan left and right, near and far, panicking that he's gone, that I've ruined my chances, but, relieved, I catch a glimpse of him crossing the road at Piccadilly Circus. He moves to the right and disappears from view again.

I run. I don't care how I look to the people around me. I charge towards Piccadilly Circus like a bat out of hell and reach the place where I saw him less than a minute ago. He's not there anymore. To my left is a classy restaurant next to which is a long narrow side street. There are a few people milling around, but no sign of Edward.

So it's the restaurant, I assume.

How to see inside without entering? Side on, I edge towards the window. There's some kind of netting in it, an afternoon-tea menu encased in what appears to be a shiny precious metal, and the window is tinted. I can't see in further than a few metres. I can just about make out a table, the white tablecloth hanging down to the floor.

I don't have a choice. I have to go in.

Cautiously, and moving as slowly as I can without drawing attention to myself, I open the door. Stepping inside, I'm relieved to find a hostess's lectern, with a tablet perched on it, within a metre of the entrance. Most of the restaurant is shielded from where I'm standing.

'Can I help you?' a pretty young eastern European lady asks from behind it. Her accent sounds Hungarian. She has jet-black hair and olive skin.

'Can I help?' she repeats when I don't speak. I have to catch my breath.

'I wonder if it's possible to make a reservation for the twenty-seventh,' I say to her, selecting a date arbitrarily, hoping to occupy her on the tablet for a few moments while I reposition myself to scan the restaurant tables.

'One moment while I check.'

I step to the right, lift myself on tiptoes and twist my neck as much as is necessary to get a good look around, scanning the tables.

There's a sea of heads, many people facing away from me, and I can't see Edward. But just as the hostess straightens herself up and speaks to me, he appears – he must have been using the loo or something – and sits down opposite a blonde woman. The back of her head is all I can see. I'm certain she's attractive.

Edward pulls in his chair, shifts to get comfortable and smiles at her. It's the kind of smile he used to offer me. Then he lifts his eyes from her, allows his gaze to drift over her head and, after a brief glance around the room, it lands in my direction. For a moment, our eyes lock.

I freeze, unsure what to do. He can see me. I don't hear the words the hostess is saying, but there's an echo, a muffled sound in my ears, and then they start buzzing and, pulling down my sunglasses to cut off eye contact with Edward, I turn around and shuffle out of the restaurant without a word to the hostess who calls after me, 'Miss? Miss?'

Dizzy, I leave and don't look back.

He saw me.

40

The whole way home, my mind races with thoughts of Edward and that blonde woman. Holding hands, a romantic walk by the River Thames, giggling and rubbing up against one another, in bed together. She and Edward by the Golden Gate Bridge. She and Edward on the roof of the Chrysler Building. She and Edward shopping in Milan. Those are my memories and she's stealing them from me.

How could he?

As soon as I re-enter our house, I charge to Edward's office and try again to open the door, forgetting that I already know it's locked. I have to find the answer. I have to know who she is. I have that single purpose in mind. There must be something else in that room that will lead me to the truth.

When the door doesn't budge, I turn the handle and push my shoulder against it. Then repeat, pushing harder. It still doesn't give. I start pushing against it repeatedly, harder and harder, knocking it with my body, until I'm certain my shoulder must bruise and bleed, and then I shake the handle, thinking of Edward touching her, kissing her, having sex with her, and then I kick the door and shoulder-barge it and kick again, and suddenly there are hands on my shoulders, then they wrap around my chest, and I feel a face press into the crevasse between my neck and shoulders, and there's a shushing sound, and I'm turned around against my will, and Edward pulls me in and hugs me, squeezing.

I cry. Clinging hold of him, I clench a fist and start ineffectually pounding against his back while keeping a tight grip of him with my other hand.

The bastard.

But I love him. He saved me. He gave me life. He renewed me after my father had destroyed me.

Why were you with that woman? Who is she?

The words I so desperately want to say won't come out.

He's shushing me, but my sobbing only intensifies.

'Amelie,' he says, but nothing else. It's supposed to soothe, but my name is an empty word, or the sentiment behind the pronunciation is vacant. It's not my real name anyway. I don't feel like me anymore.

'What is going on, Amelie?'

I don't answer. I can't.

'What's going on?' he repeats.

What's going on? With whom?

Suddenly, and to my surprise, I manage to release the words that have been trapped inside. 'Who is she?' I look him squarely in the eyes. 'What's going on between you two?'

'What?' he guffaws. 'You mean Barbara?'

'Her name's Barbara!' I screech.

'Calm down, Amelie, she's a colleague. It was just a business lunch. I have them all the time, with many different people. Including women.'

'Attractive women.'

'Yes.' He laughs. 'All kinds of women.'

'Did she call me?'

His shoulders rise. 'What are you talking about?'

'You know what I'm talking about! What are you doing, Edward?'

'I'm doing the same as I do every day, Amelie. I'm working. I'm moving day to day, trying to provide us with the life we've always wanted.'

'It's not the life *I* wanted.'

'That's nonsense.'

'You don't want me anymore, do you?'

'I don't know what you're talking about.'

'I saw the CCTV, Edward. I know you saw it.'

'Saw what, woman?' I can tell he's becoming exasperated with me.

'That car. The car that tried to fucking run us down.' I swipe at him, but he manages to sidestep my hand.

'Amelie, please, stop this—'

'The car that tried to kill me!'

He grabs me by the shoulders, desperation in his eyes. 'I don't know what you're talking about.' His voice is high-pitched.

'Yes, you do!'

'For God's sake, you're speaking in riddles!' He shakes me, too hard. My head hurts. 'Amelie!' And flings me, letting go, and I fall back against his office door.

There's silence for a time while he stares at the ground and then he shakes his head slowly. 'What is happening to you? Tell me what's going on inside that head of yours.'

'That's what I want to know from you.'

He shrinks. 'You need help.'

'I need a husband!' Then more softly, 'Or, at least, I *needed* a husband.'

He holds out a hand. 'You have a husband. I'm here for you. I always have been. Remember? I said I'll always be here for you.'

'I don't know who you are anymore.'

'I'm Edward.' He adds in a whisper, 'Your husband.'

'My husband,' I repeat, automatically. 'And who am I?'

He whimpers. 'I'm not really sure. All I know is the Amelie I married wouldn't behave like this.'

I screw up my face. 'I don't know either.' And the tears silently start flowing again.

There's a look of horror on his face. 'I'm sorry,' he says, and he unlocks his office door. 'I'm so sorry,' he repeats, and without looking back he walks inside, softly shutting the door, and shutting me out.

X Marks the Spot

I'd got into the habit of making myself comfortable. One day, almost four months after I first entered the house, I was in the bathroom, sitting on the toilet. I might have been reading a newspaper.

My guard was down, and suddenly I heard the front door open.

I sprang up. I remember holding my breath, as if I might never breathe again, but I don't remember much else about what happened.

Suddenly, I was back in her bedroom. And then I was deep inside her wardrobe.

I prayed it wasn't her. And, if it was her, I prayed she wouldn't come into her bedroom.

God didn't answer: it was her, and she did come up to her bedroom.

Sweat was dripping off my forehead and down my nose. My palms were clammy. My armpits were soaked. The shirt I was wearing was stuck to the line of my spine.

And without so much as a moment's notice, she opened the wardrobe door. Even though I knew she was in the room, I wasn't expecting it. I wasn't completely hidden by the clothes. She screamed.

I switched off, leaping out and grabbing her. Once I had hold of her, the momentum took me forwards and her backwards, and we travelled across the room. We only stopped moving when we collided with the wall, her back hitting it hard. She doubled over, winded, gasping for breath. I grabbed her beautiful blonde hair, how I'd wanted for so long to be able to touch it, but I didn't have time to enjoy the sensation. Instead, I wrapped it around my hands and brought her head crashing against the windowsill ledge, again and again and again, until there was a loud crack and blood sprayed and then it started spreading, and presently she stopped making any sounds.

Eventually, I don't know after how long, I let go of her body and she collapsed into a heap on the floor. I sank to my knees.

It was while I was on my knees that my vision regained focus and I realised exactly what I'd done.

I saw Megan, and what I had done to her.

I reached out to touch her, my hand brushing the skin of her thigh. The skin was so soft. It was everything I'd imagined.

I wanted her.

I knew it was all over. I would never see her again. I was angry with myself and punched the carpet in frustration.

Now she was out of my life forever.

But it couldn't end like this.

So it was there, in her bedroom, before I left the house for the final time, that I finally had her. It was the best sex I'd ever had. And it got me thinking. Maybe this was the way it should always be.

41

The following morning, by the time I wake up, Edward has left the house. I glance at my watch and realise I'm late for work. I promised to meet Hillier for a catch-up at nine. I grab my phone from the bedside table and call him. 'Sorry, running late. Just having to make a few stops on my way,' I lie. 'Shouldn't be too much longer. Have there been any new leads?'

'Nothing,' he says, his voice deflated. 'And to top that off, three new cases have landed on my desk.'

'I shouldn't be more than an hour.'

'I'll keep your seat warm.'

I know I should laugh, but I don't. 'You do that,' I say and mean it, before hanging up.

It takes me twenty minutes to pull myself out of bed and into the shower. For some reason I can't identify, there's something sloth-like in how I'm moving, like I've developed a disability, no matter how much I try to pick up the pace.

As the falling water massages my back, I close my eyes and see Edward walking through Leicester Square, then in the restaurant with the blonde, then hailing a cab with her, then they're in a hotel room, and then they're in bed together. I let the falling water cover my face, bring my hands to it and press my fingers into my eyes. *What did I do to deserve this?* I've always been a committed wife. I've always been true to Edward. I've always loved him. I've never done anything to hurt Edward.

Except . . .

No, it can't be. Disappointment, yes, but surely he can't resent me for it. There was nothing I could do. It's biology, it's who I am as a woman, it's not my fault.

Edward was devastated when we learnt I couldn't have children. For two years he hinted, then attempted to persuade me to try, telling me that having a child would make us complete. The truth was, I didn't want children – I was focused on my career – but when I eventually acquiesced and we tried and failed, we were both deeply hurt. Equally, I thought. I discovered I had actually wanted children, wanted them very much, but now it was too late.

I've always needed Edward, but I especially needed him after we learnt I'd never be able to have a child. All the attention focused on me. Now that I think about it, I could see the pain in his eyes, but I was so wrapped up in what I was going through – it was my body, after all, that had failed us – that I failed to even check how Edward was coping.

And now there's every chance that he's turned to another woman. I don't know if I can believe his excuse – a work colleague? That's an easy answer, the obvious one. So if she isn't a work colleague, who is this Barbara? If she's the mystery caller, she knows my name. That means he's told her about me. Or maybe she's found out somehow, stealthily; in the way I've been trying to be. I need to see Edward's diary again. I need to search through it more carefully, methodically, and I need to find her in it. But I know how unlikely it is that there will be an opportunity for that now.

I try to think of some way I might be able to get Edward to leave the house without locking his office. He could go on an errand. Something that would need a man's involvement. Some DIY – something to do with the garden, maybe. If I can think of something that would require a visit to a shop, that might provide me with enough time to look carefully through his diary. But the office would have to remain unlocked, which is something that simply never happens when he goes out.

After I have finished in the shower, I grab a quick coffee, then lock the house and drive to the station. I place my bag on the floor behind my desk and turn on the computer. Hillier walks in with a mug in his hand. He smiles. 'I'll grab one for you,' he says and skips off.

'Hi,' I say, but he's gone.

There's a lot of activity in the major incident room, a lot of toing and froing, so there's constant chatter and a bustling noise in the background. Sitting here, I feel warmer and calmer than I have for a couple of days, perhaps because this place is like a home to me, somewhere I feel like I belong.

I realise my warrant card, which I normally keep in my jacket pocket, is in my bag, so I reach down, unzip it and root around for it. My hand catches my notebook. I pull it out and, smoothing it open on my desk, study it carefully.

18 September; 25 September; 6 October; 11 October; 12 October; 21 October.

The dates I copied from Edward's diary but in number form.

There is nothing marked on this week's pages, so Wednesday, 16 October, the date of Laura Randall's murder, isn't marked with an **X**. But the two most recent dates that were crossed match the dates of Fiona Cunningham's and Rachel Adams's murders. That points to Edward being a possible suspect.

I'm not sure about the dates in September or the significance of 6 October. This case didn't exist then. I turn on HOLMES and search the dates 18 September and 25 September. I read the crime log to see if anything similar occurred on those dates. I check a day either side of them.

Nothing that's vaguely similar. One death resulting from a violent crime across the four dates I check and that was a fight in a pub – which will probably end up as manslaughter. Three car accidents, one hit-and-run. A domestic fire.

And 21 October – what about that? I have no way of seeing into the future, but clearly Edward has something planned for that day.

'Here you go,' Hillier says, appearing with two mugs. He places one on my desk and, seeing the piece of paper I'm looking at, asks, 'More lottery numbers? Thought you'd have given up by now.'

'No,' I shake my head, 'just some dates I'm thinking about.'

He twists his neck and looks at them. 'Oh yes,' he says, 'and I think we'll be thinking about *them* for quite a long time to come.' After an extended look at the page, he sighs to himself and walks over to his desk, sinking deeply into his chair and sipping his mug of tea. 'Not going to forget those two dates in a hurry, that's for sure. What are the others?'

'I'm not sure yet.' I'm not lying, but I still feel awkward – what possible reason could I have for writing them down on the same piece of paper as the dates of two known murders? 'Do you know how the tip-offs are going after the press conference?' I say to change the subject.

He leans in his chair. 'Wright's working through them. Last night, she said her team was on number twenty-five of one hundred and thirteen. And twenty-five nothings from what she can see. God knows how many more have come through since then. It's like a dog trying to catch its tail. Almost seems pointless to ask for the public's help.'

'It just takes the one good one.'

'I know,' he says. 'I know.'

As I reach for my mouse, my arm knocks my coffee cup and some of the liquid spills on my desk. 'Shit,' I say.

'You okay?'

'Yes, thanks.' I grab the tissue box that's on my desk, but it's empty. Opening my drawer, I pull out a packet of pocket tissues and start to extract one. But my eyes fall on the piece of paper that's in my drawer, face up.

Numbers.

Or dates?

I stare at it for a moment.

Yes, dates.

Ignoring the spillage, I grab the piece of paper from the drawer and place it on the desk next to my notebook. I gaze down at them both.

6 October; 12 October; 13 October: three of the dates I copied from Edward's diary.

The numbers given to me by the female voice during

the second phone call are dates: *10, 6, 10, 12, 10, 13* is the same as *6, 10, 12, 10, 13, 10*. The same numbers but in reverse, in the American style: '*10, 6*' – October sixth; '*10, 12*' – October twelfth; '*10, 13*' – October thirteenth.

Two of them, the dates of the murders, confirmed by the phone call.

So the phone call, Edward and the murders are definitely connected. There's no doubting that.

I wanted answers. Now I fear I have them.

'Edward,' I mouth.

Do you really know your husband, Amelie?

42

I stare at the words and numbers and the connection is unequivocal. They're a perfect match. I don't know why I didn't see it instantly; the link was right there in front of me.

I try to think about everything in a disconnected way, attempting to remove my emotions, to remain level-headed and see clearly, but it's impossible.

Can Edward really be the man I'm hunting? My Edward, the kind, considerate man I married. The man I love, the man with whom I vowed to spend the rest of my life.

All the dead girls are sixteen and seventeen, the same age I was when I was violated by the person I should have been able to trust more than any other. My father betrayed me. Now is Edward, my husband, the second man to betray me?

Those poor girls. I came out from the other side of hell, but they'll never have the chance to emerge.

I don't know what to do. Turn him in? On what, the evidence of two untraceable phone calls made by an unknown voice, as well as a diary with marks in it? A diary I may never have the chance to see again.

That's not proof.

The woman I saw Edward with, Barbara – if she was the caller, why would she have gone out for a meal with Edward after she had alerted me to his awful crimes? It doesn't make any sense.

My head's spinning. Nothing's clear, nothing makes any sense. And the car – why did the car try to run us over? Did Edward pay the driver to try to kill me, to get me out of the way so that he can continue his fling and his killing spree unhindered, remove the unsuspecting wife and investigating officer at the same time? But the car aimed for him as well; he was only unhurt because I managed to push him out of the way. He couldn't have timed it that well. He couldn't be that good an actor. And he saved me, too.

No, I know him. I'm his wife. He loves me. He saved me. He couldn't. He wouldn't.

After I'd already lived for so many years truly believing I couldn't ever trust another man for the rest of my life, Edward showed me a different kind of man. He showed me that my father was not a representation of all men.

And yet, I know I've got to act; I can't turn the other cheek, no matter who Edward is and what we've been through together. I'm a police officer and it's my responsibility. It's what I do, it's who I am.

But can I stop the man who is my husband? Can I accuse him when maybe this woman caller is setting him up? I can see him. In my mind, it's just him and me. He's holding me by the hand, like he always does. He loves me, I know that, and I love him. He has done for me what can never be repaid. I owe him everything. In fact, I owe him my life.

I lean back and open my mouth to scream out of sheer frustration. I manage to exhale with the force of a mighty wind, but no sound leaves me. I breathe in, swallowing the air, sucking it into the pain that already exists deep inside me.

I look again at the dates, focusing on the final one: *Wednesday, 21 October.*

That's in four days' time.

If it's Edward, I've got to stop him, and if it's not Edward, I have to find out who's setting him up.

I've got four days.

X Marks the Spot

Initially exalted, I then became, after a time, shocked by what I had done. Not repulsed, though. Never repulsed. It had been such an out-of-body experience, and I kept reliving it. I re-watched myself grabbing her, bashing her head against the ledge, how the blood splashed over the windowsill and dripped onto the floor, the stain that spread over the carpet. And having sex with her. Finishing inside her nubile body.

I was excited each time I replayed the event, and the urge to get into another young girl's house to do the same thing started to run rampant over me. When I thought about what this made me, I knew I had to fight to suppress the desire. I didn't want to be a killer, I had a moral compass, I was not a killer, although I had killed. Killing seemed like it would be an inevitable requirement if I wanted girls like Megan. I wanted them so much. I wanted, but I didn't want to be a killer.

Traces of me would have been left at the scene. We had had sex without a condom. Traces of me would have been all over her. I knew I was now a wanted man. If I killed again and left more traces, the police's search for me would only intensify. After killing one, surely I could disappear. With more murders, I'd only endanger myself. I had no idea how to evade capture. I couldn't risk being caught, so I did the only thing I could think of to quash it once and for all. I had to start dating. I would try to find a mate, a life partner, someone who might help me suppress that rage and desire. Someone who was able to distract me from those desires. And it wasn't long before I met a lady who fit the bill. She was perfectly acceptable, so I did all I could to woo her, to encourage her to fall for me, and I breathed a sigh of relief when she did.

When we were married, I was determined to be happy. On some days, I was. On other days, there was a rage within me. But I had to make it work. To never go back. A child, I thought. Maybe a child would be the answer.

If I had a child, maybe I would never be able to go back. Or, sometimes I feared if I had a child, maybe that would become another danger.

43

When I arrive home, the house is still empty. As I enter the kitchen, my jacket in my hands, I spot a piece of paper on the worktop.

It's a note from Edward. The first time he's written me one like this.

Unexpected business trip. Trouble with my mobile. Sorry.

It says he'll be back on Monday. The day when **X** marked the spot. The day after another girl may have died.

I pull my mobile phone out of my jacket pocket, expecting to see a missed call from Edward. Surely he's tried to call me since writing the note. But there's nothing. It feels like he's abandoned me.

There's no word about where he's gone. I select his name on my phone and press the call button. I wait for a connection. Straight to voicemail, phone off.

I ring his office. 'I need to know where Edward is,' I tell the receptionist. She puts me through to his personal assistant. 'Where has Edward gone?'

'I'm afraid I don't know. He booked the trip himself.'

'I need to know where he's gone.'

'I'm sorry, Mrs Davis, but I don't know. I can call him and ask for you.'

She's lying. I hang up without another word.

I try Edward's office door and, as expected, it's locked. *Sod it*, I decide. I go into the garage, searching for some tools. I find Edward's toolbox, but just as I'm about to open it I spot a crowbar in the corner. I grab it and return to the office. I slide the crowbar into position and put all my weight behind it, trying to destroy the door frame so that I can open it. I strain and strain, pressing my body up against the door, and finally it gives. A few more pulls with the crowbar and then I use my hands to tear the remaining parts of the frame from the wall.

The door drifts open.

Edward's office looks no different from the last time I was in here. I head straight to the desk. He's taken his netbook with him, so there's no way I can try out the numbers to see if they're the password. The drawers remain locked shut. I force the crowbar into a gap, wrestle with it for a moment, and then push my weight downwards. I hear wood splintering, but the drawer doesn't release. I push down further and then up and down again and repeat, more splintering, scraping, cracking sounds, and finally I win the battle. The top drawer pops out. I remove it completely and pour its contents onto the top of the desk. Then the second drawer and finally the third, larger one. When I'm finished, the desk is covered with paperwork and notebooks and other stationery.

I start sifting through what's there, flipping through the pages of the first couple of notebooks. A lot of numbers and company names, product names, nothing about people. I want his diary, but it's not here. I need some kind of clue about where he is and who he's with, where he's been and when.

Four victims so far. I can't let there be a fifth. I need to know where he is!

After I've clawed through Edward's belongings without success, I drop into his chair, exhausted, breathing heavily. There's got to be something else I can do.

I've destroyed Edward's office and learnt nothing. Even if I'm wrong, I don't care what he thinks anymore. I don't care what will happen when he returns to find this mess. I'm not going to try to cover up that I've been in here again.

My eyes land on the phone on his desk. I'll give it one more try. Lifting the receiver, I dial.

It rings.

This time, he picks up, but there's only silence at his end. I wait, willing him to speak, my body tense, but he doesn't say a word.

'Where are you, Edward?' I blurt out.

No answer.

'What kind of mess have you got yourself into? What are you doing?' I give him time to answer; he doesn't. 'I want to know. If you're looking for someone, please stop now. Or if you're with her, please don't do it.'

I listen carefully but am unable to hear a connection any longer. I glance at the receiver. At the same time, my mobile phone buzzes. I glance at it.

A text message. I open it.

It's from Edward.

Sorry, called away suddenly. Am in Madrid. Major contract problem. Will call in the morning after everything's settled but didn't want you to worry. Didn't even make it to office today so was worried they wouldn't be able to tell you where I am. Sorry again, darling. Sleep well.

I put the desk phone receiver to my ear again and listen carefully. 'Hello?' I say. Nothing.

But there was a connection, I'm sure there was. Someone was on the other end of the line. It must have been Edward.

Now this message. *Is it genuine?* He sounds so caring. He sounds just like the old Edward.

His trip means I have a bit of time. I have to figure everything out and I have to find a way to bring this to an end.

By either stopping him or helping him.

44

'You have nothing to be afraid of. I will never leave you. Ever.' Edward gently takes the sides of my face in his palms. He caresses soothingly. Like magic, I feel instantly calm. 'I'm here for you, ready to listen whenever you want to speak. I'll wait for you for as long as you want. But just remember this: whoever has hurt you, I am not that person. I am nothing like that person. I won't ever be that person. I am here for you now, today, tomorrow and every day afterwards. I will never let you down.'

We lie down on the sofa, he on his back, me with my cheek pressed against his chest. I can hear the regular beating of his heart. It's slow and controlled. I believe him. I've never felt this way before, never thought I could ever feel this way.

'I love you,' I murmur.

'And I will always love you,' he says, his arm holding me tightly, reassuringly.

My eyes drift closed and, content because of a man for the first time in my life, I sleep. I sleep next to a man, one who isn't hurting me, for the first time in my life.

When my eyes open, I reach out to Edward. He isn't here. I sit up. 'Madrid,' I whisper, and I realise Edward wasn't with me last night, that I was dreaming of our early days. Our happy days, before everything changed.

I stay where I am for a time, sitting still, reliving memory after memory with Edward. Reliving what my life was like before he came along, before he said he wouldn't give up trying to win me over, before he persisted and won. If he'd have given up on me, no doubt like other men would have . . . No, Edward is unique. He's the only one.

My loyalty lies with my husband. I'm afraid he's trapped somehow. Either through his own choice or because of someone else. Maybe because of that woman.

I know what I have to do. And I will do it for Edward.

I will do it for my husband.

He saved me. Now I will save him.

And if he isn't what the woman on the phone suggested, perhaps she's the one – maybe she's a danger to *us*. I have to find out who she is and I have to stop her.

But first . . .

I call Hillier. 'When's the latest progress report due?'

I hear some clicking. 'This morning. Arrived an hour ago.'

'Super. I'll be there in an hour or so.'

'I'll be out. I've got some appointments booked in.'

'Okay, I'll catch up with you later.'

When I arrive at the station, I speak to a few colleagues for additional progress reports – a social media search update, a DNA search update, a response to press conference update – and then I settle at my desk. I print off the latest progress report summary and log on to HOLMES for an updated report, one now containing details of all four murders and victims, including the latest, Laura Randall. I print off several more pages and move to the conference room to update the information board.

On the updated whiteboard are pictures of all the victims, when they were alive and then when they were on Emerson's bench, pictures of the corpses at the crime scenes, maps of the locations, and the same information on each girl that I'd listed about Fiona Cunningham several days ago. There are other piles of paper all over the room. Some to be filed, some to be read.

I settle at the conference table to work my way through the updated documentation, drawing my index finger slowly down each line of text. One of the first names is Dean Wicks, the result of his DNA being found inside Fiona Cunningham. For a moment, I wonder whether Hayley Turner has tossed him. I hope she has.

Keen to find something, I return to the lines of information. I look down each page slowly, even though I want to scan at a greater pace. I can't miss anything. I scan top to bottom, frustrated that this is all I can think of doing. Page after page after page. I'm irritated that nothing has yet come of all the angles that are being investigated, that no one on the team has made any more connections. *There must be something.*

I turn more pages. More reading, not scanning. Intricate, careful checking.

Several pages further in, I stop.

There's a name I recognise. A name I know all too well.

Steven Barr.

Instantly, I'm transported back seven years. Back to the case – a double missing persons' investigation, two teenagers, both fifteen-year-old girls, who lived only a few miles apart. The investigation, the suspects. One was a man named Steven Barr, a thirty-five-year-old who worked in a bar and had sold both girls alcohol in the months before their murders. The arrest and subsequently the trial.

Steven Barr was guilty, there could be no doubt. Hairs and fibres from his clothing were found on both girls' bodies, which were discovered in woodland towards the back of Primrose Hill Park. But shortly after the trial commenced, the defence team put the arresting officer on the stand. The lead barrister took great pleasure in the questioning and did it slowly and methodically; it came across as an elaborate performance, because it was: he built up the tension until he asked his final killer question. And with that question, he revealed the flaw in our actions that would set his client free.

The senior investigating officer, Detective Chief Inspector Jan Harris, had failed to read the suspect his rights during the initial interview. She believed he was going to cave in and admit to the murders. Which he did.

But by omitting the first line, *You have the right to remain silent*, she failed to advise him of his basic rights. She failed to act within the law.

Steven Barr walked free due to that ridiculous technicality.

We were all, all of us who had worked on the case, devastated. It wasn't Jan's fault; she did what many of us would have done. She thought she was going to obtain a confession, so she broke the rules. But by doing so she jeopardised the prosecution. It ruined her career and destroyed her personally. The last I heard of her, she'd been forced into an administrative role before quietly taking early retirement.

Steven Barr deserved to be sentenced. He deserved to be punished.

So perhaps now I can put that right . . .

I return to the computer system to see if any more information about him is available. Listed is his last known address. His arrest picture is also there. I don't need it; I remember his face too well. And a person's eyes – they never change.

Standing up, I switch off the computer. I take one long look around my office. *Yes, a place I could easily call home.*

Yet I'm about to risk it all.

45

I wait outside Steven Barr's last known address, which is in a cul de sac in Barnet, for almost an hour before a car pulls up. A woman, most likely in her twenties, gets out. I hop out of my car and cross the road. 'I'm looking for Steve,' I say casually. 'Steven?'

She shakes her head. 'I don't know anyone called Steven or Steve, sorry.'

'Steven Barr?'

She shakes her head even more vehemently. 'No, it's still no. But I think Barr was the surname of the previous owner. I can't remember for sure, but I think it was the name that was on some letters we forwarded on after we moved in.'

'Do you still have that forwarding address?'

She smiles. 'We've lived here for five years.'

'Do you remember anything about him?'

She eyes me curiously. 'Sorry, and you are?'

I pull out my warrant card. 'Police. I'm trying to locate him.'

She shakes her head slowly. 'I'm sorry I can't help more. I never even met him. It was just a handful of times those letters arrived and a long time ago at that. I don't even remember what town or city it was. When we moved in, there was a note on the kitchen unit with an address on it, asking for any post to be forwarded. That's all I remember. Like I said, five years passed this past July.'

'Do you remember which estate agent was responsible for the sale?' I ask.

She tells me. I write down the name and thank her.

Next, I call the DVLA, identify myself, and ask if there are any cars listed under the name Steven Barr. The operator tells me there are several Steven Barrs in the UK.

Ideally, I don't want to go back to the station to search the licence plate database in case I'm seen by colleagues, and I can't call in with the request because that will involve creating a potential witness, so I decide to try the estate agent first. I ask the receptionist if I can see the person who sold Steven Barr's property five years ago.

'He's due back from a viewing any moment,' she says after looking up the address, and she offers me a coffee when I say I'll wait.

I sip slowly on the drink and flick through one of the glossy magazines that have been displayed in the waiting area. After a time, a tall man with a well-kept beard comes in, shaking the drizzle from his coat.

The receptionist tells him I'm waiting. Dropping his coat behind her desk, he comes over to me, tidying his jacket collar and flicking the lint from his shoulders as he walks. 'Detective, I'm Neil Fletcher,' he says through a beaming smile that reveals stained and crooked teeth. 'This way, please.' He leads me to a desk and I sit opposite him.

I show him my warrant card, which he casually waves away. 'That's not necessary. A pleasure to help.'

'I'm looking for an individual I believe can help with my enquiries into a number of serious crimes. It's very important, otherwise I wouldn't be disturbing you right now. I'm afraid I can't say anything more than that. It's a tricky situation and the last known address I have for the person in question is no longer valid. But it turns out you sold that property to the current owner, so I'm here to ask whether you arranged the next sale in the chain or if you have the details of what that was.'

Neil Fletcher leans back in his chair. 'So you basically want to know where he or she is?'

Slowly, I nod my head. 'That's right.'

'I shouldn't really. GDPR and all that.'

'I know you shouldn't. I can get a warrant. I'm just very conscious of time and how this man could disappear. This would save me that time and eliminate that danger. I really need to locate him.'

'There's data protection to worry about . . .'

'Perhaps you have a good memory instead? No formal checking that way. It's a name you may already have been familiar with, and his face too. He was on the news a few years before you sold the house.'

He leans forward, interested, and smiles knowingly. 'Perhaps I can help as a caring citizen, not as an employee of this company.'

I nod and say, 'Steven Barr.' Then I recite his last known address.

'Oh, yes. How could I not remember that one? He was all over the news for ages.'

'What do you remember?'

'That sale must have been . . . what, five years ago now. We didn't arrange his purchase, just the sale. I don't know who dealt with the follow-on in the chain. He moved out of town. I don't know much more than that, but I do remember the area he moved to.'

'Where would that be?'

'Oxford.'

46

I return to the station, reluctantly but without any other option, and casually enter a quiet office off the major incident room in an attempt to use a computer out of the eyeshot of others. But I understand the need to appear casual. Even when what happens to Barr happens, there's no reason anyone should check my computer records. I've got to act as if today is the same as any other day.

The computer takes an age to load before I can log on. The whole time, I keep my eye on the closed door, expecting to be interrupted, preparing my relaxed smile for the moment when, or if, someone comes in.

When the computer is finally ready, I open the vehicle registration database and enter the name *Steven Barr* along with the city reference *Oxford*. The system searches and after a few moments some lines of text emerge as if from behind clouds.

I grab my notepad from my bag.

The name Steven Barr.

A registered address.

A licence plate. Make, model and colour.

What the hell?

A blue Ford Mondeo.

No . . . How is that possible?

A Mondeo. Could it have been Steven Barr at the restaurant? Did Steven Barr try to kill me?

I quickly log off, replace the notepad in my bag, and leave the station. Getting into my car, I set the satnav and begin the fifty-mile-plus journey to Oxford. There's something disturbing in realising I'm going to see Steven Barr for the first time in seven years.

During the journey, I recall the details of the case against him and his trial. I recall the destruction he left behind. The two beautiful young girls, their families. I can still see their faces. My face as a sixteen-year-old fits in beside them, as it does beside the recent girls, Fiona Cunningham, Rachel Adams, Niamh O'Flanagan and Laura Randall. I belonged with the two girls back then and I belong with these girls now.

I remember the pain I endured during the investigation as I learnt about their suffering, and how I understood exactly what they'd been through right before he killed them. How I was desperate to hide my own personal scars that had never truly healed, how I had managed to suppress them, but how the investigation turned me back towards my own past. The same as now. How I was desperate to find a way to bring healing to their families. Also the same as now.

The ultimate help for the families would have been to arrest and prosecute Steven Barr, then to convict him. We did the former, but we failed with the latter.

I hated that we failed. I felt so bloody useless sitting in that courtroom while the judge read out that ridiculous statement, how the barrister moved for a mistrial and the judge agreed with him.

In releasing Steven Barr, the girls' families were forever imprisoned.

In releasing Steven Barr, we, the officers involved, were forever bound in guilt.

And now this, perhaps, could be my opportunity to make amends for all that injustice, to say sorry for the additional pain the system that's supposed to bring justice inflicted on the innocent families and the memories of the murdered girls. I can save Edward, yes, but at the same time I can bring Steven Barr to the end he deserved all those years ago.

After an hour of not being able to think about anything other than the past, I pull into Langley Meadow, relieved and exhausted. The car crawls as I scan the door numbers. I'm looking for number 85.

When I see number 81, I pull the car over on the opposite side of the road. Barr's house is the third along in a row of six terraced properties, narrow yet tall buildings.

I'm pleased there isn't a car in the driveway. I need to rest and I need time to plan.

First I need to switch off my thoughts and push away the memories because I have to focus on the here and now. I have to act carefully. I can't mess this up.

But above all, I'm determined to get him. For the girls. For their families. And for Edward. For my own future.

All I need is to see him, to make sure this is *the* Steven Barr, and once I've done that, I'll be ready.

He won't suspect a thing.

47

A loud noise startles me.

It's raining heavily. A downpour. It takes a moment before I realise where I am. The car windows have steamed up, I can't see anything outside the vehicle, so I switch on the engine and put on the windscreen wipers.

I squint through the rain on the windscreen as it clears and falls, clears and falls. Yes, Langley Meadow. I try to see the door to number 85.

Steven Barr's house.

I'm drowsy. I don't know how long I've been sleeping, so I check my watch. Not that that helps, as I'm not sure when I arrived. The light's fading and I can't see at all well, even when the windows are completely clear. I can't really see the time on my watch. Instead, I look at the dashboard, expecting to see illuminated numbers spelling out the time, but all I can make out is a green blur. The numbers are there, but I can't see them. Squeezing my eyes shut, I rub them. That done, I open them again, but somehow my vision has become worse. The steering wheel is in front of me, I know it is because I can see its outline, but I can't see any detail on it. Maybe because it's dark. Maybe it's the fading light. Maybe I've got a migraine coming on. Maybe I've been drinking again. I peer into the footwell but can't see anything there. Not even my legs. The rain is relentless, pounding on the car, so much that it's shaking. It's windy too. I feel under attack, suddenly small and helpless. Wind strikes against the sides of the car and I'm knocked left and right. A larger gust hits and I fall towards the passenger side. Using my arms for leverage, I drag myself back into an upright position. The windows are completely steamed up, but they're porous and the rain starts streaming into the car. It's covering me. And then I'm aware of a pounding. There's a hammering noise, it's coming from the side. I spin to the right, but the door isn't there anymore. I'm exposed and a wave washes over me. As its effects dissipate and a sense of clarity emerges, a figure stands just metres away from me. It's outside the car, in shadow. Its hand reaches out towards me and it takes a step, two steps, forward, and then it's in the car, and it's grabbing me, and it pushes me onto my back, and it leans right over me, and suddenly I see clearly.

I see my father's face.

I scream.

'Jesus,' I gasp, my heart hammering, and I take a deep breath, relieved to see it's still daylight and not raining. I check inside the car, just to make sure. There's no one here. I glance at my watch. I can see its face. Everything is clear. I take a deep breath as I try to relax my pounding pulse. I must have dozed off, and only for a few minutes because it's still early afternoon.

I don't have a good view of the front door of number 85 from where I've parked, so I switch on the engine and edge the car forwards. When the red door comes into view, I stop.

It is red. I try to shake off the dream. That doesn't mean anything. *Concentrate*, I tell myself. *Just concentrate*.

Patience. Give it time.

48

It's an hour later and I'm desperate to pee. I can't hold on much longer. I use the satnav to search for the nearest coffee shop. There's a Starbucks just over two miles away. Switching on the engine, I pull away from the kerb and try to make the journey as fast as possible.

Traffic is light, so I arrive within five minutes. It's a standalone building in a retail park, near a computer retailer and some discount fashion shops.

I jump out of the car and head straight for the loo. There's only one, a large toilet that caters for both sexes and the disabled. The coffee shop is unsurprisingly busy and there are two people waiting to use the loo. Well, three really: an old man and a woman in her thirties who's holding a baby that's only a few months old.

After they finish, I dash into the toilet and relieve myself. Hands washed, I leave, walking towards the door with my head down. Just as I'm about to reach it, I look up to push it open, but the door is already open and a man is entering. My eyes catch his and I stumble backwards.

It's Steven Barr. He's slightly older now, with less hair and a larger belly, but it's unmistakably him.

Startled, I twist my neck away, attempting to shield my face, and I grab the door as he lets go of it, heading out without looking back, moving as quickly as I can without drawing attention to myself. I hope to God he didn't recognise me. I have no idea. *If he did . . .*

Anxious to get away, I keep moving quickly in the opposite direction of my car. If he's watching, I can't let him see which car is mine. I enter a clothes shop and stand behind a rack of clothing, the rack that's nearest to the entrance, which offers me a sightline to the entrance to Starbucks.

I need to see him leave. I need to make sure he's gone before I come out.

The pace of time feels like a slow cog on rotation. I'm getting agitated and feel ridiculous standing here on the spot. But I can't move; if I do, I might miss him leaving.

After a while, and after having glanced at me several times, a shop assistant comes over. 'Can I help you?' she asks tentatively. She's young and extremely skinny with curly shoulder-length brown hair, and she's very pretty.

'I'm fine, thanks. Just looking.'

She doesn't back off. 'Are you looking for . . . anything in particular?'

She doesn't look like she's going to leave me alone, so I decide to drop the façade. 'Look, I'm a police officer,' I snap at her, 'and I absolutely must keep watch on the building over there. I don't anticipate being here for long, but I need to be left alone. The person I'm watching can't know I'm here and by talking to me you're potentially drawing attention to me. Please step away.'

She holds up her hands. 'Sorry,' she grumbles.

'I don't mean to be rude. It's just very important.'

'Of course,' she says indignantly and moves away at speed.

My agitation is increasing the longer he's in there. Perhaps he snuck out a back way because he saw me and maybe he's searching for me.

Fortunately, my paranoia isn't warranted. When I've been lurking here for around fifteen minutes, he emerges, no coffee in hand. He pauses on the pavement outside, turns to the left, turns to the right. *He's looking. I'm sure of it. Searching for me.*

After a few moments scanning the area, he gets into his blue Ford Mondeo. I move towards the door and watch him pull away. The licence plate number matches the one I retrieved from the computer system.

I don't know the colour of the car at the restaurant, but it's definitely the right shape.

As soon as he has disappeared from view, I run as fast as I can to my car, jump in and accelerate out of the car park, swerving to avoid a driver who reverses out of a parking space and into my path.

When I arrive back at 85 Langley Meadow, Steven Barr's Mondeo is in his driveway. I park even further away this time, but don't keep such a great distance that I can't see his car.

Yes, it really looks like the car.

He's in there, and he won't be going anywhere without me seeing exactly what he's doing.

49

When Steven Barr re-emerges from his house, I take note of what he's wearing, which I didn't notice before, thanks to the unexpected circumstances in which I encountered him. He's dressed in a uniform, a blue shirt and matching overalls. That must mean he's a manual labourer. Perhaps a mechanic. Perhaps someone who works in a warehouse. Definitely someone who gets his hands dirty. Squinting my eyes, I try to take a closer look as he walks to his car. I can't see if his hands are dirty, nor can I make out any kind of company logo on what he's wearing.

Glancing at the clock, I see it's almost 2.30 p.m. That and the fact that he's wearing work clothing makes me assume he's either about to start an afternoon shift or he's been home for his lunch break and is returning to work. And if it is lunch, he must work fairly close by. Either way, I assume he'll be gone for at least three or four hours.

Which means his home will be empty.

I keep my distance, following his car cautiously as he weaves his way in and out of traffic. He knows the area well. In under ten minutes, we arrive at an industrial area. It's full of warehouses, DIY stores and offices. He pulls into the carpark of a garage, outside of which there are about a dozen parked cars. A small number have got prices on their windscreens. I stop a little further down on the other side of the road and adjust my wing mirror so that I can watch him from where I am. I track him as he enters the building.

This must be his workplace. Could be shift work. Some kind of work that operates on a Sunday. Could equally have been a lunch break. I wish I could have seen if he was already dirty. That would have allowed me to ascertain whether he'd been at work this morning or not.

I need to know his work pattern. I need to choose the right time to do what I have to do.

After making a note of the phone number that's displayed on the front of the building, I move off, searching for a payphone. I can't use my mobile; mustn't have a record of anything that can connect me to him. It takes a while to locate a phone box, but I find one. I dial.

'Robinsons' Motors,' a male voice announces cheerfully.

'Hi there,' I say. 'I was in last week and an ever so helpful gentleman called Steve was helping me. I'm thinking of bringing my car in again tomorrow, but I'd very much like to see him as he was so kind and helpful last time. He explained everything so clearly, see, and I really have no idea about cars. Can you tell me if he'll be at work?'

'Tomorrow?'

'Yes, that's right.'

'His day off's tomorrow. He'll be back in on Monday from eight a.m.'

'Super,' I tell him. 'Wonderful. I'll see him then. Thank you ever so much for your help.'

Monday it is, then. 8 a.m.

50

I spend the next day researching Steven Barr. Is he married? Does he have a partner? Does he share that house with anyone?

That's what I predominately want to know. Could there be anyone else in the house while he's at work?

I need it to be empty.

I scroll down his Facebook page, which hasn't been updated in over eighteen months and that last post was a simple check-in-at-a-pub post. He doesn't appear to be on Twitter or Instagram.

While I'm on social media, I decide to take another look at the girls' online accounts. And a fresh look too – Micah Ainsley still hasn't turned up anything, and surely there is something between them. It's the connection that holds all four girls together.

My eyes stop while I skim through their lists of followers. I think for a moment.

I jump back to Steven Barr's Facebook page. I click on the About page. Year of birth, nothing else. I start working my way through older posts, two years ago, three years ago, earlier than that when his life appeared to be busier, or at least his social media presence was more active. Comments under pictures. Comments under adverts. Comments under services.

And that's when I see what I've been hoping to find.

Under a post about a plumbing service, Barr queried the hourly rate. The company replied, requested an email address to which full details could be sent. Barr dutifully complied.

His email address, on the screen for me to see.

Steven Barr needs to be connected to these girls, or at least to some of them. I need to create an indisputable link between him and them.

I quickly head to a local supermarket, the largest one nearby. I want to blend into the crowd and I want to go to a place that sells a lot of goods, which will make my purchase untraceable. En route, I stop at a cash machine and withdraw some money.

I arrive at the supermarket about ten minutes later, enter the store and locate the mobile phone section. There's a young man standing behind a small counter towards the other end of what looks like an alcove in the corner of the store. As I browse the walls, he calls to me, 'You after anything particular?'

I don't turn around. I just keep scanning the shelves. I say, 'No thanks, all good.'

I grab the first one that looks appropriate. Mobile phone, pay as you go, Internet capability.

I pay for it using cash at the self-service tills.

When I'm back in my car, I open the box, remove the phone and insert the sim card. I'm relieved to see it has some battery life. And the reception is clear too.

I open the Internet browser and go to Twitter. There, I create an account for Steven Barr using his email address. Feeling pleased, I click Submit.

Then a message appears: *Verify account by clicking link that has been sent to email address provided.*

Shit, I hadn't thought of that. And now Steven Barr might have an unexpected email from Twitter alerting him to the account I've just set up for him.

'Shit,' I say, this time vocalising my frustration.

Think. Think.

Frankly, Instagram is the most popular site for girls their age. I decide to open him an account there, disregarding Twitter. Hopefully that email went into his spam folder and he won't even see it. Or maybe he doesn't even use that email address anymore. The Facebook post on which I discovered it was over five years old.

First, I have to create a new email address for him. I go to gmail.com and enter the required details. I verify the account by entering the new mobile phone number I've just acquired – a phone I'll soon throw away.

Once that's done, I go to instagram.com. I enter Steven Barr's details and confirm the account through the Gmail email address. Then I go back to his Facebook account, download the only picture he has on there – his profile picture; it's an old one, but it'll do – and return to Instagram where I upload it as his profile picture. To follow anyone, I learn I need to download the app, so I download it from Google Store and then start following the girls. When it comes to the last account, Fiona Cunningham's, I decide not to follow. There's enough to connect Fiona Cunningham to Niamh O'Flanagan, so if he's following her he could easily have been aware of Fiona Cunningham.

I remove the sim card, smash the phone under my foot as best I can in the cramped conditions of my car and then I drive several miles away, spot some bins near a newsagent, and deposit the phone in it. I drive several more miles, get out of the car, grind the sim card under my heel and kick its fragments into a drain. I find another bin in which to throw the phone's packaging.

Thinking about all the girls' online followers, I'm again struck by the notion that there must be a connection that goes beyond Fiona Cunningham and Laura Randall having met.

I open Google on my mobile and search: *how can you cross reference followers between two social media accounts*.

After a bit of reading, much of which confuses me, only one result looks promising. It's the website of a company called SSS, Software Search Systems, which offers subscribers an online software that enables them to compare followers of different online accounts. It sounds exactly like the kind of thing I'm looking for. But it's necessary to make contact with the company to register interest; it's not something that can be used immediately or purchased. Which perhaps means it isn't legal. I imagine it might be a scam, but because I can't find anything else in the search results that looks like the right sort of thing, I click on the contact button on SSS's website. There's only a form to fill in, no phone number, no postal address and no email address. Disappointed, for I'd hoped for a phone number as it would be the quicker option, I recognise that it's my only hope, so I fill in the form.

I type in my request, stress that it's for urgent police

business, and ask for an immediate phone call back. I offer my work email address, even though I understand there could be risks involved with doing so, but it'll surely carry more weight than my personal Gmail account; it'll make my query appear more official.

Realising I'm at a temporary dead end, I try calling Edward. His mobile is switched off, so I call his office where his secretary promises she'll send him a message on my behalf. I really want to speak to him, need to hear his voice.

Before I . . .

I need to feel sure about what I'm going to do.

After Edward doesn't call me back, and having tried calling him several more times, his voicemail picks up. I speak calmly, slowly. 'Edward, I hope everything's all right and that it's going well. I really just want to hear your voice. Please call me. I hope you're okay.'

A short while later, the phone rings. I grab it and my pulse races when I see who's calling.

'Edward,' I say, unable to contain my enthusiasm.

'How are you?'

'Without you,' I say, 'not so good.' Then I mouth inaudibly, 'Not good at all.'

'Won't be long now. I should be back tomorrow.'

I pause. I don't know if I should say it. Then I realise I should. 'I miss you.'

'I miss you, too.'

'I—'

'Sorry, got to dash. I'll see you soon.' There's a pause and I want to fill it by saying so much, but I can't.

And then he's gone.

51

I'm doing this for Edward. *It's the right thing to do*, I keep telling myself. I told myself the same thing the whole way here.

It's Monday. I left the house at 4 a.m. Now it's half five and I'm sitting in the car down the road from Steven Barr's house, waiting for him to leave for work. I arrived early; I couldn't risk missing his departure.

I'm doing this for Edward.

En route, I stopped at the Starbucks where I saw Barr on Saturday. It's a twenty-four-hour facility. I knew I'd need the sustenance, so as I wait in Langley Meadow I'm sipping on a cappuccino and nibbling a flapjack I purchased there.

Time passes exceedingly slowly, which gives me time to think. Thinking gives me time to picture how everything needs to pan out. Thinking gives me time to make sure I'm about to do everything right, that I foresee anything that might happen, that I do what needs to be done to save Edward. In my mind, I need to separate him from those girls, who I know too well, and from the woman on the phone, who I don't know at all, and I need to make sure that when I close my eyes it's Steven Barr who I see standing over their bodies, that I see him and believe it, because if I believe it, then I'll be able to convince everyone else of this simple truth: Steven Barr is guilty of the murders of four young women. And who knows how many others that we don't know about?

He raped and killed two girls. He's been free for too many years to do the exact same thing again. He doesn't deserve that freedom. He deserves to pay for his crimes. Even if that means paying in a different way. Paying for the things I'm going to prove he is doing now.

I've never done anything like this, but as the time nears 8 a.m., I don't think I've ever felt so much determination to see something through in my life.

I'm doing this for the man who gave me life. I'm doing this for *our* life together.

When Steven Barr exits his front door, I spring to life and watch as he gets into the Mondeo. He pulls out and accelerates down the road. I watch as he turns at the end of the road and disappears.

Which means the house is empty. All my research has indicated he's single. That's not surprising. There aren't many people his age or mine who don't know who he is and what he did.

It's tempting to jump out and get in there quickly, but I wait patiently. I have to be sure he's arrived at work before I move. I don't want to be surprised by an unexpected return.

Which means I wait fifteen minutes precisely before I get out of the car. It's cold and the street is quiet. From the backseat, I remove a sports bag.

I cross the road and walk up the path to the aged red front door. I press the doorbell. If someone answers, I'm merely a salesperson. When no one answers, I press it again, just to be certain.

Satisfied that the house is indeed empty, I look to both sides of it. There isn't a side gate leading to the back. Which means there must be another way round.

Casually, I walk away and pass the house next door and continue on. Further down, I come to a path that leads along the side of the final house in the row of houses. I make my way along it and at the end there's another path to the right. There's a wall on the left the entire way along the path, but on the right are fences and gates leading into the back gardens of the six houses.

The back gate to Steven Barr's garden is the third along. I try the gate, delicately, to be as quiet as possible. It opens and I step inside. The garden is small, so I move in haste and arrive at the back door in a matter of seconds. I keep close to the door and building so that I can't be seen from any of the windows on the neighbouring houses.

Automatically, I try the back door, but I'm not surprised when it doesn't open. Not knowing whether the house is alarmed, I need to make a decision: try to force open the door or smash a window.

From my bag, I remove a pair of gloves, a short metal pole and a bedsheet. I put on the gloves. Balling it up, I place the bedsheet against the door's window. I bring the pole towards it three times, sharply and deftly, and the window cracks. It doesn't make an excessive amount of noise. I push through a few shards of glass and reach in.

There's a simple old-fashioned twist lock on the inside. I turn it and the door unlocks. It opens like a magic trick solution. I step inside.

I find myself in a kitchen with floor tiles patterned in blue and white. Everything in here looks old and worn. Dishes lie in the sink. A half-full mug of coffee sits on the counter top.

I leave the kitchen and enter the narrow corridor that leads to the front door. Inhaling, I smell the air that Steven Barr breathes. It's musty. There are a couple of pictures on the hallway wall. Standing close to them, I see Steven Barr with a woman. They're smiling.

How could you not know? I think. *Or maybe you do, in which case what the hell are you doing with him? What is wrong with you?* I wonder who she is. They look close.

Keeping my eyes on him, I step backwards. Then I make my way upstairs. The first room I come to is a spare bedroom. There's a double bed in it, but it and all the space around it are piled high with rubbish, bags and boxes and dust. The room smells like it hasn't been aired for a long time. Next is a larger bedroom in the middle of which is a double bed. The sheets are half hanging off it. There are items of clothing on the thickly carpeted floor. *Dirty bastard*, I think. *Why am I surprised?*

I scan the room. I can't see what I'm looking for.

Next, the bathroom. And there it is. Like a precious heirloom or the genie's lamp that Aladdin discovers.

There's a hairbrush on a shelf that's above the toilet. In between its teeth are lots of short dark hairs.

From inside my bag, I remove a small plastic bag with a seal line. I carefully extract several hairs and place them into the bag, pressing the seal tightly together when I'm finished.

I'm about to leave when I think, *more, find something else.*

I return to the bedroom and glance around. *Yes,* I think, *there.* I pull open the drawers nearest to me. The third drawer contains his underwear.

Dirty, I think. *These are clean. Better to get dirty underwear.*

Re-entering the bathroom, I locate the laundry basket. I scoop larger items of clothing out of the way and find a pair of black Y-fronts. Turning them inside out, I inspect the groin area. A couple of white marks. *Perfect.*

I place them in another plastic bag and seal it.

I leave the way I came in. *Who cares if he arrives home to find a break-in? That won't prove anything. I'm being careful; I won't leave any traces of myself behind and risk sabotaging the case.*

I get into my car and only when I lean back against the seat do I realise just how much I've perspired and how tight my chest feels. I lean my head back against the headrest and breathe in deeply. And then relief floods over me.

It's exhilarating, yet worrying at the same time.

Got him. I'm finally going to destroy the bastard's life.

52

In the afternoon, when I return to the station, I put the small bag of Barr's hairs and his underwear into a larger carrier bag and store them in my locker, in its deepest recess behind several items of spare clothing. I have what I need, but I can't use it yet. I've come to the sad realisation that I'll have to wait for another victim to be discovered before I can do anything with what I've excavated.

I know there will be more deaths. We're too far from finding the killer for anything more optimistic to be the outlook. Now I'm crossing a line and, by doing so, more innocent lives may be lost. I will hate myself forever if that becomes a reality, but this is for Edward. Is he worth it? I think so. *No, I know so.* Is it worth jeopardising my career? I know of others who have planted evidence, who have been caught and consequently have destroyed more than just their careers – their whole lives, in fact. And, of course, it could all be for nothing. What if, in days or weeks or months – sometimes it's even years later – some evidence comes to light suggesting that it's not Barr or Edward, but someone else? Then all I will have done is make things worse. *Will I ever be able to forgive myself?*

But for Edward, for my marriage, I have to try. If I don't, I won't be able to live with myself. But if I do and it all goes terribly wrong, I don't know what then . . .

When it happens and I do what I've planned, at least I know Steven Barr is a bad man and deserves what will happen to him. Then I need to confront Edward and, somehow, to find out who the woman on the phone was, find out how he's involved, and, if necessary, take him far away from here. He's got the wealth; we could move, we could get away from any threats; whoever's causing this, we could start again.

As I pull into our driveway at just after midnight, I'm surprised to see Edward's car in its usual space. I forgot he was due back. Switching off the engine, I move quickly to the front door. I don't think, *I'm so happy he's back.*

The key won't go into the lock easily, my hand is shaking so hard. Finally, I manage to slot it in and unlock the door. Dropping my bag, I fling my jacket on the staircase banister and go straight towards Edward's office.

I charge along the corridor. 'Darling,' I say, delighted.

I come to a sudden halt.

Edward is on his knees, picking up pieces of the office door frame. He peers up at me.

I cringe. I'd forgotten what I did here. I'm responsible for this mess.

I bring my hands to my mouth, genuinely shocked. 'I'm sorry,' I say, not knowing what else to say.

'What happened?' he says, rising, concern straining his voice and face.

'I'm sorry,' I repeat, it's all I can do, and I stumble into his arms. I bury my head in his shoulder. Then I utter a muffled repetition, 'I'm so, so sorry.'

His hand rubs the back of my head, as if I'm a babe in arms. 'Ssh, it's okay.'

'I didn't know. I thought you were gone. I didn't know what to do. I'm so sorry. I thought you were gone forever.'

He pulls back and looks me right in the eye. 'It was work, Amelie, just work. But don't worry, I'm back now. I won't leave you again. I promise.'

53

I wake up in bed in the morning, this time in Edward's arms. My cheek is on his chest, my hand on his belly, my leg hooked around his. Smiling, I feel content.

This is my husband.

I will do anything for him.

I already have and I'm ready to do more.

I relive last night. How he led me up here. How he lifted me at the top of the stairs and carried me through the bedroom door like we had just been married. How there were roses in a vase on the dresser and petals over the bed. How there was a gift bag on the bed and inside it, wrapped in scented paper, was some black satin underwear.

How I felt so spoilt by him.

So close to him.

How I still do.

My phone vibrates, disturbing the perfect moment.

I don't know where the phone is, but I can hear it. Reluctantly, I pull myself away from Edward. The ringing stops before I locate the phone, but then I find it on the dressing-table chair, with the chair tucked under the table.

The screen tells me there's a missed call from the station. Before I have the chance to return it, the phone rings again.

'Ryan,' I say, pressing it against my ear.

'Another body's been found.'

My heartbeat instantly quickens. 'When?'

'The body was found before five. Same as the others, Amelie. It's the same guy.'

'Oh, Ryan.'

I hang up the call and look at Edward, who's still asleep on his side of the bed.

For Edward.

Now's the time, I realise.

There can be no mistakes. I will only have one chance to get this right.

54

Regents Park, London

She was found deep in the recesses of the park, behind the tennis courts, by another early morning dog walker. So often, it's unsuspecting dog walkers who discover the bodies, people going about their everyday business who inadvertently find something they'll never be able to forget for the rest of their lives.

It's the eyes you remember, that's what most of them tell me. The whites of the eyes. I call it the death stare.

Having stopped off at the station to remove the Holy Grail from my locker, I arrive at the cordoned-off area within an hour of Hillier's call. I show my warrant card and am given access to the scene.

Hillier isn't here yet. In fact, there are only a few scene investigators present. It's quiet. Exactly what I need it to be. I have to hurry, though, before they all arrive.

Long blonde hair. Blue eyes. A black thigh-length dress. Black heels. She's a stunning girl.

I stand a few feet from the body, swaying as I study her.

I feel apprehensive; the knowledge of what I'm about to do gnaws at my insides, but its necessity helps me maintain the focus I need. *There'll be no turning back after this.*

As I stare at the body, another thought mingles with my personal worry: the loss. Another family ruined. But there's a hope, the slightest hope, for my husband. *Surely that will make it worthwhile.*

I have to do this, no matter what the sensible part of my brain tells me. I have no choice.

I put on a pair of disposable gloves. Discreetly from my pocket, I remove the small plastic bag. I tip the hairs into my gloved hand and, checking that no one nearby can see, crouch down next to the body and place each of the four hairs into the girl's mouth. I ensure that one goes under her tongue. The sensation of lifting a tongue, when rigor mortis has begun to set in, makes me feel nauseous. I rise, disconcerted, and quickly back off. I want to cry, for this girl who's lost her life, this girl I've just violated, for the family that'll suffer so much, but also for myself, for what I've just done *to myself.* I'm a criminal now and I'll have to find a way to live with that forever.

When I see there's nowhere I can convincingly place Steven Barr's underwear, I decide to keep it in my bag. I'm on my knees when Ryan Hillier's voice sounds behind me. 'What have you found?' he asks.

I have no idea how long he's been there and hope to hell he didn't see what I've just done. I stuff the plastic bag into my jacket pocket and try to move as steadily as possible. 'She's so young,' I say and push past him, eventually succumbing and vomiting in a bush.

Unexpectedly, as I'm bending over, I feel Hillier's hand

rubbing my back. 'It's okay.'

'Still not . . . feeling too good,' I struggle to say. Then when I straighten up, 'Oh, she had so much life to live.'

'Haven't they all?' he says, not really asking a question but more resigned to the fact. He moves away and takes a slow look at the body. 'We have to find him, Amelie.'

I'm not ready for the stark realisation that my actions have just made capturing the real killer even more improbable. *How can I ever live with myself? Why was I so stupid, to think I could make everything better by doing this?*

The true killer will forever be free because of what I've just done.

But it could be Edward. I know him. I love him.

I *have* done the right thing. *This can end it.*

We stand back while Emerson and his full crew search the scene. After an hour of waiting around, Emerson calls us over.

'She has her ID on her,' he says.

'On her? Not dropped?' Last time looked like an accident. This sounds like a change in pattern. Changing patterns rarely make sense.

'Yeah, a provisional driving licence tucked into her bra. Her purse was on the ground.'

'Like he wanted us to find the ID,' I say.

'Looks like it,' Emerson responds.

The killer is showing us, or showing me.

Emerson says, 'She's seventeen. Her name's Kinga Nowicka. Her address is here.' He places it in an evidence bag and hands it to me.

'Let's get her parents informed,' I tell Hillier. 'See if we can make a positive ID as soon as the body can be moved.'

'I don't understand,' Hillier says. 'He's been so consistent. This seems too sloppy. It can't – God, you look faint, Amelie.'

He takes my hand in his. I peer at it and then suddenly pull it away. 'Keep me informed,' I say, handing him the evidence bag and walking away from him and the scene, fighting off the tears and struggling to think clearly.

'Amelie, where are you going? Lange will want his report from you.'

I wince. 'I've got to – It's okay, Ryan. He'll get it. Just keep me informed. As soon as the body's moved, let me know.'

'I will.'

I start to thank him but turn as soon as the sound starts to come out of my mouth. I don't want him to see my emotions. I place my fingers on my temple as I pass the officers who are standing by the police cordon and follow the paths that lead to the exit.

When I fall into my car, the tears escape as if a tempest has broken out. I peer at myself in the vanity mirror, and I hate what I see. I pray and beg not for forgiveness but to find a way to get through this. I know I'm beyond reproach and I fear there's no chance to find a way out.

Yes, I have a husband. Yes, I've saved him. And that should enable me to feel relief.

But first, I have to do everything I can to make things as right as they can be. I have to find the real murderer.

I know that social media may hold the solution, but when I check my emails, there isn't a response from SSS. I compose another message on the webpage's contact form:

I need an urgent response to my query.

Then I give it a moment's thought but ultimately decide that I don't care whether the next words I use sound unprofessional or desperate. It's the truth, plain and simple.

This is a matter of life and death.

55

After returning to the station and spending some time sifting through the evidence with Hillier, who also returned, we received a call from Daniel Emerson, who said he had something important to show us, so now we're heading to see him. As we walk through the door to the morgue, he's sitting at his desk, his eyes fixed on his computer screen. Nearby, on the raised bench, is Kinga Nowicka, the fifth victim of our mystery killer.

Or, as it is now, the fifth victim of serial killer Steven Barr.

I know why we're here before Emerson starts to talk.

'How's it going?' Hillier asks.

'Good, good, good.' Emerson rises, picking up an evidence bag from the desk. 'Very good. Something very different this time. I found these in the victim's mouth.' I hope I manage to effect a neutral look. He holds up the bag, passes it to me. I nod, trying to appear pleased as I stare at the contents. In some warped way, I am, but I'm not sure how convincing I am.

'They were in her mouth,' he adds. 'Seems he got a little too close to this one.'

'Have you run them yet?' I ask instantly.

'Results are running through the system as we speak. If he has a record, there'll be a hit and we'll know who he is.'

'Good,' I say, knowing what that hit will be. 'Good.'

'Time of death?' Hillier asks.

'We estimate between ten and eleven last night.'

I arrived home after midnight. Edward was back. That means he had time to do it and arrive home before me.

But how could he have known I would arrive home so late?

Too much convenient timing. It couldn't have been him.

I turn my head, my eyes falling on the naked body of Kinga Nowicka. *Yes, another, so pretty, just like the others.*

Like I was once.

'Is everything else the same?' Hillier asks.

'Evidence of vaginal penetration, yes, and traces of semen. We'll have to see if it's post-mortem. Nothing under her nails. Underwear around the neck. Evidence of muscle relaxant in her blood, same as with the other four. So, just like the others, she might have been incapacitated while he raped her. Perhaps aware, but unable to do anything about it.'

Good God. I lean against the bench to steady myself. 'Poor girl,' I mouth.

'You can say that again,' Emerson responds. I wasn't aware that I'd vocalised what I'd been thinking.

Hillier moves to my side. 'How long before the hair results come back, Dan?'

'How long's a piece of string?'

I've glazed over, but my words are working. 'The second you get anything,' I say, 'call us.'

'I will.'

'The very second, you hear?'

56

The following day, Hillier and I are in a boardroom off the major incident room. Lots of paperwork from each of the five murders is spread across the large table.

'Another college,' he says. Kinga Nowicka went to St Andrew's College in Hampstead. 'They all went to different schools, both private and comprehensive, and not all of them were actively in full-time education, so no connection through education. What about when you or any of the others spoke to the families?'

'We've got through the folder of lists of friends and found nothing, but I'm waiting to add some for Kinga Nowicka. Her parents promised to email them over by the end of the day. There's nothing else any of us have been able to see. It all seems so random.'

'He's psychotic. Nothing this guy has done will ever make sense to me.'

Suddenly, I think of Edward and lower my head in shame. I don't know what my face reveals, but I don't think I can hide the guilt that's stirring in me for much longer.

I don't believe the woman on the phone, but there's something about the word *psychotic.* Hearing it said aloud has startled me. *If it's about Edward . . .*

Do you think you know your husband, Amelie?

I try to ignore the question, but I can hear her voice in my head. It's as if she's in this room, sitting right next to me.

I do. I know him. It can't be, it can't be him.

Last night . . . Emerson said the time of death was between ten and eleven. Would that have given Edward enough time to return home before I arrived just after midnight, time enough also to prepare the bedroom so beautifully? Surely not. And what would have happened if I'd got home earlier than I did? There'd have been no planning for that. *No, Edward couldn't have killed those girls.*

I'm confused, questioning myself, and irritated. It's what she's done to me. The faceless, nameless woman from the phone calls.

She could be anyone. I feel a creeping unease as I think about how much she seemed to know about me. If she's his lover, how much of it did she learn from him? But if she's a stranger, all it would have taken is logging on to Edward's Facebook page. She could learn so many things about me from that. He's posted pictures of me. She could have found out my name and where I work. It was our anniversary only a few weeks ago. He posted pictures of us enjoying a meal at a restaurant in Soho and at the theatre afterwards. She could know our every move from what he revealed. She could even have been following us as he checked in where we were.

Pictures.

Facebook, Twitter, Instagram. People put them up everywhere. You don't even need words – a picture can tell a story: where you go, who you're with, what time you're there, whether you're enjoying yourself.

Maybe that's it. I've been too focused on trying to find names. Maybe the answer lies in the pictures.

If I could find something out about them by looking at some pictures, the killer could have done that too.

Fine, not their schools – I've searched for that already – but something deeper. Perhaps I haven't been looking closely enough.

After I've started scanning their Facebook profiles again, Hillier's desk phone rings. He picks it up. 'Hillier.'

He nods his head while he listens and then replaces the receiver. Then he turns to me.

'The sperm matches the others. Mr Cold Case. And we've got a match on the hairs.'

I rise, the goose bumps appearing on my arms.

'Seems like a familiar name. Steven Barr,' he reveals.

'Got him,' I say.

In more ways than one.

'Get on the phone. Get a warrant.' I head for the door. 'And make them wait. I want to be there when it happens.'

57

Four hours later, after the warrant has been rushed through, we've arrived and parked our car in almost the same spot where I parked just a couple of days ago. Hillier is in the driver's seat and I'm by his side. Another two unmarked police cars are further behind us, and the lead van is down the road on the other side of the house. The officers in that vehicle are the ones who'll move in first. Around the corner from them is another van filled with seven back-up officers.

Before we move in, we have to be sure Steven Barr is home. His car isn't in the driveway, so I doubt he is, but of course I can't mention I know anything about his movements or the kind of car he drives.

A voice comes on the radio. 'Car registered under suspect's name is a blue Ford Mondeo.' It relays the registration number.

'Not here,' Hillier responds.

'So we wait,' I say, keeping my eyes on the end of the road, eager to see Barr's car emerge. 'When he shows up, give him time to settle down inside the house, and then, on my signal, we'll go in.'

We sit in silence for a time. I'm relieved to think that this part is almost over. But then I have to begin and complete part two before I can take Edward away, before we can restart our life together. Part two is searching for, finding and stopping the actual killer from killing again. And somehow making him disappear. For if there are any more murders after Steven Barr is arrested, everything has the potential to fall apart.

'I googled the name Steven Barr,' Hillier says suddenly. 'No wonder the name was familiar. You were involved in the case, weren't you?'

'Intimately,' I say.

'I don't remember much about him. Only what was on the news and my memory of that's sketchy. I'd only just joined the force when he went on trial.'

'Seven years ago, he raped and killed two fifteen-year-old girls,' I say, swallowing hard and trying to sound neutral. 'We had him. I was a DC at the time, so I supported on the case. The DCI who led it made a choice we all understood, but it backfired and he got off on a technicality. She got a confession from Barr, the prosecution was a dead cert, but as she thought Barr was close to confessing, she didn't say "you have a right to remain silent" because she feared that might make him hesitate.'

'He got off for that?'

'You have to follow the letter of the law. We all learnt a harsh lesson that day.'

'What was he like?' Hillier asks, sounding genuinely interested.

'He was evil, Ryan.' I turn to him. 'The most cold-blooded killer I've ever known. He seemed to enjoy what he did. It gave him pleasure. He deserves to go down for this. He should already be locked up.' Then, even though I know it's false, I add, 'If he had been, then we wouldn't be sitting here with five dead girls and five grieving families.' That's not me; as soon as I've said the words, I regret it. But it has the desired effect – I can see Hillier getting worked up and sharing my eagerness to catch Barr.

A voice breaks out on the radio. 'Blue Mondeo, right registration number, approaching.'

It turns into the road and heads towards us. I lower my head. I don't want Barr to recognise me, at least not until we've broken down his front door and he's on the floor in handcuffs, glaring up at me as the spotlight of arrest is upon him.

Barr parks his car, gets out, and walks casually to the front door of his home.

'Wait,' I say into the radio. 'Give him time.'

Barr enters the house.

'Patience.'

We sit. We wait. I stare at a printout of a map of the street and its property boundaries.

'Car one,' I say after a few minutes, 'line the fence to the right of the terrace and two of you go down the path to the back of the house. Give me a signal when you're in position.'

The doors of the car opposite us open and a group of uniformed officers emerge. They line the fence. The officer at the back of the line is carrying a battering ram, a large chunk of metal with hand grips, painted red. Two of the officers turn into the path and move towards the back of the house.

I picture them walking down the path, turning right and then stealthily making their way to the rear of the house, as I did only yesterday.

'In position,' says one of the officers by the fence.

Then another voice says, 'In position at the back of the house.'

'Go, go, go,' I call, and Hillier and I jump out of the car and walk briskly across the road. We move side by side along the pavement and, just before we reach the path that leads to Barr's front door, the officers from car one cross our paths and move quickly to the front door.

The first officer bangs on the front door. 'Police!' he shouts. 'Open up!'

He steps aside and the officer with the battering ram moves forward, swinging his arms and striking the door. It buckles. He repeats the move and, after a third strike, the door gives, exposing the inside of the house. Three officers charge in and then Hillier and I follow.

By the time we enter the lounge, Steven Barr is flat on his stomach and there's an officer's knee pressing against the small of his back. His hands have been pulled back and cuffed.

'Steven Barr,' I say loudly, making sure he hears every word of the right to silence, 'I'm arresting you on suspicion of the murders of Fiona Cunningham, Rachel Adams, Niamh O'Flanagan, Laura Randall – and Kinga Nowicka, yesterday, the twenty-second of October.' Now I lean close to him and stress each word: 'You do not have to say anything, but it may harm your defence if you do not mention when questioned something which you later rely on in court. Anything you do say may be given in evidence.'

Hillier and I watch as Barr, who looks stunned, is lifted from the floor and taken out of the property.

'Well done,' Hillier says, as more officers enter and the search for evidence begins. 'He heard every word this time,' he says.

'Yes,' I answer. 'Yes, he did.'

And he deserves it, more than Hillier or anyone else will ever understand.

58

When Detective Chief Inspector Jonathan Lange suggested that Detective Sergeant Katherine Wright should lead the questioning of Steven Barr because, as he said, my connection to his previous arrest might not be helpful, I was, if I'm honest, relieved and I quickly agreed.

The less Steven Barr sees and thinks about me, the better.

'We've got him with the hairs,' Lange said, 'but there must be an accomplice. My guy from fourteen years ago. It wasn't Barr. Find a way to press him on that. They must be working together. Find out who he is.'

It's approaching 10 p.m. and Hillier is assisting Wright with the questioning of Barr. This doesn't mean I have any time to rest; instead, it offers me some time alone in the conference room.

I've spent the rest of the day filling in paperwork, much of it pertaining to Steven Barr's arrest. After a time, Hillier enters carrying a fresh mug of coffee. He places it on the desk and drops into a chair.

'How's it going?' I ask.

He sighs deeply and shakes his head. 'He's denying everything.'

'As we'd expect,' I say, perhaps too keenly. 'But we have the physical evidence.'

'Of course, but that doesn't mean he's going to be any easier to break. A confession would make things much easier. But this is hardly his first time doing this.'

'Have you mentioned the semen? The accomplice?'

'No, Wright doesn't want to yet. She wants to break him down over the hairs. She thinks it's the best route to a confession and then the semen can be introduced later. Maybe as part of a plea, if he won't break.'

'What's he like?'

'He's being combative, so it's going to take time. He's stubborn or deluded and looks genuinely confused by what's happened to him. Katherine called him a good actor to his face. He didn't like that. He's demanded a lawyer, so we've had to pause till one arrives.'

'He started without a lawyer?' I'm surprised. Someone like Barr wouldn't ever be so stupid, I thought. 'The arrogance.'

'Says he didn't have anything to hide, so he didn't need one, but when we made it clear that we didn't believe him, he closed up and demanded legal counsel.'

'Well, it's all part of the process, I suppose,' I say. 'And even if he doesn't crack, he won't be able to challenge his own hairs being in her mouth. I mean, surely there's no reasonable explanation he can offer for that. Don't let him get to you, Ryan – that's what he does. We've got him. That's all that matters. There's nothing he can do about that.'

'I know, you're right. It's just draining sitting in there, listening to his lies.'

'It'll all be worth it. You'll see.'

'I know.'

He drinks some coffee and closes his eyes, savouring it.

'I remember him well,' I say. 'He was a difficult one.'

He opens his eyes. 'He remembers you too, Amelie. He's mentioned you already, in fact.'

I cock my head in surprise. 'Me?'

'Yes. He started by asking a bundle of questions about you. About your current role, about your family. We didn't answer anything, of course. Then he said he saw you recently. He started acting really paranoid about that. If it wasn't for the hairs, I'd – well, I don't know really.'

'But we have the hairs,' I say slowly and forcefully.

'Yes, we do.' He thinks for a moment. 'You know, he swears blind he saw you at a Starbucks in Oxford the other day, that's all. And he says seeing you earlier today, seeing you in person and up close, confirms that it was you he saw. Apparently, he wasn't sure then, but he's certain now that it was you. I think he's just trying to distract us.'

I don't know what to say. Lie some more, deny it completely, or give him something in return. I don't want to incriminate myself.

It's my word against his. He's a semi-convicted felon. He's a fucking murderer and I'm a respected police officer. Who's going to believe him over me?

They could check the CCTV. I'll be on some recordings, I'm certain, although they wouldn't go that far, surely.

'I was there a while back,' I decide to say, trying to sound innocent and casual. 'I went shopping. I guess he could have seen me, it's possible, but I didn't see him. I mean, what's he suggest—'

'Nothing, I'd say. Just trying to be creative in finding a way to deflect the attention from himself. That's what Wright said it was; she said it to his face. He didn't like that. A colourful imagination, she called it. That made him really indignant, I can tell you.'

'He was convincing when I knew him. He really believed what he told us,' I say, my heart pounding. My need to try to convince Hillier is automatic.

'I don't doubt that for a second,' he says. 'If anything, I'd say his skills have only sharpened over the years. But don't worry, we'll find a way.'

'Yes,' I say, worrying, 'I'm sure you will.'

59

Sensing that I'm standing in his office doorway, Edward peers up from behind his desk.

'You're home late,' he says.

'Yes.' I linger a moment and he notices my uncertainty. 'Everything all right?'

I want to tell him, but it's surprisingly harder than I thought it would be to say the words. 'We arrested a suspect today.'

'Oh,' he says and then pauses. 'Good.'

I don't say anything else, I just stare at him. At the man I've ruined myself for.

'Tired?' he asks.

'Shattered.' I step into the office. 'But we got him. We got the man who's killed five young girls and I couldn't be happier.' I'm searching to see if there's any trace of a sign in his eyes. I don't think I see anything.

I step round his desk and behind him. He remains on the chair and I place my hands on his shoulders and lean my head against the back of his head. Then I gently rub his shoulders.

'That feels good,' he says. 'But maybe I should be doing that for you.'

He spins round and pulls me onto his lap, kissing me deeply. I clasp him by the face, stroking his cheeks and running my hands through his hair.

As I take a breath, I say, 'We've got him,' and then we kiss again.

He lowers his head and nuzzles my neck. 'Yes,' he murmurs. 'Yes, you have.'

With my arms around his head, embracing every kiss that he gives me, I mouth, 'Yes, we have,' and silent tears start to drip down my cheeks and onto Edward's hair.

60

Waking up, I find that Edward isn't in the house. This is becoming a habit. I call his mobile and get the voicemail. I don't leave a message. Instead, I check my work emails. Still nothing from SSS, the online company that claims it's possible to find connections between individuals' and companies' social media profiles by using their software service. Waiting for a response is becoming a huge frustration. An email from Micah Ainsley informs me about Kinga Nowicka's accounts, so I get to the station as quickly as I can and, once I'm online, I start searching through them and I revisit those of the other four dead girls, looking again and again at certain pages. Trying to find something important. Maybe something I – we – have missed.

Just as I'm about to log off and make my way to St Andrew's College in Hampstead to speak to Kinga Nowicka's teachers and friends, an email alert reveals that, finally, I've received a response from SSS.

The email is signed by someone called Barry. He can help, he says, and he's included his phone number, asking me to get in touch.

I look up. 'Ryan,' I say.

'What's up?'

'I'm on to a lead here. Do you have time to make the St Andrew's visit for me?'

'Yeah, I've got nothing booked in till two. Should give me plenty of time. When are they expecting you?'

'Ten minutes ago.' I smile.

He returns the smile. 'Ah, so that means leave now, then.'

'If you don't mind.'

'No problem.'

I wait till he leaves, then I grab my mobile and call the number. Too fast; I make a mistake and have to type in the numbers again.

'Software Search,' a male voice says.

'Barry Rogers, please,' I say.

'Speaking.'

'Barry, it's Detective Sergeant Amelie Davis. Thanks so much for returning my email a little while ago. I'm calling from the MIT, the police, in London.'

'Of course,' he says animatedly. 'How can I help?'

'If I give you the social media profiles of five girls, can you tell me whether they have any followers in common?'

'Absolutely. What are the account names?'

I read them to him.

'Won't take long,' he says. 'Can you hold?'

'That fast, really?' I'm surprised.

'That fast.' There's a boastful edge to his voice.

While he's gone, I open up Fiona Cunningham's Instagram page again and scroll through her pictures. Beautiful bone structure, high cheekbones, deep blue eyes, shiny straight blonde hair. A truly stunning girl.

What a waste, I think, shaking my head, struggling to believe what I'm in the middle of.

'Detective,' Barry's voice interrupts my thoughts.

'Yes, Barry.'

'No followers in common. There is one, a Steven Barr, who follows four of them though.'

'Okay,' I say, expecting this. I offer my thanks, but feel deflated. It had been my only hope. There must be some other connection, some link I'm not seeing.

'How reliable is the technology you're using? Can it be mistaken?' I hope for an answer I doubt I'll get.

'Created, actually,' he says.

'Sorry?'

'Not just using it, I created it.'

'Oh.'

'Yes, that's right, and it's infallible. It works on algorithms that search key words – in this case, usernames that are repeated in the follower lists of all five. A username won't change from profile to profile. If one profile follows two accounts, its username will be identical, so it's impossible to miss. The only way a person could follow two profiles without being traceable is if they use two different accounts, so two different usernames, in which case they'd be unidentifiable to my software, or any other, for that matter. They'd be absolutely impossible to trace.'

Of course one person could use two, or multiple, accounts. In which case, I'd have no chance of finding them. 'I understand. Well, thank you for your time. I appreciate –'

'It doesn't mean, however, that the five girls aren't all following one specific account.'

'What do you mean?'

'They have followers, but *they* are followers as well. Flip the concept around. They can all follow the same person or company account.'

'You'd be able to check that too?'

'I already have.' He clears his throat. 'And I have a result for you.'

My heart rate increases. 'All five girls were following the same account?'

'That's right.'

'How many accounts?'

'Just one.'

This is it. This is the connection I've been waiting for. 'Is it the account of an individual or a company?'

'Actually, a company,' he says. 'It's called londonteenlifestyle.'

He continues speaking, but I've switched off. While he says something, I type *londonteenlifestyle* into the Instagram search bar and click on the first suggestion.

I read the profile:

Exhibiting the hottest and most fashionable teens London has to offer. Check out what's hot – and who's hot – right here. Updates daily. Collab possible. See website for contact details.

Scrolling down the page, I see girl after girl, dressed and half-dressed. Girls sixteen, girls seventeen, girls eighteen. All pretty girls. All . . .

I stop, staggered, and scroll back up to what I've just gone past.

My eyes widen as the image comes back into view. Blonde hair, blue eyes, slim figure, bikini, lounging by a swimming pool.

It's a picture of Fiona Cunningham.

I slowly become aware that Barry Rogers is still speaking, repeating my name. 'Er, thank you, Mr Rogers, you've been a great help,' I say, ignoring him. 'If I have any more questions, I'll be in touch.'

I hang up without letting him say anything else and keep scrolling.

Blonde hair. Kinga Nowicka.

I keep scrolling.

Blonde hair. Laura Randall.

I keep scrolling.

Blonde hair. Niamh O'Flanagan.

I keep scrolling.

Blonde hair. Rachel Adams.

They're all here. All five girls. This is the link. This is the indisputable connection.

This is how he's choosing them.

I've done it. I've found the answer. But I can't tell anyone. I desperately want to call Hillier. I want to shout it out – the killer is on here somehow – but I know I can't. I don't give a shit about Steven Barr – he can rot in jail, for all I care, because that's precisely what he deserves – but it feels like control of all the different elements is slipping from my hands.

Instead, I'm alone. It'll be down to me to dig deeper. I'm the one who has to find him. And then I need to stop him.

61

I check out the website of *londonteenlifestyle*. Another company where contact is only possible via an online form. *Why do none of these web companies list physical addresses?* It's like they're all trying to hide something.

I don't want to fill it in and tell them who I am and what I'm doing. What happens if the real killer runs the company or can see the messages that arrive? I need to work out a different way to make contact or to find out where they are based. I need an address. I have no way of finding one alone. I'll have to work out an explanation for the time when I'm asked why I needed to know an address for the company, but right now I'm going to have to take that risk and ask for help.

'Tim, I need an address for a company called London Teen Lifestyle,' I say to a member of the web support team at the station. 'Web-only contact on their website and they have an Instagram page. Will you be able to find anything?'

'I should be able to,' he tells me. 'Might take a little while, but let me dig and I'll come back to you as soon as I have something.'

Sign up, I think. *Get them to contact you.* I click on the sign-up button. When the form opens, it requests my name, age, date of birth, town or city and country of residence, and a picture sample. It tells me I'll either be accepted or declined within twenty-four hours.

Twenty-four hours – not long to wait.

I provide fake details and a stock photo we use for online situations such as this.

After I click submit, I'm asked to set up an account. Username, password, repeat the choice of password.

I click submit.

Then it asks for two security-question answers.

Favourite singer or band.

I enter *Justin Bieber.*

Then the second security question. Surprise makes me double over, like I've rear-ended the car in front.

Now I know how he gets to them.

62

'Amelie, I need to see you. Come to my office now.'

It's DCI Jonathan Lange. His call interrupts my online search for more information about *londonteenlifestyle*. I tell him, 'I'll be there in five minutes.'

I'm nervous as I head to Lange's office; there was something unusual in his voice.

'Sit down,' he says after I enter, not a request he usually makes.

He looks drawn and angry. He sits opposite me and sinks into a deep chair. 'I'm going to be direct and I want an honest answer from you, do you understand?'

Of course I understand. I already know where this is going.

'Yes.'

'Steven Barr says you were in Oxford just days before he was arrested. He says he saw you in a Starbucks. Is that true?'

I breathe deeply, considering for a moment whether to reveal the new connection I've made between the five girls. *Tell him about* londonteenlifestyle, I think. *Take the focus off yourself.*

But I need to find the killer.

I swallow. 'I have been there recently, yes, that's true. I don't remember when exactly.'

He doesn't look pleased. '*Why* were you there?'

'I went shopping. I had some lunch.'

'So it's just a coincidence that a man whose case you assisted on seven years ago and who has now been arrested for crimes you're currently investigating says he saw you in a Starbucks not long before he was arrested *by you*?'

'Yes.' When I see he's about to protest, I add, 'He may have seen me, I don't know. I went to a Starbucks, yes, but not just Starbucks. I went to a number of places. I needed the loo and Starbucks was the closest place that had one. Coincidences can happen, you know.'

'He also says his house was broken into two days later. Are you aware of that?'

'No, not at all.' I need to be outraged here. I need to look truly shocked. The problem is I'm not. 'Look, excuse me, sir, but I hope you're not suggesting –'

'It's what *he*'s suggesting that's my problem, Amelie, not me,' he says, leaping out of his seat and pacing. 'For Christ's sake. Do you not see what's happening? It could make the entire investigation go tits up. He's accusing you of setting him up. He insists he hasn't done anything wrong. And he's got a pushy lawyer who loves a good scandal. What I'm suggesting is, this is going to be a big problem for me. Which means it'll be a big problem for you. And I don't want a problem. If you have gone and done something very stupid, you need to tell me right now.'

'Sir, there is no problem. You have the evidence, it's indisputable. Steven Barr's DNA was found on Kinga Nowicka. Case closed. This is simply a sideshow, a distraction. He's trying to get us to back off. We had him once, remember, and he got away with it because of a mistake we made. He's trying to make us make another mistake so that he can get off again.'

'What mistake?' he snaps.

'He wants you to doubt me. And it sounds to me like he's doing a fairly good job in that regard.'

Lange stares at me for a moment. He looks furious, but he's thinking about what I've said. I think I'm getting through to him. 'I need your word, Amelie, and I'll tell you now, if it turns out that you aren't being straight with me, you're finished.' He holds me in his death stare. 'You'll get jail time. I'll make sure of it myself.'

I try not to break eye contact, even though I want to shut my eyes and scream. *What am I doing to myself?* 'I understand, sir.' I know I'm shaking, so I try to steady myself before I say in a way I hope sounds unequivocal, 'You have my word.'

'I'm old enough to remember when that meant something.'

'Which is now. My word means something *now*.' After a pause, I add, 'You know me.'

'Yes, detective sergeant.' Then he says very slowly, maybe too slowly, 'I know you.'

63

As I reach my office door, I pause. My body's quaking. I'm in too deep. I've passed the point when I can change what I've said and done. Even though I'm so close to discovering the real murderer, I can't suddenly start saying *yes, I was there, I was searching for Steven Barr in order to set him up to save my husband who may or may not actually be the murderer.*

There's no answer. I was there, it's that simple. One look at the CCTV footage from Starbucks will show that. But one look at the CCTV from the clothes shop and I'll be ruined; they'll see me loitering near the door and watching the building across the road. Watching for Steven Barr.

A lawyer can't access CCTV based on a client's accusations, I know that. It has to be the police and a warrant has to be requested. Surely I'm protected enough. But I can't help feeling worried. If I'm looked into properly, there's no way my lies will add up. And everything's being said behind closed doors, so I don't know what's going on and what's being said.

Pushing the door open, I enter my office. I'm surprised to see Hillier behind his desk packing some things into a bag. He looks flustered.

'Oh,' I say, 'you're back.'

'I'd barely left. A call came through while you were in with Lange, so they phoned me and told me to turn back. Another body's been found, Amelie. A young blonde. Teenager. It looks the same.' He winces. 'I mean, Jesus, how can that be? We've got Barr right here with us.'

I fall into my chair. 'Another?' A ball of emotion swells up within me and feels like it's going to explode.

It's because of me.

'Either Barr's got an accomplice or we've made a terrible mistake, Amelie.' His head tilts back and sinks into his shoulders. 'How can this be?'

'I don't know,' I lie, my eyes glazed over. Inside, I'm trembling. This is what I feared. 'I have no idea.'

But I know. Oh God, I know. I know exactly how. Because the murderer is still at large.

'We should leave. You are coming?' When I don't answer, he says loudly: 'Amelie?'

'Yes?' I say, snapping back to reality.

'We have to get there. Now.'

'Where?'

He tells me where the body was found. Now I visibly start shaking. He's still talking, but I can't hear him. I remain in my chair, stunned.

The place.

It can't be.

'What's the matter?' Hillier asks. When I don't answer, he says, 'Amelie, are you okay?'

The location.

I turn and stare at him, swallowing deeply.

'How is that possible?' I whisper.

'How is what possible?'

'Oh my God,' I mumble. 'Hillier, don't you see?'

'What are you talking about?'

'The body . . . He's playing with us.'

64

Primrose Hill, London

We arrive to find all the roads closed and the entire area in the process of being secured by uniformed officers. We're waved through after Hillier lowers his window and shows his warrant card.

During the entire journey here, Hillier kept asking me what was wrong, whether he could help in some way, but I told him I wanted quiet; I needed silence to process what's happening.

Steven Barr is in custody, so who could have done this? It must be someone who knows Steven Barr, or someone who is working with him while he is being held.

This has everything to do with Steven Barr. I'm certain of that now.

Getting out of the car, we enter the park and head up the hill. 'It's the far side of the park,' he says.

I know.

As we reach the hill's peak, I stop for a moment, as though I've reached a wall, and I stare at the bench. It's a bench I've often shared with Edward.

'Lots of trees down there,' Hillier says, gazing down the hill to the other side where the body is hidden. 'Plenty, so it can't be seen.'

I know.

'When was she found?' I ask. He's probably already told me, but I've struggled to process anything he's said.

'Just over an hour ago.' There's concern, not frustration, in his voice.

He heads down and, after a moment to try to clear my head, I follow.

As we approach, Daniel Emerson spots us and comes out from the brush. He nods in greeting. 'Who'd have thought we'd be here again, huh?' he says.

'I can't believe it,' I whisper.

'What's that?' Hillier asks. 'What do you mean?'

'This is where Steven Barr's victims were found seven years ago,' I say, gazing at the spot where now a third victim lies – or the eighth, depending on how the scenario is viewed. 'It's the exact spot in the park where Steven Barr's victims were found seven years ago.'

'No shit,' Hillier says.

'Yes, shit,' Emerson says.

'How long has she been here, Daniel?'

'This is where this one's different. I estimate that she was killed around five this morning. Much fresher than the other five. He took a great risk in killing her here at that time.'

'Is . . . everything else the same?'

'Pretty much, from what we can tell at this point, yes.'

'How was she found?'

'Those houses over there.' He points. 'A woman cleaning the upstairs windows in her house saw something that looked unusual. It was the blonde hair, she said. When there was no movement after some time, she came down to take a look. Didn't expect to find a dead body, but that's what was waiting for her.'

'Show me,' I tell him.

Before entering the cordon, we get kitted up, as usual, in blue suits that cover everything from head to foot. We enter the brush and come to the body. Two large trees shield her from the view of the main field area.

Another pretty blonde. Sixteen at most, I'd guess. Maybe even younger. *Christ*, I think. She's wearing a black skirt. The lower end had been lifted to her waist, exposing her blood-stained underwear. The colour, once white, is now blood-red. Her thighs and lower stomach are also smeared in blood.

I reach out a hand and press it against one of the tree trunks to support myself. *It's my fault.*

'Are you okay?' Hillier asks, spotting my discomfort.

I nod my head, too vigorously, but don't speak.

This is because of me. I've caused this to happen. The poor girl. How can I ever be forgiven?

I close my eyes. I am, once again, in my bed. It's dark. There's a light on somewhere in the distance, further down the hallway. A figure approaches and creeps into my room. Onto my bed. Onto my body.

Touches me where this poor girl has been touched.

Violates me as this poor girl has been violated.

I shriek at the vivid vision. Hillier grabs me by the arm. 'Amelie?'

'Oh, Ryan,' I say. 'No, no.'

Hillier and Emerson share a concerned glance. They're confused and troubled by my behaviour – there's nothing I can do about that now. 'I'll be back,' Hillier says to Emerson, and he takes me by the arm and leads me away.

As we cross the police cordon line, I say, 'You need to find out who she is, Ryan.'

He shushes me. 'I will. Listen, Amelie –'

I hold out a hand. 'Promise me. Promise me the second you know who she is, you'll tell me her name. I need to know who she is.'

'Okay,' he says softly, stepping towards me.

'No, just back off. I don't need your help.' I start to remove my protective clothing.

'Aren't you staying?'

'No, you take care of this.'

'What about you? How are you going to get back?'

'I'm fine, don't worry about me. I'll take a taxi. You just get her name. Leave the rest to me. This can't go on.'

'Let me help you, Amelie.'

But I'm walking away and I don't answer and I won't look back.

I can't.

'Amelie,' he calls. 'Amelie.'

65

As I leave the park, I turn into the high street. There I find a coffee shop and quickly make my way to the toilet. Behind the closed door, I sit on the toilet and gasp for air, struggling to breathe. Where's the hope? I'm trapped. I can never forgive myself for what I've let happen.

I might as well have killed that poor girl myself.

I remove my mobile phone from my pocket and glance at the screen: two missed calls; one from DCI Lange and another from a number I don't recognise.

Even though I know I need to return Lange's call, I call Edward. *I need to know.*

The phone rings.

He picks up and speaks before I can say anything. 'Amelie, I'm home. Sorry I missed your call this morning, but I was called to the office unexpectedly very early. There's a problem. I'm just running out of the door again. I'm sorry, but I've got to go to Berlin for an emergency meeting. A deal's falling apart and I've got to sort it out. Otherwise we could lose a fortune.'

I shake my head. He can't leave, not now. 'No. I need to see you. Now, Edward. I need to see you at home.'

'I've got to get back to the office, darling, and then straight to the airport. I'm so sorry, it can't wait.'

'Edward, you can't –'

'Listen, I'll call you when I get to the hotel and we can talk on the phone.'

'Where did you really go this morning?'

Either he doesn't hear me, or he pretends not to, or the words don't actually come out of my mouth.

'It'll only be a few hours, I promise. Look, must dash.'

'Edward –'

He's gone.

I need to know if you killed this girl.

The phone, a moment ago dead, rings and startles me. I glance down at the screen. I shouldn't be surprised to see DCI Lange's name appear. I press the phone against my chest.

I can't speak to him, not now. Which means I can't go back to the station.

I need to hear from Hillier. I need to find out who the girl is.

I need more time.

I reject the call.

I need to find out for sure where Edward was this morning. I phone him again. It rings and rings. No answer.

I check the time. I'm about twenty minutes away from his office. If I rush, I might be able to catch him before he leaves for the airport.

Dashing out of the park, I scan the street for a taxi. Frustrated that I can't spot one, I start walking at a fast pace in the direction of the West End, all the while twisting round so that I can see if a taxi is approaching from behind me, spinning back to see if one's approaching from ahead.

Eventually, one comes into view. I hold out my hand, eager, shouting out, but it passes by. Then another. This time, I step into the road, but it also passes.

Now I pull out my warrant card. I keep walking on the road, unwavering, despite the traffic and ready.

When the next taxi approaches, I stand in its way, stretch out my hand and shout, 'Halt, police!'

The taxi slams on its brakes.

I open its back door. 'Police emergency,' I tell the passengers. 'Get out!'

The frightened-looking Chinese tourists, with cameras around their necks, nod quickly and jump out, attempting to press cash towards the driver.

'Go!' I shout at them, and then to the driver, 'Drury Lane and fast!'

He nods and doesn't hesitate, pressing his foot on the accelerator, and we move off at pace, weaving in and out of the traffic. Reaching a queue of cars at a red light, I tell him, pointing, 'Go around them, just go around.' So he veers onto the wrong side of the road and jumps the red light, swerving to avoid a motorcycle that attempts to cross our path.

'Fuck!' he says.

'Don't stop, keep going.'

The way he's driving intensifies the urgency I'm feeling. My desperation to see Edward is increasing by the second. I can't let him leave without talking to him. I can't keep this to myself anymore. I need to get everything off my chest and find out what the hell, if anything, is going on with him. The phone call. The car at the restaurant. What I've done. Whether he's responsible for these girls' deaths.

I have to ask him everything.

And I have to tell him everything.

66

The taxi pulls up outside the coffee shop opposite Edward's office on Drury Lane. I remove my credit card from my bag and press it against the card payment reader.

As I open the door and put a foot onto the pavement, I glance in the direction of the office and see Edward exiting. He's moving quickly to the edge of the pavement where a car's waiting.

'Edward,' I call out, but he's already in the car and it is speeding off.

I jump back into the taxi. 'That car,' I say, pointing, 'the black one. Follow it.'

He presses on the accelerator and the car lurches forwards.

'It'll be City Airport or maybe Heathrow. Nowhere too far.'

'Heathrow – not far? This time of day?' he says. 'Have you ever been in London midweek before?'

I don't answer. I sit on the edge of the seat and watch eagerly through the front window to make sure Edward's car doesn't disappear.

We reach Marylebone Road. So it's Heathrow. This will be a longer journey and traffic is heavy. He's too far ahead of us for me to signal to him. 'Don't lose him,' I say to the driver.

My hands squeeze so hard they might press through the seat. Then Edward's car turns left off Marylebone Road.

'Maybe he's taking a shortcut,' the driver says. 'Looks like there's some kind of jam up ahead.' He signals his satnav.

'Get after him,' I say.

He struggles to weave through a few cars and makes the turn.

This can't wait. 'Look, catch up with him, will you?'

'And do what exactly? You know, this isn't a racing car.'

'Block him off.'

'This is Central London and we're in rush-hour traffic. What on earth are we doing here?'

'Just do it!' I say. Then more softly, 'Please.'

The driver manages to pass a couple more cars and then within a minute or so we're behind Edward's taxi.

'Now,' I say, seeing our chance. 'Go round him, now!'

The driver veers into the other side of the road, but a vehicle appears from a side road, so he has to swerve back behind the other taxi.

'This is dangerous, what you're asking me to do.'

'We have no choice!'

'No, it increasingly feels like I haven't.' He's trying to find an opportunity to pull out again, but there are too many cars coming in the opposite direction. 'Unless,' he says to himself.

I can't see what he's doing, so I lean forward until my head is pressing against the Plexiglas that divides the front and back of the cab.

'What are you doing?'

'I can't get past him.'

'Try!'

Then I see what he's doing. He's signalling the taxi in front by flashing his main beam lights and putting on his warning lights. 'Stop doing that! Just drive round.'

'I'm trying to get him to stop,' he says. 'It's the safest option. If I do it your way, I could kill us both.'

'Look, there's a gap. Do it! Do it now!'

He turns the wheel sharply, which propels me sideways. He floors the accelerator and the cab lurches forward. We're side by side now, the two taxis, and I turn to the left. Edward comes into view. His face is down, he's doing something, but he can sense something unusual, so he looks up. As his eyes meet mine, my cab passes his and starts to edge to the left. Suddenly, there's an almighty braking sound and the cab skids to a halt. I'm thrown, shaken, but I pull myself up and get out of the cab. One of the front wheels of Edward's taxi has mounted the kerb. The driver's shouting, 'What the hell are you doing?'

My driver is out of his cab and is shouting back. But as soon as I see Edward slowly emerging from the back of his cab, I can't understand anything either of the drivers are saying.

Edward pulls his wheelie suitcase onto the kerb, his eyes fixed on me the whole time. He's either as shaken as I am or he's seething with anger.

He doesn't say anything, so I speak up. 'What time did you leave me this morning? Or was it last night? I need to know, Edward. I need to know if you did it?'

Again, he doesn't speak, but I can see lots of incomprehensible words on his face.

'Were you in Primrose Hill, Edward?'

'I'm sorry,' he says softly. He steps towards me. 'Amelie, I'm so sorry.'

'Why?' I gasp. 'What have you done? Tell me.'

He looks solemn, closes his eyes slowly and rubs his forehead. 'Not here. Please. Can we do this somewhere private?'

'There is nowhere private and there is no time to go anywhere!'

He looks from left to right and then back again. 'Come here, please.' He takes me by the arm and awkwardly tries to move me and his suitcase into the doorway of a building.

The driver of Edward's cab appears behind us and pulls at my shoulder. Edward pushes him. 'Back off!' he warns, pulling a few notes out of his pocket and thrusting them at the driver. He does the same with my driver who also comes towards us, shouting.

'Tell me,' I say. 'Were you in Primrose Hill this morning?'

He looks sick. Deathly sick. I brace myself for what I know is about to come. The revelation. I know what he's going to tell me.

'No,' he says. 'No. But I was with Barbara.'

'What?' Suddenly, I'm confused. I was so sure. *You're a killer. You were about to confess to me.* 'Who – who's Barbara?'

'The woman you saw me with at that restaurant.'

'Barbara?'

'Look, Amelie, I'm sorry. I will never be able to express to you how sorry I am. The truth is . . . I've been having an affair. I've been seeing Barbara for several months now. Like you – like you thought. I can't tell you how sorry I am.'

67

An affair. Now it all makes sense. Horrifying sense.

'What have I done?' I whisper.

'Amelie?'

'What the fuck have I done?'

'Amelie.' He tries to take my hand in his.

'*For you.*' I snatch my hand away from him. 'Do you have any idea?' I snap. 'Any idea what I've done for you?' *I was completely wrong.* 'My God, what have I done?'

'Amelie, just stop and listen. Let's go home and we can talk about this in private. This isn't the place –'

'Maybe in the hotel room where you've been fucking her?' I slap him.

He rubs his cheek. 'Please, Amelie, don't, let's not do this in front –'

'What I've done for you . . .' I'm sickened. I've ruined everything. I've destroyed myself. I've placed myself in an inescapable hell. 'How long have you been fucking her?'

'I told you. Several months.'

'I want a date. When did it start?'

'In June or thereabouts. Look, it was a mistake. I was a stupid fool. Now let's go home and talk there.'

'Home? No chance. We don't have a home anymore. Soon enough, you'll never have the chance to speak to me again.' He thinks I'm suggesting divorce, but what I'm thinking about is prison. 'When they find out what I've done.'

'Who?' he asks. 'Who are you talking about? *What* are you talking about?'

If he's capable of such deception, if he could have fooled me for all this time, what's to say he isn't fooling me in other ways too? What else is he capable of?

'Were you in Primrose Hill this morning?'

'I was with Barbara, okay?'

'Did you do it?'

'What are you talking about, Amelie?'

'Did you kill those girls? Because I did it for you. *For us.*'

'I don't know what you're talking about?' Now he sounds irritated.

'The marks in your diary. The crosses. Two of those crosses marked the dates when Fiona Cunningham and Rachel Adams died. What were the other dates?'

He sighs and steps closer to me. I'm against the side of the entranceway, so there's nowhere to go. Suddenly, his breath smells rancid. 'You really want to do this here?' he whispers. 'Think before you speak, for God's sake!'

With tears falling, I nod. 'Yes, I want to talk about it right now,' I say as firmly as I can.

'Listen, you've got to believe me when I tell you I feel terrible and I can't possibly show you how sorry I am –'

'Your diary,' I repeat. 'Those dates. What were those markings for?'

'Those were the times I was with Barbara. I mark – oh, really, if you insist, if you must hear it. I mean, if you want to torture yourself with the details. If you must know, those are the times when I met up with Barbara.' He looks into the street. 'Sometimes we spent the night.'

The bastard. 'You mean you fucked her?'

'Well, if you must be so crass about it all –'

'Yes, I must!'

'Okay, then, yes. Happy now? Look, it was an affair, it was stupid, I see that now. I wasn't thinking straight.'

'You were thinking with your dick! Like all fucking men!' I push him and step out of the entranceway. 'I thought you were different! You tricked me.'

'God, can we just get the hell home? What is wrong with you, putting on a spectacle like this?'

He takes me by the arm and tries to lead me to the kerb edge. I pull back. 'You were – with her?'

'Yes.'

'All those times?'

He looks ashamed. 'Yes. And you need to believe that I am so sorry.'

'All those times . . . What you've done – what *I've* done – I did it because I thought –'

I turn around and look back into the space where we were just standing. In my imagination, I see Steven Barr there, framed by the entranceway. *Framed by me.*

'What?' Edward asks with a pained expression on his face. I can see it reflected in the glass in front of me. 'What have you done?'

I can't do this alone. I need help.

Steven Barr is going to destroy me.

'Take me home,' I mouth. 'I need to tell you everything.'

68

When we arrive home, Edward says, 'Sit tight. I'm going to make us two strong drinks.'

Good, I think. *I want to feel the sting. I need something that will help me forget.*

While he's in the kitchen, my phone starts to ring. I see on the screen that I have three voicemails.

'Ryan,' I say, trying to sound as bright as I can, cutting him off. 'Listen, I'm so sorry about earlier. I wasn't feeling well. Some kind of sickness bug.' I lie again. 'I came home for a rest and have slept it off. I'm feeling much better now.'

'Oh, good. I'm glad to hear that.'

'What's news?'

'I've got the girl's ID,' he says.

'Go on.'

'Her name's Sarah Blythe. Seventeen years old.' There's an awkward pause, then he adds, 'And Amelie, I'm sorry, but Lange's been saying he needs to see you again. He's very concerned.'

'I have some voicemails. Probably him. I've only just seen them. I was – sleeping. I'll call him.'

'Barr's solicitor has lodged an official complaint.'

'Ah,' I say. 'As I feared.'

'Lange thinks it could lead to an IOPC investigation.' The IOPC is the Independent Office of Police Conduct.

'Whatever must happen must happen, Ryan. Don't worry about me. If you see him, tell him I understand and I'll call him soon. I'm just in the middle of something important right now.'

'I believe in you,' he says. 'For what it's worth, I'm on your side.'

I smile. 'It's worth a lot, Ryan. Thank you. You're a good man, Ryan.' I end the call.

You're just the kind of good man I need right now.

69

Using my phone, I type *londonteenlifestyle* and *Instagram* into Google. When the page opens, I scroll down, looking at the pictures.

It doesn't take long. I knew I'd find her.

Sarah Blythe is pictured on a picnic blanket, leaning back in a tight low-cut top. She has a beaming smile.

Long blonde hair. Beautiful eyes.

It says in her bio that she's seventeen years old.

Was.

I start typing an email to Hillier.

All six girls were members of London Teen Lifestyle, a teen model company that uses Instagram to share pictures of its models. To register, the girls have to identify their place of education. That's the link, and that's how the killer has been locating his victims. The killer must be someone at London Teen Lifestyle who has access to the registration data. It can be no one else. I'm still waiting on Tim at tech to find out who the company's registered to. That could be something significant. Give him a push for me, Ryan. I'm certain the answer lies there. It must be someone at the company.

Edward walks in before I can reread the email, so I switch off the screen and drop the phone in my bag. I'll send the email later after I can check it.

Edward hands me a glass filled rather high with whisky. I sip it. It's a familiar friend. It helps. As he sits down, he swallows a large quantity, sighs and murmurs, 'What a day.'

I don't answer. I look at him closely. He looks different somehow. I always thought he was different from other men, but now I realise I was very much mistaken.

'You know, Amelie, I do love you.' He pulls an odd face, there's something matter-of-fact about it, and he nods his head. 'I love you very much.'

'But?'

'No buts. I just wanted to say that at the start because I've no idea where this conversation is going to take us and what tomorrow will look like for us. You're being very cryptic, so I don't understand much at all about what's going on inside your head, and your behaviour has been more and more – well, odd, recently.'

'That's because you've changed, Edward. I've been suspicious about you for some time now. You saved me,' I tell him, 'but now I don't know if I'll ever be able to forgive you for what you've done. You've betrayed me. You're now another man who's hurt me. I never thought you could do it.'

'I know.'

'So it's been going on since June?'

He shrugs. 'I think so. I wasn't really counting.'

Every word hurts. 'How many times?'

'Sorry?' He laughs.

'I said how many times?'

'Oh, come on.' When he sees I'm serious, he adds, 'Look, I don't know.'

'When I saw you in that restaurant, was it just a meal or was there going to be something more afterwards? Did I interrupt something?'

'Oh, Amelie –'

'Tell me. I want to know what was really going through your head when you came back here right after me.'

'We had a hotel booked.'

'Bastard.'

'Yes. I know I deserve that. Say what you want. I'll take whatever you have to throw at me. But I'm going to be honest. If it proves to you –'

'I received two phone calls recently. A woman's voice. Disguised. One of those distortion devices. She told me not to trust you.'

'Phone calls?'

I nod. 'The first one woke me up in the middle of the night.'

'A woman's voice?'

'Yes.'

'Barbara,' he says. 'It must have been her.' He leans forward and takes a sip of his drink. 'Listen, that was around the time I tried to break it off with her. I felt terrible for doing what I was doing. When I said that, she threatened to get in touch with you. She said she'd tell you what had been going on between us. She said she'd tell you *everything* and ruin us. I couldn't let that happen, so I gave in. I've kept giving in ever since. Believe me, I didn't want to do it. I haven't for a long time. I tried to stop it, tried very, very hard. But I believed she'd do it when she threatened to tell you and I feared that would destroy our marriage.'

'During the second call, she gave me some random numbers: ten, six, ten, twelve, ten, thirteen –' I have them memorised now; they've become so familiar – 'I couldn't understand what they meant.'

'She was probably trying to confuse you, so you wouldn't know what to believe. To make you suspicious.'

'Yes,' I say, 'that's how it went. I became so confused and suspicious. If that's what she wanted, it worked perfectly. I didn't know what it meant. Didn't know if it was real, even. For a while, I thought maybe it was all in my head. But then I saw inside your diary. There were lots of marks in it. An "X" to mark all these different dates.'

'Then she was telling you when she and I saw one another.'

'Two of those dates were the dates when the girls were killed. There are six now, the latest last night. Her name was Sarah Blythe. On all these dates, you've either been away or disappeared.'

'There are lots of dates marked in there, Amelie, okay. It's been going on a long time. Too long.'

'You know, I looked just like those girls when I was their age. Seeing them, getting to know who they were, it all brought back memories of when I was their age. Memories of my father. I was sixteen when he started to abuse me. Every feeling associated with him that I've managed to escape for so long and have managed to keep buried has returned. It's been almost two weeks and those memories have come back at me, stronger than ever before.'

He says simply, 'I'm so sorry, Amelie. I didn't mean to make it worse.'

I nod. 'I know. And so am I.'

'For what?' When I don't answer, he asks again, 'What for, Amelie? You keep speaking in riddles. What is this thing you needed to tell me?'

Silent tears start to form in my eyes.

He looks like he's about to come over to me. I hold up my hand and he stops. Instead, he says, 'Don't. I'm the one who should be ashamed. I've done wrong, not you.'

'I convinced myself you were in trouble, that she must have been blackmailing you or something.'

'Who?'

'The woman on the phone.'

'Barbara?'

'Yes, Barbara. Now I know. Barbara.'

'Well, in a way, she was. But we don't really know about the phone calls and we can't. They're not important anyway. It's over. I won't be seeing her again, so you see, the phone calls don't matter anymore.'

'Oh, but they do. *Everything that's happened matters.*'

I can't bring myself to confess.

'Why does it have to matter?'

'I thought, could you have been responsible?'

'I wasn't.'

'But I couldn't be sure. The crosses in the diary, you weren't around, all those business trips –'

'I've always gone on business trips. It's part of my job.

You know that.'

'I know, but so many things were pointing towards you. The phone calls. The mud in the shower.'

'I went for a run, I told you.'

'But you don't run.'

'*But I did.* For once, I did. I wish to God I hadn't, but I did.'

'And that car – I saw the CCTV footage and it looked like you turned towards the car before it came at us.'

He shakes his head vehemently. 'I promise you, I never saw that car.'

'Like you were signalling it.'

'I came out of the restaurant, just like you. It aimed at me as well, remember.'

'I know. I understand. I see that now. I was just – overwhelmed by everything. And I've made a very bad choice.'

'What bad choice? What do you mean?' And now he comes near me and I don't stop him and he goes onto his knees so that he can look into my face as I speak.

I shake my head slowly. 'I set someone up for the murders, Edward. Someone we couldn't convict seven years ago. Someone who deserved it. His name is Steven Barr.'

'Steven Barr?' He pauses. I think I see a sign of recognition on his face, but he manages to contain it. Then steadily: 'I remember him.'

'I broke into his house and planted his hair on the fifth victim. He's been arrested. He's being questioned right now. But he saw me in Oxford and then his house was broken into two days later. By me. Now he's accusing me of framing him. And he's right. His lawyer's making an official complaint. Lange wants to see me. And now another girl has been killed. While Barr was being held. So now it's obvious he isn't the killer, but how can I explain the hairs on the fifth victim? It's obvious he's been set up. And I'm the only one who could have done it. I'm finished, Edward. I'll end up in prison because of this.'

He stands up and spends some time inside his own thoughts. He empties his glass and leans down, kissing me on the forehead.

'I'm not going to let that happen. Let's just think for a moment, Amelie. Now you know the truth about what I've been doing, you can brush off those concerns and think more clearly. We can think together. If we put our minds together, we can find a way through this. First, you have the power of denial. That man Barr is a cold-blooded killer, everyone knows that. He can deny being the killer, but DNA is DNA. It can't be challenged, it was found on the body, that's a fact. You can deny and you can keep denying. What can he prove? Nothing. You just have to be able to lie with a clear head and determination. Be convincing. Anyone can lie convincingly, Amelie, if they are determined enough. Can anyone place you at his house on the day you broke in?'

'I don't think so. I was careful.'

'And you say he saw you?'

'Yes, at a Starbucks.'

'Did you go anywhere else?'

'I ran into the clothes shop opposite and hid till he came out. I'd walked past him in the doorway and reacted. I was worried he'd seen me, so I hid.'

'And he had seen you. Okay. Did he also see you go

into the clothes shop? They'll have CCTV.'

'I wasn't sure, but now I don't think so. Hillier told me he wasn't sure it was me till two days later when I arrested him. So it doesn't feel like he had reason to watch me as I went. I don't think he was suspicious at the time, only after the arrest.'

'Anywhere else?'

'No.'

'Is there anything else that can tie you to him or his house?'

I stand suddenly. 'I can't believe I forgot about it.'

'What's that?'

'I took some of his underwear. It's in my bag upstairs.'

'Get it,' he says. 'I'll light the fire and we'll burn it. Right now.'

'Okay.'

I grab a carrier bag, go upstairs and return with the underwear in the bag. When I re-enter the lounge, the fire is alight.

'Is that it?'

'Yes.' I nod.

'Nothing else that might link him to you?'

'That's all.'

Edward snatches the bag from me and drops it straight into the flames. For a moment, we watch as it catches light and slowly starts to burn.

'Then, so long as no one thinks to look at the CCTV in the clothes shop – and why would they if no one knows you went in there? – it's your word against his. And your word counts for something. Look at everything you've achieved as a police officer. You've had a distinguished career. You've received awards, for goodness' sake. And everyone knows what he did. Everyone knows what he is. No one's going to care if he goes down for these murders. In fact, I bet most people will be pleased. I know I will. He's done so much wrong in his life and you've never done anything wrong. You just need to remember that, convey that and stick to your story. It's the DNA versus his denial that way, and the DNA's going to win the argument.'

I grimace. 'I don't know if I can do it. I don't know that I've got it in me.'

'Hey,' he says, holding me, 'you've got this far. You've entrapped him perfectly.' He smiles. 'You were devious. You were callous. *You can do anything.* So I think you can do a lot more than you realise. And I can tell anyone who asks that I knew you were going to Oxford for a shopping trip or something like that. We're a happy family. We can make them see that. Show them happiness, show them confidence, and you can't lose.'

'I'll try,' I say.

'I *am* sorry,' he says, suddenly hugging me. Then he squeezes more tightly.

It's clear I can't do this without him. 'I know,' I say.

'Let me make you a lovely meal, then. And let's have another drink. Or several, what the hell.'

'Fine.' The side of my face starts to warm against his chest as we continue to gaze down at the fire, as the underwear burns and starts to disintegrate.

'Everything will be all right,' he says. '*Everything.*'

70

While Edward prepares our meal, I nurse another whisky as I sit in the armchair and watch the flames eradicate the final remnants of the carrier bag. I sip from the glass, trying to relax. The whisky is sharp, just what I need. That and Edward's calm and collected instructions about what I need to do have helped a lot.

Yes, I think, *I can do this. With Edward by my side, I can do anything. I need to be consistent and steady. Steven Barr can say what he likes, but he can't prove anything. He will go down for this.*

I call DCI Lange. His secretary tells me he's gone home. 'Can you let him know I called and that I'd like to do everything I can to challenge Steven Barr's accusation? Tell him he can have full faith in me and that I'm not going to let that guy lie his way out of the trouble he's in. He's not going to get away with it again.'

'Will do.'

'And please ask him to call me as soon as he can.'

Making that call and saying those words makes me feel better. It proves I can convey an impression of confidence. Knowing that makes the world of difference.

I lean back in my chair and take a few more sips of the whisky. The alcohol helps too, no doubt about it; it makes me feel more alive. As I'm drinking the whisky, I open my emails on my phone and proofread the message I composed to Hillier. It contains everything I want to say, so I press Send.

I'm just about to switch to a news site when a new email arrives. It's a message from Tim in tech support. I open it and instantly lower my glass.

The Subject Line: *Your query, contact detail request, IP address 172.16.254.1.*

I scroll through the details in the email. Then I read and reread every word carefully.

'No,' I mouth.

'What is it?' Edward says, re-entering the lounge.

I glance up at him, then I look back down, in shock, at the screen and the words in the body of the email: *IP address 172.16.254.1. is listed to Edward Smith, 48 Bridge Lane, Chorleywood, Herts WD44 4PQ.*

'Amelie,' Edward says, 'what is it?'

Not his genuine surname, but it's our home address.

71

Edward can read in my eyes that something's the matter. He must be able to. There's no way I can hide the turmoil that's suddenly spinning me out of control. My heart's pounding. I fear it'll rip out of my chest.

'Is everything all right?' he says, nodding towards my phone.

'Oh, yes, this,' I say, lifting up my phone and almost dropping it. 'Yes, it's, er – just some work emails. Nothing I have to deal with right now. They can wait.'

He approaches me and I flick my finger across the phone screen without looking at it, hoping the movement will close my emails. He stands over me for a moment. I feel so small. Then slowly he leans down and I prepare myself to feel pain. As his face comes in line with mine, he says, 'Thought maybe you . . .' and he keeps moving his head closer. I squeeze my eyes shut, my breathing unnaturally heavy, bracing myself for whatever he's about to do. Then he places his head between my head and shoulder, nuzzling my neck.

I feel disgusted. I want to push him off. I want to run away from this house.

But I can't.

He mustn't suspect me. He mustn't think anything is wrong. I have got to pretend. But I worry I won't be able to.

The man I love is a killer.

'Maybe I what?' I say, staring intently into the fire.

The pause is painfully long.

His lips stop brushing against my neck and he comes into view, blocking the fire. 'Could help me with the table. Dinner's almost ready. Here, let me top you up.'

He takes my glass, stands upright and smiles. There's a menace in his smile.

Trying to hide both the surprise and relief I feel, I say as casually as I can, 'Absolutely,' and try to effect a smile.

He stares at me for a long moment. 'You know I love you, don't you?'

'Of course,' I manage to say.

There's a pause as we each wait for the other to say something more. I can't bring myself to say any other words, though.

There's something awkward in his eyes as he says, 'And you still love me.' It should be a question, but it doesn't sound like one.

I nod my head, slowly. 'Yes,' I mouth, but the sound comes out hoarsely.

'Good.' He leans forward again and kisses me on the lips. Then he moves back a couple of inches and smiles, looking me right in the eye. He's so close his face is partly out of focus. 'Good,' he repeats.

And he walks abruptly out of the lounge.

Wondering what I should do, whether I can call anyone without him hearing, I glance at my phone screen.

No. The screen. It's still lit up, and the email from Tim in tech is still on display.

Shit! Could he have seen it?

I know the answer is yes.

I wonder if I can quickly pretend to use the loo and make a phone call or send a text or an email. Ask someone for help. But he's waiting for me. Every second I sit here will make him suspicious – that is, if he isn't already suspicious, thanks to my reaction.

And he might have seen the email.

I glance at it again and check how it looks upside down. Numbers and words, all indecipherable. Surely, he wouldn't have been able to read anything coherently while he was leaning towards me; he only had a few seconds and the text was upside down.

No, I should be fine. I should have time. I'll go and set the dining table, trying to act as normal as I can, make him relax, and then I'll say I need the loo. That's when I'll text Hillier.

I shut my emails, place my phone in my jeans pocket and head to the kitchen.

'Mm, smells great,' I say as I walk into the kitchen.

Edward is standing by the sink, his head peering into it. The tap's running but he's not washing his hands. He must be cleaning something.

'Salmon,' he says.

I open a drawer and remove two knives, two forks and a few spoons. Then I grab some table mats and move across the kitchen to where the dining table is. It's a large wooden table and I place the items I've collected in its centre.

'Cloth,' I say. 'I'll give it a wipe.' I approach Edward at the sink to get a wet cloth, but before I get close he holds one out. 'Thanks,' I say, taking it from him. I return to the table, wiping it carefully. When that's done, I lay the table.

'Wine?' he asks. 'Or more whisky?'

'Wine,' I say. I need to have a clearer head. I have to keep my focus.

'Would you do the honours?' he asks, his hands still in the sink.

'Of course.'

I go to the fridge and open it, pulling out a chilled bottle of white wine.

'I was thinking red,' he says.

'Good idea,' I say, and step towards the cupboard where Edward keeps an extensive collection of red wines.

'Take out something vintage,' he says. 'We are celebrating, after all.'

I crouch down onto my knees and open the cupboard. 'Celebrating?'

'You still love me,' he says. 'Despite what I've done.'

I turn and look at his back. For a moment, neither of us says a word.

Despite what *you've done.*

'I feared you'd kick me out when you found out about Barbara,' he says after a long time. Then after another pause: 'You know, we've both done wrong, Amelie.'

'Yes,' I say. 'I know.'

I turn my attention back to the cupboard. It's dark where the wines are stored.

When I turn around again to stand and switch on the lights, he's staring at me. I feel so self-conscious and exposed, I'm certain he can see through my performance. *He can see through me*, I think. *He knows*. I should just run, try to get out of the front door before he can catch me, I'm nearer to it than him, after all. But I'm frozen stiff and can't move.

'What?' I say softly.

A smile suddenly beams on his face. 'You still love me.'

I return a smile, much smaller than his.

He cocks his head. 'Say it.'

'Sorry?'

'Tell me.'

'Tell you what?'

'Tell me you still love me.'

I need to keep my breathing regular, but I'm struggling. I can't tell if he's toying with me, or whether he's truly deranged and needs some kind of reassurance. *Psychotic*, as Hillier said. I reach out and put my hand on the sideboard. It's silly, but I need some kind of support as I speak. 'You know I do.'

'Then say the words to me.' He speaks his words slowly, crisply, and steps slightly forwards, away from the sink. 'I want to hear you say the sweet words.'

'Edward . . .' I try to compose myself. I have to make this work. *Think about how you'd normally speak to him. How you'd have reacted to him before you found out he's a killer.* I gently clear my throat. 'You saved me. You made me feel human. I owe you everything. Without you, there'd be no me. So yes, I love you. I love you with all my heart.'

Loved, I think.

He places his hands on his temple, closes his eyes, massages his skin and breathes out heavily. Then opening his eyes again, I can see they're moist and he says, 'You know all the right words,' and he shakes his head slowly. 'You know the right words indeed.'

Our eyes remain locked, then I step back and switch on the lights.

'Ah, yes,' he says, chirpily. 'The wine.'

I pull out a bottle of French red wine with the year 1987 printed on the label. I don't know much about wine – that's Edward's domain – but it seems to be vintage enough to me. 'Is this one okay?' I ask, standing and holding it out so that he can see the label.

As I turn around, I almost bump into him; he's unexpectedly standing right behind me. 'Oh,' I gasp. Then, 'Gave me a fright.'

'Need to get the butter,' he says. Then he looks at the bottle and adds, 'Good selection.' He steps around me and opens the fridge.

I collect two red wine glasses and a corkscrew and head back to the table. I remove the plastic cover from the top of the bottle and insert the corkscrew. I turn it and try to pull out the cork. It's snug. I'm struggling with it, so I lift it from the table, step back and place it between my legs as I try to pull harder.

Once, and it won't budge.

A second time, and it still won't budge.

On my third attempt, a really hard pull, the cork pops out with a noise. 'There,' I say, straightening up, suddenly pleased, and that's when something heavy collides with the side of my face, the open wine bottle falls from my hands and smashes as my body careers into the wall, the other side of my head striking it, and I fall down in what seems like slow motion, my head spinning and my vision starting to blur. As I collapse, I manage to see Edward dropping the cookbook he's just used to strike me and grabbing a ball of thick string from the kitchen sink.

Then I only see black, and then I see nothing at all.

72

I start stirring because of some sort of sound. Then the same sound again. A third time and I recognise it: *the doorbell*. My head's pounding and it's a struggle to open my eyes; they feel bruised. After a few moments, on hearing the doorbell again, I manage to prise open my eyes.

My body won't move. I can't feel my hands.

I'm drowsy but can see clearly enough to know I'm in the lounge, tied up on a dining-table chair. My hands are wrapped behind my back, my legs are tied to the chair legs and I know I must have been in this position for a long time because my hands have gone numb.

I turn my head and can see along the corridor. Edward is standing at the far end, peering around the corner towards the front door. Suddenly, he turns back and sees me.

'Oh,' he says, 'you're awake. Good. Your bloody detective friend has arrived. Poking his nose around, no doubt. I wonder what else he's been poking around. Hmm? Has quite an unhealthy interest in you, I'd say.' He pauses for a moment. 'I'd say I'm a pretty good judge of character when it comes to unhealthy obsessions with other women.' He sniggers.

I try to say, 'Ryan', but my mouth won't move. That's when I realise it's taped shut.

'This is going to be interesting,' Edward says, and he disappears from view.

I hear the front door opening.

'Ryan,' he says cheerfully. 'Good to see you again. Sorry you've been waiting, was in the loo.'

'No problem,' I hear Ryan say. 'Is Amelie in?'

'No, I'm afraid not. She went out. Said something about some interviews she had to conduct.'

'Oh, that's a surprise,' Hillier says. 'It's just that she sent me a message and asked me to meet her here.'

I didn't. I'm sure I didn't. That means Hillier's lying to Edward. *Does that mean he knows? Has he also somehow figured things out? Maybe Tim sent him the same details he sent me.*

'Oh,' Edward says, sounding surprised. And I'm sure he genuinely is. 'Well, er . . .' There's a rather lengthy pause while I hear some movement. 'Well, then, erm, maybe she won't be too long. She didn't say. Why don't you come in and wait for her? Have a warm drink or something. Be nice to catch up a bit. Fancy a beer?'

I want to scream, *No, don't!* but I can't open my mouth. Struggling, I make muffled sounds as loudly as I can, but Hillier's probably too far away to hear. I try to move, try to rock my body. If I could only fall over, the noise might cause a distraction and alert Hillier to something being wrong.

Something is very wrong.

'Maybe just a coffee,' Hillier says.

'So come in,' Edward says.

I hear the sound of a foot stepping up into the house, but only one step before there's a swinging sound, a creaking hinge, and a crashing noise, glass shattering and a heavy thud. Then several more thuds.

I try to scream again.

I know what's happened: as Ryan was coming into the house, Edward swung the front door at him. The tempered glass window probably shattered on his head. *Oh God, Ryan . . .*

There's some grunting and then the front door slams shut. Then a sliding sound and Edward comes into view, pulling Ryan towards the kitchen. I shuffle, desperate to get out of the chair. I attempt to revive my hands, get the blood flowing, try to kick out with my legs. There's slight movement, ever so slight. I can't get the damned chair to move any more than that. I can't free myself.

Edward returns, walking back along the corridor towards me. When he enters the lounge, he circles me, like a tiger stalking its prey. Then he comes to a stop in front of me. 'Well,' he says, 'this isn't exactly what I was expecting.' He looks down at the ground. 'Shit,' he mumbles. He walks over to the cabinet, unlocks one of the doors and pulls out a decanter of whisky. Removing a glass, he pours a large shot. Quickly putting the glass to his mouth and leaning his head back, he empties the contents. 'What am I supposed to do now, hmm?' he says, suddenly smashing the glass on the floor and lunging towards me. 'You've really gone and fucked this all up for me, you know that, Amelie?'

I try to speak again, but no sound comes from my mouth. I open my eyes wide, trying to tell him with my eyes that we need to talk. He has to let me speak.

He sees. 'Are you afraid?' he asks, almost casually. Now he grabs another glass and pours himself another whisky, this time filling the glass halfway. He takes it and perches on the arm of the armchair. 'You know, I never wanted to hurt you. I've had these urges, see, since I was a teenager, but with you I was able to keep them in check. I could have done it to you any time, if I'd wanted to. The number of times I've watched you fall asleep at night or stood behind you while you were at the kitchen sink. Or while you were sunbathing in the garden. So many moments when you were completely unaware, and your life was in my hands each and every time.' He laughs momentarily to himself, almost looking pleased. 'I spared you,' he whispers, leaning menacingly towards me. Then he straightens his back and knocks back half the whisky. 'Because I wanted to. Not because I felt a sense of duty or anything, but because when we met one another, I liked you and, when we got married I liked the sense of normal you brought to my life. Normal was necessary. Otherwise, being so young, I knew I'd soon get caught and be locked up. It's taken me years to gain the confidence of knowing I could get away with it. The truth is, Amelie, there hadn't been much normal in my life before we met.' He drains the rest of his glass. 'No, don't worry, you've been perfectly safe with me.' He stares at the glass. 'Until now.' He points at me. 'Now you've gone and fucked everything up for us.' He shakes his head slowly. 'Stupid nosy bitch. Why couldn't you just keep on not seeing? Being a blind drunk. You know, Steven Barr was the perfect scapegoat. You'd actually gone and done one thing right. It was perfect, and it was your idea. Think about the headlines: *Steven Barr imprisoned after seven years of freedom.* Fucker deserved it. I could almost have applauded when you told me. I was delighted. I knew him, did he tell you that?'

Stunned by the revelation, I shake my head as vehemently as I can.

'Good. For a moment, I was afraid he did. Only for a moment, mind. I suppose, deep down, I knew if he's one thing, he's not a grass. Because we're similar, see. After he was acquitted, I became very interested in his story. He'd done what I had wanted to do, and I managed to find where he lived. It wasn't far away. He had done what I had only done once, when I was very young. Fine, I'd gone one step further, but he'd chosen two beautiful girls, just the right age. Two.' There's some sort of excitement in Edward's voice. I'm horrified by its sound. 'I was lonely. You could never be enough for me because I could never show you who I truly am. I needed to know someone who understood how it felt.

'Oh, he was difficult to get through to. When I told him who I was, he was sceptical at first, didn't want to know. The husband of one of his investigating officers making contact and trying to befriend him . . . When I told him who *you* were to *me*, he thought you'd put me up to it. That you were trying to entrap him through me. But he was curious about me, I could see that, so I persisted. I'm good at finding a way inside a person's head, like you found out when I managed to get through to you. You know, I think he was even harder to crack than you were.

'We were good friends for a time. Shared the same hobby, the same interests, see. He told me his fantasies, I told him mine. It always involved girls like my sister, her age from those days, and black underwear, like the underwear I saw my sister wearing, wrapped around their throats because my sister had suffocated me with those images of herself in similar underwear for so many years. Then I asked him. I wanted us to do it together. If someone was with me, it would have made me stronger, and in the beginning I was certain I'd have to rely on his experience. But he was too afraid to do anything else after almost being sent down. He was filled with this huge sense of paranoia that he was being followed by people like you, and no matter how much I tried to reassure him that he was safe, that I knew what cases you and your colleagues were working on because when I asked, you told me, he wouldn't let himself believe it, even though I could tell he so keenly wanted to.

'We did a lot together. But all planning, no action. The thrill from talking about it, saying the words aloud with someone else, that was good for a time. The words had finally been allowed to come out of my head. But he could never move beyond the fear he felt. It paralysed him and caused inaction. *I wanted action.* And then one day, after two years of planning and my desperation to get started, my patience waning thin, somehow he found God. The Holy Spirit took him off and the fucker abandoned me. Told me to rot, when I got angry with him. Then he moved away suddenly. He wasn't at his house when I went to see him. I was going to persist, see. And then poof, he was gone, just like that. Five years ago now. How time flies. And here we are together, today, and Steven Barr has been arrested again. So you see, he deserves to go down for this.'

X Marks the Spot

Finally, after two years of hinting and then trying outright to persuade her to have children, she agreed to try. I was so relieved. It could have been the answer. It could have prevented me from reaching my final destination.

But she couldn't conceive. I mean, the bitter irony. I wanted a child in order to save myself, but the news that it would never happen damned me and put me on a path that meant one day I would take what I had wanted for so long. I just needed the confidence and I needed support.

The timing couldn't have been better. Steven Barr was being convicted of killing and raping two fifteen-year-olds. I followed the case like a hawk. I asked question after question and received answer after answer. I read article after article. I got to know Steven Barr so well, in the end, I may have known him almost as well as I knew myself.

When he was released and I tracked him down, I used every power of persuasion I had so that he would let me into his life. It took time and effort, but it worked, and I cannot describe the thrill when I finally broke through to him.

I had found someone who knew what it was like to take what they wanted, who knew the thrill of the kill. I thought my life would change forever.

When he broke away from me after almost two years, I couldn't let that be the end. But I knew it couldn't be the beginning. How could I once again become the thing I had fought to resist for so many years? How could I become a murderer? No, I would find a way to resist again. All the urges, all the inspiration from my conversations with Steven Barr, would have to be put on hold. I would still plan. I would still dream. But I wouldn't act. I had a wife. She was a police officer. There was no way I could get away with it.

But then one day, almost five years later, thanks to you, Amelie, I was ready to begin.

73

I brought Steven Barr down for Edward. And in doing so I've brought down an innocent man. A reformed man.

But he's Steven Barr, for Christ's sake. Steven fucking Barr. He's a sick psychopath. Steven Barr is as bad as Edward. If what Edward says is true, and he reformed himself, that doesn't negate the fact that he raped and killed two fifteen-year-old girls and destroyed their families forever. *No, nothing can ever erase what he did.*

He deserves it. He needs to be punished, and so does Edward.

'The final motivation,' Edward says to me now, 'I bet you're wondering what finally made me start. It was urging me all the time, but I kept it at bay, I couldn't quite bring myself to begin even though I had planned intricately and even though I felt confident I could keep hidden from you what I was doing. But there was this voice in my head saying don't do it to her. She's a good woman. She loves you. That fucking conscience. So I kept resisting. But over the past year, since you started being partnered more with that clown in there, all I hear from you is Ryan this, Ryan that. You spend too much time with him. You run around him like he's some fucking Adonis. If she can't resist, I thought, well, then, why the hell should I? Oh, I know, he's younger than me and prettier and he makes you feel oh so good. I know, I've seen you together. I've seen how you look at him, his pretty-boy features. Well,' he laughs, 'not so pretty anymore, now I've smashed his face in. I've ruined that for you as well.'

He leans his head back and breathes in deeply.

'I hated you for the way you behaved around him, you know. And so I watched and watched, I waited and planned and, finally, I started. And I cannot tell you the thrill was worth the fucking wait. Now I don't want to hate you for it; instead, I want to thank you. You were my great motivator. Without you, I couldn't have done it. And now, dear motivator, you and I, we need to find an exit.'

He returns to the decanter and refills his glass with whisky. He's thinking. 'Unless,' he says to himself, eventually nodding. 'It could work, you know.'

He sits down again on the arm of the armchair. 'You've already framed him, Amelie. There's no reason why he can't still be the one who killed them. Otherwise, you'll go down for planting evidence and obstructing justice. You'll lose your job, you'll end up inside. Imagine that, your life over, ending up inside where you've put so many other people. People who deserve it. You don't deserve it, Amelie. And I would end up inside, too. Or I'd be forced to kill you to protect myself, but who knows whether the fiction I'd create to explain the circumstances of your death would be believed. So I might not get away with it; I could end up inside either way. Or I could disappear, but then I'd have to be on the run for the rest of my life. A man who disappears leaving behind a dead wife doesn't exactly look innocent, does he?'

He puts his glass on the carpet, then comes and stands over me. He peers down at me and then lowers himself to his knees. He places both his hands on my cheeks. 'Yes, Steven Barr did it. Steven Barr killed those girls. It's your word against his, remember? Why should anyone believe him over you? That hasn't changed. His DNA was on Kinga, after all. He won't be able to explain that. So Steven Barr can pay for his crimes and you and I can go on living our life together.' He squeezes me slightly. 'What do you say?'

I make a small noise and again try to message him through the widening of my eyes.

'Oh,' he sniggers, 'you can't speak. Sorry. Do you want to answer me?'

I nod.

He moves his hands to the tape that's covering my mouth. 'Easy and slowly,' he says. 'No sudden movements, okay?'

I nod again.

'This might hurt – just a little.' He pulls quickly, unexpectedly, and the tape rips off, stinging my lips and skin. I wince in pain.

'I never wanted to hurt you,' he says, toying with me, leaning forward and kissing me on the lips. Then he draws back and adds chirpily, 'So how does that sound to you?'

'What about Ryan?' I manage to say, my voice now hoarse. I twist my neck so that I can see along the corridor, but I can't see Ryan. I can only imagine him on the kitchen floor, bleeding, suffering, dying.

'Nice that you care about him so much. He's a lucky guy,' he mocks. 'Come on, Amelie, you're more creative than I ever gave you credit for, so I'm sure you'll think of something.'

'What do you mean?'

'You know precisely what I mean, Amelie. You can decide how it happens.'

Death. 'I can't do that, you know that. He's a good man. He's my friend.'

'Fuck buddy?' he sneers.

'No,' I say. 'Never.'

'Sometimes in life, Amelie, we have no choice. Sometimes we have to do things we never thought we were capable of. Hasn't your Steven Barr experiment shown you that yet? Some kind of accident will have to befall him, and time really is of the essence, so you'll need to hurry up and make your decision.'

'Why?' I ask, a sense of pleading in my voice.

'What do you mean, *why*? Why do you have to decide how your little boyfriend dies? Because then your hands are as dirty as mine. Because maybe you have been fucking him and wouldn't that then be a poetic touch.'

'Why does he have to die?'

'The answer's obvious.'

'My hands are already dirty,' I say through gritted teeth. 'Don't make me do it.'

'Not dirty enough.'

'Can I ask you something else?'

He stands still. 'By all means.'

'Did you have an affair? Is Barbara your lover?'

'Oh, that woman. An affair? No, she's a client, like I said. I mean, I have fucked her once or twice, but I don't think you can call that an affair.'

I try to remain calm. It takes all my training to succeed. 'So what are the marks in your diary, if not times when you met with her?'

'Well, one or two of them will have been when I met her. Or one of the other women. You know, there have been a lot of women, Amelie. But most of the "X"s mark dates relating to my current project. The latest, when I killed the girls. The earlier, stakeout days. When I did reconnaissance. I told you, it took a lot of planning and preparation. And practice runs. Future marks – well, they're for the future. See, I've only just begun.'

'Why, Edward?' I try to keep the pleading from my voice but think I fail. 'Why did you kill those poor girls? They were completely innocent. They had their whole lives ahead of them.'

He tilts his head and gives me a sardonic glance. Then he shrugs. 'Why do some people get cancer? Why do others get knocked over? Life is full of curiosities, isn't it?'

'That isn't you, Edward, and this isn't about something random. These are all choices you've made.'

He shakes his head slowly. 'No, if you knew what was in my head, telling me, urging me, how it's been there since I was fucking thirteen, you'd understand it is random. I didn't ask to feel this way. I didn't ask to *have* to do this. It just *happened* to me.'

I want to shout but stifle the desire. 'What happened?'

His eyes glaze over and he appears to be staring at nothing. 'Life is . . .'

'You don't have an answer, Edward, because there is no point.'

'There is every point,' he says, regaining his focus on me. 'I never wanted to hurt other people. You think I'm a monster? No, this is something – out of my control. The first time, I just wanted the girl. But life is . . . sometimes there are circumstances that make that impossible. Desire is something . . . it swells, it grows till you can take no more. I couldn't have her, but I liked her. And I think I deserved her. I didn't mean to kill her. She caught me in her room. She wasn't supposed to be there! I had to act. But when it was over, it made me realise something that I could never forget, even though I did try. Especially by marrying you. You see, I learnt that the best sex is actually with a dead teenager. Well, right before and after as well.'

'Oh,' I moan, more repulsed than I've ever been, even than the time my father was violating me. 'You sick –'

'You know, you never did wear that sexy black underwear I gave you. Remember?' He reaches into his trouser pocket and slowly removes it. 'Ta-da, here they are. They belonged to Sarah Blythe. I took them from her bedroom a few days before I killed her, when I was researching her. Try them on now. Go on. Now.'

I scream and try to wrestle free. 'You bastard! You motherfucking bastard! I want to kill you!' I'm gasping for breath as tears fall down my face.

He laughs. 'There, there,' he says. 'You see how easy it

is to want to kill? Doesn't take much, Amelie. It's human instinct. Perhaps you do understand me a little, after all.' He glances at his watch and taps its glass face. 'Now, time is ticking. Tell me what's going to happen to Ryan in there?' He stands up and starts edging to the doorway. 'It'd be better if it came from you. You never know what I could end up doing to him if the decision's all mine. He might suffer more.'

My tears are real, no acting, but I also wonder whether I might be able to use my genuine emotions to my advantage. Get a psychological advantage, or at least make him pause. I force back the tears. 'Don't you love me?' I ask him.

He pauses. 'Oh, darling.' He places his hands on his hips. 'Of course I do. You were so troubled. So lonely. You gave me the outlet I needed, and I gave you the outlet you needed. We were right for one another. At that time. Like an eighties' one-hit wonder. But we can still find a way to be right for each other if you tell me how to get rid of him and promise me that Steven Barr will remain responsible, no matter what anyone says or does. You just have to hold your nerve. It's exactly like I said before. *Nothing has changed.*'

Everything has changed, I think. 'Untie me,' I tell him, 'and I'll come and help with Hillier. You have my word. We'll get through this together. If you love me.'

He lights up. 'I do.' Edward looks like my old Edward for a moment. He looks so . . . happy.

'Together?' he asks.

I nod. 'Yes, you and me. Let's begin the rest of our lives together, right now.'

'You really mean that?' he asks, delighted.

'You know it,' I say. 'You've been my rock all these years. You saved me. I can't ever forget that. I won't let you go. You mean everything to me. Love is stronger than – anything else.'

He walks towards me. 'I do love you, Amelie. Do you understand that?'

'Yes,' I say. He runs his hands along the sides of my face. 'Yes,' I murmur, quivering. 'And I love you, too.'

He kisses me. It's repulsive, but I return the kiss. Long, slow, deep. *Remember, genuine emotion.*

Just a few more steps.

'Untie me,' I murmur again, when the kissing subsides, 'and let's begin our new life together. We can move away if necessary. We can do anything for the chance to start again once Steven Barr is sentenced to a very long time behind bars.'

'Steven Barr?' he says cheerfully.

'Steven Barr,' I repeat, seriously.

He moves behind me and starts to rub my shoulders. Slowly, his hands come to the sides of my neck and I tense my body as his fingers linger, waiting for the moment when he starts to squeeze. He could kill me in a matter of moments. His fingers trace the sides of my neck, then they rub gently, then harder, and he massages, and then his hands move down to my shoulders, then they come together at the centre of my spine, and then they make their way down to where my hands are tied.

Where he unties and releases me.

I stand slowly, unsteady on my feet. Needing to get the blood flowing, I shuffle from left to right. It takes some time.

He lifts my hand and leads me to the corridor. As we're

in the doorway, I pull him towards me and kiss him. Disgusted, but knowing it's necessary, I put my tongue in his mouth. As he sighs deeply, I kiss harder, more sensually, and I rub his body with my hands. As I lean in, I feel his arousal, and lift my knee, in a short, sharp movement, into his groin. His body doubles over and I bring another knee, hard and fast, to his face. His body propels backwards, his head smashing against the wall behind him. As he's falling down, I charge to the kitchen, where I find Hillier face down on the floor with his hands tied behind his back. He's breathing, but when I shake him he doesn't respond.

I start to untie his hands and, just as I'm releasing the final loop of rope, I'm grabbed from behind. Now I'm propelled backwards and I stumble over something – Edward's foot – and land on the floor. My head bounces off the tiles and I feel dizzy. Then there's a heavy weight on my chest. I manage to open my eyes and see Edward on top of me. He's sitting, dead weight, on my chest. I try to kick up to push him off, but all I manage to do is lift my legs into the air. He remains firmly in place, his hands clasped around my neck.

He squeezes hard and immediately I struggle for air. My hands clutch his wrists and I try to pull, but to no avail. He looks like the devil preparing to drag me into hell. I try again with all the energy that's left in my body to pull his hands away from my neck, but my fingers are weakening. I'm feeling faint. I can't take in any air. My head's spinning. My legs stop moving. I try to move any part of my body, a finger even, but nothing.

I know what that means. *I'm dying.*

My chest rises as he presses my neck even harder against the floor tiles; I think my body is going to crash through them.

It's over. Time has run out. There's nothing I can do. I can only die.

My eyes shut.

Then he's not on top of me anymore, and I gasp for air, surprised but automatically sucking in every ounce of sweet air I can grab, and I cough, spluttering, desperate to curve my body and clutch at my aching skin, but my body won't move, even though my mind tells it to, and I hear Edward say, 'Maybe just one more time, huh,' and I hear him unzipping his trousers, and then he's pulling my jeans off, and I try to kick him but my body won't move, and then he's on top of me and his hand is where it shouldn't be, where it's not entitled to be anymore, and I see my father in the doorway, my father on my bed, my father on top of me, and I manage to scream, a piercing scream, a scream so frightful that for a moment he freezes, hesitates, seems to snap out of it, realise, *truly realise*, and I manage, God knows how, to punch his face, skin connecting with skin, and the sound of cartilage snapping, and blood spraying on my face, and then he's up and off me.

At first, I think it's because I've hurt him, but then I realise there's a scuffle in the room and something smashes, a chair is overturned. Still gasping for air, I manage to lift my head. Ryan is clutching Edward in a chokehold, their bodies careering around the kitchen, colliding with everything in their path.

There are growls and grunts and sighs and gasps and then more items smash and shatter and crash; the kitchen is being turned into a crash site.

Bright red and struggling, Edward forces Ryan backwards so that his back is pressed against the kitchen sink unit. Edward brings his body forwards, then pushes back sharply. Ryan's lower spine strikes the unit. Edward repeats, again and again, then snaps his head back and connects with Ryan's cheek. Edward keeps forcing their bodies backwards, repeatedly, the air being knocked out of Ryan, but somehow he manages to keep hold of Edward's neck. Edward swings his arms sideways and backwards, still ramming his body back repeatedly so that Ryan's back is pounded time and again. I see Ryan's grip of Edward weakening.

Realising that my opportunity to help him is running out, I claw my way to my feet and pull myself along the side unit, quickly fastening my jeans. I open a drawer and scramble for a knife. I glance over at them and see Ryan finally letting go of Edward. Edward swings his elbow back and cracks Ryan on the side of the face. He takes hold of Ryan's hair, pulls him round and smashes his head against the draining board. I stumble towards them as Ryan collapses to the ground and Edward turns around. He sees me coming towards him and steps forward. But he doesn't see the carving knife I'm holding. He steps onto it and I try step through him. His eyes widen as the knife slices into him. Our eyes lock and I twist the knife as far round as I can. His face erupts in surprise and then his body topples forwards, his head coming to rest on my left shoulder.

For a moment, I remain still, propping him up. His body is limp, but I can feel he's still breathing. My hand is still gripping the knife that's inside him.

'You'll never – get away with it,' he whispers, struggling to get the words out.

I pause and think. 'We'll see,' I say. Then in one great swoop, I push the blade further into his stomach and twist it again using both hands. He exhales and then I step back, letting his body topple to the floor.

74

I've been checked carefully by a medic and then in the hospital. The cuts on my face and body have been cleaned. There are bruise marks around my neck and my cheekbone is tender to the touch. My lip has been split and there's tape on one side holding the stitches together.

I'm sitting in an interview room at the station, only this time I'm on the wrong side of the table.

Detective Chief Inspector Jonathan Lange, my senior investigating officer, has taken it upon himself to speak with me. He didn't want to call it an interview. *Just a chat*, he said when I arrived here twenty minutes ago. *See if we can't get to the bottom of what's happened.*

I knew how important the conversation would be, of course. I knew I would have to speak carefully.

'Why didn't you share your findings regarding London Teen Lifestyle with anyone sooner? With Micah Ainsley, for example?' he asks me after we've been through the details of Steven Barr's complaint in full. The complaint is clear, makes compelling reading and is very, very true. But only Steven Barr and I know that. I've explained my trip to Oxford. I've defended myself against the allegations. I've reinforced my belief that Steven Barr is lying to try to get himself off.

DNA can't lie, but Steven Barr can.

What Edward said before he died was true.

'I wanted to be sure first,' I say. 'As soon as I received the information from Tim, I wrote an email to Hillier, but Edward was there and I couldn't send it. I had to wait until I was alone.'

'Talk me through how you found out about London Teen Lifestyle.'

'As you know, we kept hearing from the parents and friends that the girls were trying to become social media influencers, and Instagram is a central platform for that. I wanted to see if there were any patterns in who was following the girls' accounts.'

'And did you find any?'

'It was very difficult,' I say. 'Ainsley was trying to find the same thing. But I was able to find a company called SSS that has developed software that's able to identify patterns between accounts, like which followers accounts have in common. It took a few days for the guy who runs it to respond to me, but when he did, he couldn't find anyone that was following all five of the girls. He found that Steven Barr was following four of them.'

'Steven Barr? Why didn't you say? Barr's name wasn't on any of the lists Ainsley pulled off. She checked back.'

'It's in the paperwork in the conference room. I told Hillier. But, look, Steven Barr was only following four of the girls. The guy at SSS didn't find anyone following all five, as I said, but he did find that the girls were all following one account.'

'London Teen Lifestyle,' Lange says, lighting up.

'Yes.'

'Okay, Hillier told me about it. He read me your email.'

'I was stunned. We already had Barr pinpointed at the scene of the latest crime, his DNA. That can't be disputed. I tried to find a connection between Steven Barr and London Teen Lifestyle. Then we found another body and suddenly the claims he was making about me had more weight to them because how could he have killed Sarah Blythe when he was already in custody? So I thought that must mean he had help.'

'Edward?'

'I was putting the washing away and at the back of one of Edward's drawers I found some underwear I didn't recognise. I didn't think too much of it, but they were stained and dirty and it just seemed . . . so odd, is what it seemed.' I replay last night in my mind: Edward telling me to get the underwear, me going upstairs and taking a pair of his own the same colour as Barr's and placing them in a carrier bag, us watching them burn. I wasn't sure I could trust Edward – he'd already lied so much, and my instinct had been right.

'I was going to ask him about them, but something made me hesitate. Some kind of intuition, I think. That's what so many years on the job gives you. You become curious, suspicious even. The email from Tim in tech came shortly after, confirming that London Teen Lifestyle was listed under Edward's name and our address. He'd used a fake surname, but it was his first name and our address. I was . . .' I shake my head. 'Bowled over. I couldn't believe it. And everything fell apart from that moment onwards.'

'You had no suspicions that he could have been the killer?'

'Not at all. Edward had been behaving strangely for a time. I suspected an affair. I saw him with a woman. It looked like an affair. What I could never have guessed is that he was probably with Steven Barr. Both sexual deviants, both sex killers. Both God knows what together. Edward walked into the room when I was writing the email to Hillier explaining what I had discovered and must have been able to see that something was wrong. I suppose I couldn't fully hide my surprise – and disgust.' I look away, moisture building in my eyes. 'He was my husband, sir, and he killed those poor girls. Edward and Steven Barr.'

'That was when he attacked you?'

'I was trying to buy time, trying to find a way to get out of there. I managed to email Hillier and tried to act normally. I wanted to wait for him to be distracted so that I could escape from there and call for help. We started to get the table ready for dinner. He hit me over the head and tied me up. Fortunately, Ryan arrived, otherwise I suspect we wouldn't be having this conversation. He attacked Ryan while I was tied up and gagged. I managed to get free, but he caught me and started to choke me. Ryan woke up and wrestled him off me. Edward was going to kill Ryan, I could see that, so I grabbed a knife, and in the confusion Edward walked onto it. It all happened so fast. It was like . . . the blink of an eye. I'm not sorry it happened; I'm glad it did. If it hadn't, Hillier would be dead now, and so would I.'

'Is that when you put the call in?'

'Yes,' I nod, tears now fully formed, 'I didn't hesitate. I could see Ryan needed medical attention and I was in pretty bad shape. I could tell that Edward was dead.'

'Did you touch the body?'

'I checked his pulse,' I say. 'And as I was crouching down next to his body, I looked at my husband and couldn't believe that somehow the man I'd loved had teamed up with Steven Barr. When we were investigating the original Barr case, he'd shown so much interest in it. I remember clearly, he asked me so many questions. But he did that with much of my work – he was always so curious, so it didn't strike me as abnormal. And with these girls now, he kept asking, and now I understand why. I had no idea that his initial interest in Barr would develop into some kind of – I don't know, reciprocal fascination. Or fixation. A warped sexual pleasure they shared from their crimes. And together they've destroyed so many lives. All those young girls. But no more.' I look Lange straight in the eye and slowly shake my head. 'No more. It's over and now neither of them can cause any more pain.'

Confident, Edward had said. *Don't waver. Have a narrative and stick to your story.*

He was right. He gave me the perfect advice. This is only possible because of him.

I was wrong about Edward. I didn't know him at all. But now he's dead, he can't hurt me and he can't take the lives of any more young girls. They can live life to the full, they can thrive, they can get wherever their ambitions take them in life; they can be what I never managed to be.

'And with Edward's death, we can also put Steven Barr where he rightfully belongs: behind bars. He also won't be able to hurt anyone ever again.'

'Steven Barr's DNA being on Kinga Nowicka is undeniable and makes for a strong case. And Edward's DNA –'

'Yes?' I ask.

'An initial test has shown a match. Edward's semen was found in Fiona Cunningham, Rachel Adams, Niamh O'Flanagan, Laura Randall and Sarah Blythe.' He stares at me for a moment. 'And he's a confirmed match for Megan Goldman. Which means Edward killed Megan Goldman. We finally got him, after fourteen years.'

I shake my head slowly. 'And four years after that, I stupidly married him.'

'You couldn't have known, Amelie.' I look at Lange who, for the first time in a decade, I think has tried to offer me some comfort. He won't admit it, of course.

'It's over now, Amelie. For both of them, and for both of us.'

75

Two days after being placed on administrative leave while the IOPC investigates the claims made by Steven Barr and his solicitor, I'm sitting in the living room nursing another drink. There's little I can do to fill the days other than think about what's happened these past couple of weeks and what might happen next. All I can do is wait.

And be consistent, of course.

I've removed all trace of Edward from the house. There are no pictures on the walls, all his belongings have gone, and I threw out other items I associated with him. His favourite armchair, for example – the one he perched on while I was tied up. I've torn up the carpet here in the living room and am waiting for a replacement to be laid.

The room is much emptier. It feels almost barren. But it is mine, and only mine.

I finish the whisky and pour another. Settling back into my armchair, I hear a noise at the door. Not someone knocking but something being pushed through the letterbox. *Probably some takeaway leaflets*, I think, ignoring it. Although it makes me think that later on I might order a pizza.

I'm hopeful that the IOPC investigation won't lead anywhere and that I'll be able to return to work soon. Police work is all I have left and it's the best way I think I'll be able to keep moving forward. Edward is out of my life and I will have to learn how to compartmentalise my memories of him, like I did with my father. But I can't stop thinking about Steven Barr; he's still very much a part of my life. Once he's sentenced, if it gets that far, and once the investigation ends, that's when I will finally be able to rest.

Until then, however, I can only *maintain*.

I haven't been able to eat much and drinking on an empty stomach won't do me much good, so maybe a pizza or something isn't such a bad idea. Pulling myself up, I slide on my slippers and head to the front door to see what leaflets have been delivered. But when I turn the corner, lying next to the brand-new front door is only a single letter. A white envelope. I pick it up and turn it over. No stamp. No address. Just one line of handwriting in thick block capitals:

DETECTIVE AMELIE DAVIS

Odd. I open the front door and look into the street. Pointless, I know, because the letter was dropped through the letterbox at least fifteen minutes ago, but it feels like the right move to make nonetheless. I step into the driveway and slowly walk down it. When I come to the pavement, I scan the street in both directions. It's empty.

I take the letter back inside and my instinct is to open it at the kitchen table. It's only when I enter the kitchen that I realise I threw out the table and am awaiting the delivery of a new one. So I head back to the lounge.

After I've sat down, I cautiously open the envelope. There's a single sheet of folded A4 paper in it. I withdraw it and drop the envelope onto the floor.

I unfold the sheet. The words on it are handwritten:

Detective,
You may be surprised to receive a letter from me but there are one or two things that need to be said. After all you and I both know the truth about what has happened.

Seven years ago detective I made a terrible mistake. I took the lives of two young girls who now would be grown women if I hadn't met them. The idea that I snatched their futures from them is something I have to live with always. And it's something that's a struggle to live with. I'm not looking for sympathy. Not at all. Because it's my fault that they died. Only I am to blame so only I am responsible so only I should suffer for that. And I do suffer detective. I want you to believe that. I will never forgive myself for what I did. I was a different person back then and I made a terrible terrible mistake. There's no changing that. That's one thing I have learnt. You can never do anything about the past however much you might want to. You can only change things about the future. A wise man taught me that. A priest. I met him about a year after I was acquitted. He showed me that yes repentance is important but it has to actually mean something. It has to mean you change as you move forwards. At first I thought he was talking nonsense but something made me go back to him and I saw him again and I listened really listened. I kept seeing him and he kept making absolute sense.

So I turned my back on the kind of life I was living and I stopped thinking the horrible things I was thinking. It was much easier than I thought it would be. I was sorry for what I did genuinely sorry and I changed genuinely. I made myself a better person not to make up for what I had done because that was unchangeable but to make sure I did only positive things in the future. I tried to get someone else to change as soon as I started to change. We had been great friends for two years. We were alike and we thought alike but then I started questioning everything we were thinking. I told him we were wrong and that we had to stop. He had to change like I was changing. That made him furious. I couldn't convince him to change and he couldn't convince me to stop changing. So I stopped trying and left and didn't tell him where I was going. We never spoke again. He's someone you know only too well. Edward. Knowing he was married though I promised myself to keep an eye on you from afar. I was worried that he might one day turn on you. I decided that would be my first good deed but it would be one that would never stop. My ongoing almsgiving. I would keep an eye on you and make sure you stayed safe. For five years I came back and forth. Followed his career and business and read about your service and the cases you had been involved in. For five years you stayed safe. After the first murder I knew it was him. The way the girl was found. I read about it in the newspapers. The underwear around the throat and the rape and on the internet there were rumours that the rape was before and after she had been killed and it was exactly as Edward had described to me what he wanted to do. I didn't know why he had waited so long to start. Maybe he hadn't waited. Maybe I was mistaken. Maybe there are others we don't know about but I knew this was him and that is why I called you. I got some voice recognition software on the internet and it was able to make me sound like a woman when I connected it to a phone. I thought if you became suspicious of him you might at least be on your guard. Of course my main hope was you would leave him. But you didn't. He had you well and truly tricked. Wrapped around his little finger.

After I saw online reports about Fiona Cunningham and the graphic detail people wrote about what had been done to her I decided to call you and give you a warning. I thought it might kickstart you. Then after Rachel Adams's death I knew I needed to say more so I called you with the numbers. The dates. The first was the date when I received a message from Edward. Somehow he managed to get my number and he asked me to get in touch with him. I didn't but now I'm sure I understand why. He probably wanted to try again to convince me to join him once more before he began. He called from your home phone. I thought if you could work out the numbers were dates you might notice a phone call from your own home made to an unknown Oxford number on that date and then look into who that number belonged to. Then you would have found out it was my number. If you knew you hadn't made that call then Edward was the only possible caller. And that would have made you suspicious of him. It would have tied him to me. Plus the next two sets of numbers related to the dates of the first two numbers. I hoped with all six numbers together or three sets of dates I'd be able to provide you with the ultimate clue. I couldn't risk identifying myself in the calls because I thought you wouldn't take what I was saying seriously. You probably would have put the phone down and reported me for harassment. And I wouldn't have blamed you. I thought something cryptic might get you involved and thinking. And I must confess I thought if my previous connection to Edward was revealed that could bring back a lot of problems that I'd spent years trying to exorcise.

I followed you to Francois's restaurant because at that point it looked like things were getting out of control. Stupidly I thought maybe if I could hurt Edward put him in the hospital or something the killing spree would end. I didn't want to kill him but someone had to do something. It might have worked but you pushed him out of the way. And then I panicked. I was going to come back for another hit but without the lights on the car I couldn't see. I saw only a figure and realised only after you jumped out of the way that I almost hit you. Believe me when I say I had no intention of hurting you and I'm sorry I came so close to hitting you. After that I knew he'd be on his guard so I didn't try again. I felt like I just had to wait and give you the time that was needed to figure it out. And then I saw you in Oxford. And then my house was broken into. And then I was arrested. Everything had fallen apart. I had to defend myself. I didn't want anyone to know I knew who you were so I said I only recognised you after you had arrested me. The truth was I knew you very well and I was trying to help you.

When I realised I could go to prison for the rest of my life I couldn't think of an alternative so I spoke the truth about what had happened in Oxford. I had to speak the truth but the last thing I wanted was for you to get in trouble. I was trying to save you not hurt you and you'd put me in this position where my only defence was to bring you into it. I really didn't want to. Believe me. I've deserved punishment for a very long time and if it comes then so be it. But I don't want you to suffer any more than you already have. You were married to him after all and now you know who he was I'm sure it's incredibly painful for you. So I want to help you again. I've spent many hours these past few days sitting in silence and thinking. I have told my solicitor to drop the complaint against you. I was mistaken. I didn't see you in Oxford. I was confused and panicking after being arrested.

Edward is the one to blame. Not you. He killed the girls and planted the hairs on Kinga Nowicka to get his revenge on me for abandoning him five years ago. He must have broken into my house and planted the hairs. His semen was found at each scene. You knew nothing and had nothing to do with it. I will admit I knew him but I will be truthful about what we did together and when. I have not seen him for five years and there will be nothing to prove that I have. That will be our new line of argument and hopefully it will work. I realise the combination of my hair and Edward's semen at one murder scene will make things tricky for us but we will try and my intention is that you will be removed from the equation. You see, sorry is important detective but what comes next is more important. This is my Act of Contrition and whatever comes next will be my Penance. I will accept. My ultimate way to apologise to you, to the girls I killed, to their families and to atone for my mortal sins. I wish you well detective. I have always wished you well.

SB

I lower the letter.

I tried to protect a guilty man by framing an innocent man. An innocent man who had tried to protect me, not harm me. I feel so unbelievably stupid.

Even though I've spent many years of my life hating Steven Barr, I'm hit by a pang of guilt that I struggle to explain. Then that guilt turns to shame. *I did this.* And then remorse.

Finally anger. *Damn Edward for this. And damn my father. He is the root cause of everything.*

I am sorry. My Act of Contrition.

And now for my Act of Penance. Damn my father.

76

I've known the address since I joined the police force. Since I was able to access the national address database. I've checked it intermittently over the years, to make sure the address was still correct. I took some kind of comfort in knowing what the address was, although it always felt strange to know that, for so many years, he'd lived within an hour's journey of my own home, a place where I felt safe even while I struggled to push the memory of him away.

I've sat in a car in this street many times over the years, but I've never hung around for long enough to actually see him. I never thought I'd see him again.

Today is going to be different, however. I'm going to do more than see him. I'm going to make him suffer. He ruined me and now that I'm inexorably ruined somebody has to suffer. It's his fault. He has to pay for what he did to me. Without him raping me, I doubt I'd ever have moved away, I doubt I'd ever have met Edward, I might not have become a police officer, and then I would never have known a man named Steven Barr.

I would never have framed a man who had tried to help me.

I've parked the car on the other side of the road but parallel to the front door of the house. Even if he sees me, he won't recognise me and he won't know who I am.

The front door is red, the paint worn and faded. The front of the house looks shabby, the small garden overgrown and devoid of colour.

I can't focus on anything except the house. I don't know how long I've been sitting here when the front door opens. For a time, no one exits and all I can see is a dark, empty space. Then, finally, a man emerges. The fury boiling inside me, I leap out of the car and stand next to it, staring right at him.

He has to pay. I'm going to hurt him the way he hurt me all those years ago. The way the pain has remained, even though he's been out of my life.

This is my Act of Penance.

He steps out. I'm surprised to see he's a frail figure, his body hunched over, and he's using a walking stick. He's so . . . different. Simply stepping down from the house and onto the path is difficult for him. He must be in his mid-seventies, yet he looks significantly older. He's wearing an oversized anorak and a pair of dark trousers, even though it's a pleasantly warm day. He turns to lock the front door.

The man who raised me. The man who violated me.

As he turns and walks along the short path towards the pavement, I slowly cross the road. He shuffles onto the pavement, closing the small metal gate. From my bag, I withdraw a kitchen knife, the one I bought to replace the one with which I killed Edward. I hold it by the side of my leg as I walk. He turns to the right, just as I step onto the pavement in front of him and block his path.

He glances up at me. His face is wrinkled, his brow permanently creased, and walking clearly causes him discomfort. *Good,* I think, *let him suffer. And now let me make you suffer even more.*

As our eyes meet and I stand still, I think for a moment that I can identify a faint glimmer of recognition in him. My arm starts to shake.

I've thought about this moment for years. This opportunity. What I'd say or do.

What I'm going to do to him now. My grip of the knife tightens. There's perspiration on my brow.

I say nothing.

'Beg your pardon,' he mumbles, lowering his eyes and shuffling forward.

I don't say anything because *he is nothing.*

I don't move, so he has to walk around me. As he passes me, I can smell him. Something stale. I turn slowly as he passes, following him with my eyes, willing my hand to lift. I drift after him as he shuffles on. He steps, I step. Lift the blade into the air. As his hand presses against the walking stick, his entire arm shakes. It quakes. *Press it into his back.* I'm quaking. I can hear his heavy breathing. I try to suck in as much air as I can. Can't. Life is a struggle for him. *Thrust and make him bleed.*

I stop, peering down at the knife. I use my other hand to try to stop my knife hand from shaking so violently. Then I raise my eyes and watch him as he drags himself to the end of the road.

This frail, pitiful man, someone who is no more than a stranger to me.

Someone who can't hurt me anymore.

He is nothing.

And suddenly my hand stops shaking, and I can breathe clearly, and the anger inside me has dissipated.

I watch him as each step leads him further and further away from me. He doesn't look back. He is merely a shadow retreating from me. And when he reaches the corner, I watch as the shadow finally disappears from view, and I know I don't have to kill him, because he has finally gone.

Acknowledgements

I'd like to thank the kind authors who have offered me encouragement and supported my work as A.J. Park: Martina Cole, Sophie Hannah, Alex Marwood, Simon Lelic, M.W. Craven, Cathy Kelly, Susan Lewis, Luca Veste and Chris Mooney.

Thanks to Lucy Frederick and Tom Witcomb for their useful editorial input.

Thanks to Laura Turner for adopting the role of creative consultant.

Special thanks to Corrina Hentschel, the names of whose family members – Amy, Emily and David – inspired the character name, Amelie Davis. Corrina won the opportunity to name a character in *Don't Speak* by bidding at St Michael's Catholic High School's annual fundraising auction. St Michael's Catholic High School in Hertfordshire has for the past fifteen years raised more than £500,000 to support life-changing projects at home and abroad in numerous countries including Rwanda and the Philippines. The efforts of St Michael's students and staff are simply astounding year on year.